Bride
Needs
Groom

Also by Wendy Markham
in Large Print:

Hello, It's Me

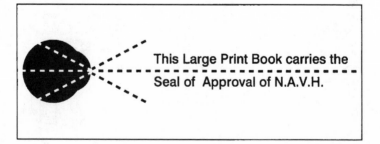

Bride
Needs
Groom

✵

Wendy Markham

Thorndike Press • Waterville, Maine

Published in 2006 by arrangement with Warner Books, Inc.

Thorndike Press® Large Print Basic.

The tree indicium is a trademark of Thorndike Press.

The text of this Large Print edition is unabridged.
Other aspects of the book may vary from the original edition.

Set in 16 pt. Plantin.

Printed in the United States on permanent paper.

Library of Congress Cataloging-in-Publication Data

Markham, Wendy.
    Bride needs groom / by Wendy Markham.
      p. cm.
    "Thorndike Press large print basic series" — T.p. verso.
    ISBN 0-7862-8385-8 (lg. print : hc : alk. paper)
    1. Las Vegas (Nev.) — Fiction.   2. Large type books.
I. Title.
PS3569.T336456B75 2006
  813'.6—dc22   2005033416

In loving memory of my uncle,
Paul Staub
10/25/25–2/18/05
who will be remembered not just
as a legendary American war hero
but as a kind, loving family man who
truly made the world a better place.

And for my boys, Morgan and Brody,
and my husband, Mark, with love and a
heartfelt *Cent'anni.*

With deepest gratitude to my editors,
Karen Kosztolnyik
and Michele Bidelspach,
and my agent, Laura Blake Peterson.

As the Founder/CEO of NAVH, the only national health agency solely devoted to those who, although not totally blind, have an eye disease which could lead to serious visual impairment, I am pleased to recognize Thorndike Press★ as one of the leading publishers in the large print field.

Founded in 1954 in San Francisco to prepare large print textbooks for partially seeing children, NAVH became the pioneer and standard setting agency in the preparation of large type.

Today, those publishers who meet our standards carry the prestigious "Seal of Approval" indicating high quality large print. We are delighted that Thorndike Press is one of the publishers whose titles meet these standards. We are also pleased to recognize the significant contribution Thorndike Press is making in this important and growing field.

Lorraine H. Marchi, L.H.D.
Founder/CEO
NAVH

★ Thorndike Press encompasses the following imprints: Thorndike, Wheeler, Walker and Large Print Press.

Prologue

July 3

"Another Fourth of July weekend without fireworks," Mia Calogera pronounces with a sigh as she and her friend Lenore emerge from an air-conditioned movie theater onto the Manhattan street.

The sun went down while they were inside, but the twilight air remains steamy. Lexington Avenue is far less crowded with traffic and pedestrians than usual, thanks to the summer's initial blast of oppressive heat combined with a long holiday weekend and mass exodus for shore and mountain breezes.

"I thought we were meeting tomorrow night to watch the fireworks," Lenore responds, removing her wire-rimmed glasses as they fog over in the humidity.

It's a long-standing tradition for the two friends to climb the stairs to the rooftop of Mia's four-story apartment building, just across the East River in Queens. From that vantage point, they can view the nationally televised fireworks display against a dazzling backdrop of city skyline.

"I didn't mean that kind of fireworks," Mia tells her friend. "I meant the romantic kind. You know . . . sparks."

"Like in the movie?"

"Like in the movie." Mia smiles faintly, recalling the romantic comedy they just saw. In a running gag, skyrockets exploded every time the hero and heroine kissed. And they kissed a *lot*.

When was the last time Mia kissed anyone that way . . . or even met a man she was slightly tempted to kiss that way?

She can't even remember. But the odds of it happening tomorrow are nil, considering she's spending the better part of Independence Day driving her elderly grandparents to visit her great-aunt and uncle out on Long Island.

The most excitement the day can possibly hold is a visit to an orchid grower's greenhouse to check out some new hybrids.

"Well, last year, Fourth of July weekend had plenty of fireworks for me," Lenore says wryly. "And not the movie kind *or* the patriotic kind. Remember? Stavros and I had that big fight about his flirting with my cousin at the beach party. That was the beginning of the end."

"I remember." Mia shakes her head. Her friend's soon-to-be-ex-husband has ruined many a holiday get-together, whether or not he's physically present. Last year's rooftop fireworks were marred by Lenore's inconsolable tears over a failing marriage.

"You're going to be okay," Mia assures her. "Better than okay."

"I guess . . . I just wish it didn't have to take so long getting from the beginning of the end to the *end* of the end . . . let alone a new beginning. I'd love to meet somebody new. Do you know how long it's been since I've had any kind of romance whatsoever?"

"Tell me about it," Mia says ruefully, lifting the weight of her long dark hair off her sweaty neck and futilely wishing for a gust of wind to cool things off. "And you'll get there. I promise."

"What about you?"

"What *about* me?"

"You deserve fireworks, too. We both deserve to meet Mr. Right."

"You know I'm not in the market for Mr. Right."

"Well, *I* am."

"Don't you have to get rid of Mr. Wrong first?"

"Any day now. Who knew a mutual divorce could be this complicated?"

"I did." Mia pushes aside the bitter childhood memory of her parents' endless court battle. If that wasn't enough to make her swear off marriage, Lenore's ongoing saga is.

"I just wish I knew for sure that I'm going to find somebody again," Lenore says wistfully. "I loved being married." At Mia's incredulous look, she adds, "Not to *him*. Just being married, in general. I'd sleep a lot better at night if I knew for sure that I'm not going to spend the rest of my life as a divorcée."

Mia opportunistically spots a neon sign in the second-floor window of a small brick building on the opposite corner. *Madame Tamar, Psychic and Spiritualist.*

"You know what, Lenore? Let's find out!"

"About what?"

"About your meeting Mr. Right in the future."

"What do you mean?" Following her gaze, Lenore's eyes widen. "Are you serious?"

"Let's go. My treat," she says before her perennially cash-strapped friend can protest. "If you can't sleep at night, I can't sleep at night."

"Okay, but . . . you really believe in this

stuff?" Lenore asks as Mia propels her across the street against the light — which doesn't matter, considering the smattering of traffic.

"I don't know . . . do you believe in it?"

"That depends on what she tells us."

"Us?" Mia echoes. "You mean *you*."

"I mean us. I'm not doing it unless you do. And you have to go first."

"Why?"

"Because I'm scared."

"Of what?"

"What if she tells me I'm going to get hit by a bus tomorrow? Or worse?"

"What could be worse than that?"

"What if she says I'm never going to fall in love again?"

"Plenty of people live long, fulfilling single lives," Mia pontificates, feeling like Oprah.

"Name one."

"Me."

Lenore dismisses that with a wave of her hand. "You're not going to be single forever."

"Oh, yes I am. No way am I going through what my parents did. Or what you did."

With a wince, her friend points out, "Not every marriage crashes and burns, Mia. Look at your grandparents."

"Look at my parents. And you. And half the people we know who are married. *Were* married."

"Look at the other half," Lenore counters.

They've reached the entrance to Madame Tamar's building. Mia presses the bell beside the door. Almost immediately, a female voice says, "Come up," and the lock is released with a click and a buzz.

"Do you think she saw us coming?" Lenore asks, looking disconcerted.

"You mean in her crystal ball, or out the window?" Mia cracks. "Come on, let's go."

"Remember, you first," Lenore hisses, following her up a steep, dark flight of stairs.

Mia expects Madame Tamar to be an exotic, eccentric gypsy type clad in a turban or flowing robe or, at the very least, earrings, bangles, and rings.

What they find on the second floor is a pleasantly plump middle-aged woman in shorts and a T-shirt. Her salt-and-pepper hair is tied back in a ponytail, and her plain features are unenhanced by makeup. Her only jewelry is a gold wedding band.

Her apartment is equally unimaginative. Unadorned white walls, hardwood floors, beige furniture that looks as though it came from IKEA.

"Have a seat," Madame Tamar offers, gesturing at a couple of chairs pulled up to a wooden table that contains today's *New York Post* and a paper Starbucks cup rather than tea leaves or tarot cards.

"Which one of us?" Mia asks.

"Both. I have a two-for-one holiday weekend special," Madame Tamar adds with the air of a happy-hour waitress. "Seventy-five dollars."

"For how long?" Lenore wants to know.

With a shrug, the woman sits across from them and replies, "That depends on what I see. Give me your hand."

Mia watches her grip Lenore's fingers, close her eyes, and begin to spout information. Most of it is general: Her heart has been broken in the past (whose hasn't?), she has a strong desire to succeed (who doesn't?), and she's wishing she were higher paid (who isn't?).

But Lenore is clearly impressed with the woman's psychic abilities, blurting, "Yes!" after almost everything she says. Her face lights up when Madame Tamar informs her that she will have a long and happy relationship with somebody she already knows.

Obviously satisfied, Lenore thanks Madame Tamar profusely.

"Your turn," the woman says, turning to

Mia with a gleam in her eye.

"Oh . . . that's okay. I don't —"

"It's two-for-one." Madame Tamar grabs her hand with sweaty fingers, clasps it, and they're off.

Mia is informed that she can be stubborn (who can't?), that she loves the finer things in life (who doesn't?), and that her heart is fickle (whose isn't?).

Then Madame Tamar clutches her hand a little tighter and says, "You'll be getting married before the year is out."

"Married? Me?" Mia snorts and tries to pull her hand away.

Madame Tamar squeezes it. "Yes, definitely married. To a man . . ."

"That's a relief," Mia mutters when the so-called psychic trails off. "Considering that the other kind of marriage is pretty much illegal."

"Shh!" Lenore shoots her a warning look. "Listen to what she has to say, Mia."

What Madame Tamar has to say, more decisively than she's said anything else, is, "This man's name starts with a *D*. D . . ."

Despite her amusement with the psychic's little game, Mia's mind races through all the men she's ever known whose names start with *D*. Devin . . . Douglas . . . David . . .

"It starts with a *D*, and it ends in a *k*

sound," Madame Tamar elaborates triumphantly.

"You mean like Dick?" a befuddled Mia asks the woman, who nods.

Definitely not encouraging . . . if she chooses to believe it. Which she doesn't. But if she did, she'd be thinking in dismay that the only Dicks with whom she's acquainted are AARP card carriers. In her own generation, men are called Richard, Rick, even Richie — but not Dick. Not in the nickname capacity, anyway.

"Maybe you're going to marry an old guy — you know, a sugar daddy," Lenore suggests a few minutes later, when they're back out on the street and Mia's wallet is seventy-five dollars lighter.

"Yeah, and maybe that psychic couldn't predict the future if it had already happened," Mia retorts.

"Huh?"

"Never mind. It doesn't matter. Like I said, I'm never getting married. Period."

Lenore just shakes her head. "I give you six months."

"Six months?"

"Till the end of the year. Mark my words, Mia . . . and Madame Tamar's. You'll be walking down the aisle before the year is out."

"So now that you know every last detail about our family trip to the Hamptons, what are *your* big plans for the Fourth?" Maggie Kennelly asks Dominic Chickalini as she tosses yet another unflattering maternity bathing suit into the open suitcase on her bed.

"Just a barbecue at my sister's," Dom replies, seated in a nearby chair and bouncing her gleeful two-year-old daughter on his knee. Maggie's oldest child, four-year-old Julia, is sprawled on the rug nearby, playing with her Polly Pocket dolls and pausing every so often to gaze adoringly up at Dom.

Dom is quite accustomed to the effect he has on females, even pint-sized ones. With his thick dark hair, chiseled Mediterranean features, lean, broad-shouldered build, and easy laugh, Dominic Chickalini is the kind of man who commands female attention without even trying.

Not that he doesn't try. Dom has always been just as magnetically drawn to women as they are to him.

"You're spending tomorrow at a family barbecue? Yeah, right." Maggie shakes her head. "No offense, but hot dogs and firecrackers in the backyard is not exactly your speed."

"Who said anything about hot dogs? I just sent over a cooler of filet mignon from the new butcher shop on Astoria Boulevard." He smiles, imagining the look on his sister Rosalie's face when she got the package.

"Still . . . I was expecting something a little more upscale and glamorous than that."

"Like . . . ?"

"Like last Fourth of July, you watched the fireworks from a chartered yacht near the Statue of Liberty. With a supermodel as your date."

"Vera wasn't a supermodel," Dom amends, setting a squirming Katie on her feet and watching her make a beeline for her big sister. "She was a swimsuit model. Still is, the last I heard."

Maggie raises an eyebrow. "You're actually keeping in touch with an ex-girlfriend?"

"No, but when I went on this job interview the other day, the person who interviewed me had her picture tacked up on his office bulletin board, and we got to talking, and it turned out he knows Vera, too. Small world, you know?"

"Nope, big world; Vera just seems to get around."

He watches Maggie turn her attention to

her closet, where she rummages through a row of hangers and holds up a long flowered sundress.

"Male opinion, please. Does this scream maternity?"

Dom gives the garment an unenthusiastic once-over. "Well, it doesn't scream *rip me off and ravish me,* if that's what you're hoping. But Charlie can always use it for a mainsail if he buys that boat he keeps talking about."

"Funny." She sighs and tosses the dress aside, hugging her swollen middle. "I can't wait until this pregnancy is over and I can get back into my cute summer clothes. Even though I won't fit into them until at least February."

"Maybe Charlie can take you to Florida for Valentine's Day. Isn't that when you met?"

It is, and he knows that very well, having been an eyewitness the night Maggie met Charlie on a blind date. Ironically, the date involved Dominic and Charlie's former neighbor, Julie. Maggie and Charlie were officially there as chaperones, but wound up hitting it off. The fact that both Dominic and Julie are still single six years later doesn't say a lot for Maggie and Charlie's repeated matchmaking efforts.

"Flying to Florida in the middle of flu and blizzard season with a two-year-old, a four-year-old, and a newborn doesn't sound great, Dom."

"I didn't mean the whole horde of you," he says, watching her toss a pair of flip-flops toward the open suitcase, and miss. "I meant just you two."

"Spoken like a true single man who has no concept of parental responsibility."

"What do you mean by that?"

"In February, the baby will still be too young for me to leave for the weekend." She bends to retrieve one of the flip-flops from under the bed skirt and groans at the effort. "Ouch. I swear, this is the last pregnancy for me."

"What if it's not a boy?" Dominic asks, knowing Maggie's husband is desperate for a son. The whole world knows Maggie's husband is desperate for a son, thanks to the monthly column he continues to write for *She* magazine despite his newfound bestseller status.

"If it's not a boy," Maggie says, "we're naming her Charlotte, calling her Charlie for short, and forcing her to play Little League. Don't laugh, Dom. I'm totally serious. Three kids is more than enough."

"Oh, come on, Maggie. Between this

fancy spread and the beach house, you guys definitely have the room for a couple more."

"It isn't about room for more," Maggie says ruefully. "It's about preserving Mommy's sanity. And anyway, this place isn't *that* big."

Dom, who a few months ago helped the Kennellys move into this five-bedroom, three-and-a-half bath Upper West Side brownstone and witnessed Maggie's every *ooh* and *aah* over how spacious it was, merely rolls his eyes.

"Oh, who am I kidding?" she asks with a laugh. "It's a freaking palace compared to where I started out. Remember my tiny apartment in Astoria?"

"Yeah, I just heard it went co-op. And I also remember Charlie's studio in the Village, which is probably worth close to a million by now." Dom sighs. "Manhattan real estate is out of control. Unless, of course, one happens to be an internationally renowned author whose breakout book is about to become a major motion picture starring Ben Stiller."

"Or the charming wife of said author," Maggie reminds him.

"Right. You don't know how lucky you are, Mags. I mean, I'm still sleeping in my childhood bedroom."

"Oh, please, whose fault is that?"

"You know I'd buy a place if I could afford one, just to get out of my father's house. Cripes, I'm almost thirty."

"On your salary, you could afford a place in Manhattan if you didn't spend every cent you make on wine, women, and song."

"Song?" He quirks a dark eyebrow at her.

"All right, wine and women."

"And song," he admits. "I just snagged two tickets to that sold-out Jimmy Buffett concert at Jones Beach on Labor Day weekend."

"Which day that weekend?"

"Saturday."

"I hate to break it to you, but you aren't available then," Maggie tells him.

"I'm not?"

"No. That's Carolyn's wedding day." Carolyn is Maggie's best friend and Charlie's editor. "Invitations go out this week."

Dom scowls. "Between weddings and bachelor parties and showers, every weekend of my summer is booked."

"Showers?"

"Yes, God help me. My sisters got the brilliant idea of having a couples shower for Ralphie and his fiancée. I'm sure you and Charlie will be invited."

"That sounds like fun."

"Well, I don't think so, and Charlie won't think so, and my brothers-in-law don't think so, and Ralphie doesn't think so. But you know Nina and Rosalie. Once they get something in their heads, they're full speed ahead."

Maggie smiles. She does know Nina and Rosalie, and he's right. "Well, look at the bright side, Dominic. By the time you get married, they'll probably be retired in Florida so you won't have to worry about them taking over the plans."

"Who said I'm getting married?"

"Dom —"

"I don't want a wife. But I could use a new job, if this interview doesn't pan out."

"Where was it?" Maggie asks, familiar with Dom's latest goal to get out of the agency and into the more lucrative field of advertising sales. She has no doubt he'll succeed in landing a plum position someplace.

"It's a start-up cable television network. It's called MAN."

"M-A-N?"

"As in *man*. Their programming is strictly male oriented."

"Featuring what? Wine, women, and song?"

"More like beer, babes, rock and roll . . . and trucks. And I'd be the perfect sales rep for them, so cross your fingers I get a second interview. Their sales conference is in Vegas in September, and I'm so there."

"Speaking of September, it would be nice if before then, you and whatever swimsuit model you happen to be dating could have dinner with me and Charlie. Although by the time September rolls around, I'll probably be wishing for an entire weekend away, not just a night out."

"So forget dinner with me and go away for the weekend with Charlie. Just the two of you. Go out to your house in the Hamptons without the girls, or wherever you want to go. I'll stay here with them."

Maggie's jaw drops. "You're kidding."

"I'm not. You guys deserve a break from the kids, and I promise I'll take good care of them. Right, guys?"

"Mommy, go!" Julia begs. "We want Uncle Dom to babysit!"

"Don't worry, guys, Mommy's going," Dom assures her.

"Dom, you can't possibly handle the girls for a weekend."

"Sure I can. They'd be fine. Do this,

Maggie. You guys need it, and I don't mind helping out."

"What the heck has gotten into you?" she can't help asking.

"What do you mean?"

"First the barbecue, and now you're offering to play Mary Poppins. It's like you're suddenly . . . turning into a responsible adult. Not that it isn't about time, but . . ."

"I've always been a responsible adult."

"You certainly have not. I can't believe it, Dom. Next thing I know, you're going to be introducing me to Ms. Right."

"Does she look like a cross between Catherine Zeta-Jones and Angelina Jolie? Because if she doesn't, she's Ms. Wrong."

Ignoring that comment, Maggie insists, "Someday soon, you're going to meet a woman who'll have you picking out your everyday china pattern before you can say, 'Adios forever, swimsuit models.' Stop looking at me like that, Chickalini. I guarantee it."

"China pattern?" His horrified expression is so exaggerated that Maggie's girls burst out laughing.

"I'll be getting married right around the time you're getting pregnant with your next kid, Mags. In other words, like you just said, *never*."

"Listen, you never know. Charlie was once called the most eligible bachelor in New York City, and now look at him."

"Yeah, look at him, poor sap. And anyway, somebody has to carry the torch all the way to the finish line. It might as well be me."

"What torch, Uncle Dom?" Julia asks. "The Olympic torch?"

"No, the Single Guy torch, and it's even better than the Olympic torch." Dom grins. "With any luck, I'll be carrying it all the way to Vegas in September. I'm going to need a decadent getaway after all these weekend weddings on my calendar be-tween now and then."

"I'd be willing to bet," Maggie insists slyly, "that it won't be long before one of the weekend weddings on your calendar will be your own."

Chapter One

September

"Champagne?"

Mia glances up from the open Louis Vuitton carry-on she's been fruitlessly searching for an emery board, thanks to the security officer who grimly confiscated her prized sapphire nail file at check-in.

"Would you like some?" A smiling female flight attendant is brandishing an open green bottle of fine champagne and a crystal flute.

All right, probably not Cristal — or crystal. But undoubtedly a fine vintage nonetheless, and the flute is glass. Definitely glass.

Glass beats the plastic glassware they use back in coach, as Mia recalls from her less-privileged past, and she greatly prefers champagne to weak coffee that isn't offered until somewhere over Indiana. Or Illinois. Or one of those Midwestern vowel-starting states that Mia has never seen in a closer proximity than twenty thousand feet.

Which is absolutely fine with her, of course.

"Yes. I'd love some champagne. Thank you." Mia smiles back at the flight attendant, who compliments her on her simple tulle headpiece as she pours the bubbly.

"Where did you get it? I'm getting married next summer, and I still haven't found a veil I like."

Mia tells her the name of the Madison Avenue bridal salon where, in the last forty-eight hours, she bought everything from her white satin shoes to the corset that enabled her to effortlessly button the low-cut gown's snug and exquisitely beaded bodice.

"Oh, I've heard of that place. It's outrageously expensive, right?"

"Not necessarily." Not if one is worth millions.

All right, it's her beloved elderly grandfather, Carmine Calogera, Jr., who's worth millions. But she's under his roof, on his payroll, and in his will. And she's going to do whatever it takes to stay there. Which is where the wedding gown comes in.

"I've heard you have to order more than a year in advance at that salon to make sure your gown is ready on time. Did it take forever for yours?" the flight attendant wants to know.

"Not really," Mia says, wondering how one defines *forever.*

"How many fittings did you have?"

Not enough, she thinks, considering that the corset she was forced to wear beneath the too-snug bodice leaves little room to breathe properly.

"Um, I had a few fittings," she tells the flight attendant.

Two qualifies for a few, right? And it doesn't matter that they were both held on the same day, in between mad dashes up and down the Avenue for Vegas-suitable clothing and wedding night lingerie. The woman doesn't need to know the nuptials haven't been in the works for months. Or even weeks.

"Well, you look beautiful. Cheers." The flight attendant's modest diamond engagement ring sparkles in the September sunshine streaming through the window as she hands the flute to Mia. "And good luck."

"Thank you," Mia says again, lifting her glass in a toast with her right hand, lest the attendant notice her left isn't even sporting a diamond. "Same to you."

Ah, champagne. Perfect! What else would a bride-to-be sip en route to her wedding?

The flight attendant smiles her way across the aisle to the next passenger, an attractive businessman who's been shooting curious sidelong glances in Mia's direction ever since she boarded.

She's been tempted to say, "What's the matter? Haven't you ever seen a bride before?"

But that would open the door to conversation, and Mia isn't in the mood to spend the next few hours chatting. She'd much rather rehash the incredible series of events that led to her elopement. She still hasn't had much opportunity to absorb it all.

Leaning back in her seat, Mia sips from her flute, swallows, and makes a face. Okay, so it isn't as fine a bubbly as Cristal. But the Cristal will surely be flowing tonight in the bridal suite.

Holding her flute in her right hand, careful not to spill any on her white silk gown, she resumes rummaging in her carry-on with her left: the hand that also happens to have a ragged edge on the fourth manicured fingernail. In other words, *on her bare ring finger.*

Mia's Sicilian grandmother would probably say that's a bad omen. Nana Mona would undoubtedly tell her granddaughter to get off the plane, jump into a cab back to Manhattan, and forget all about getting married.

Fortunately, Nana Mona isn't here.

Unfortunately, neither is an emery board.

Mia zips her bag closed, sips more champagne, and looks around the first-class cabin for a fellow passenger who might have successfully smuggled a nail file on board.

Her gaze collides with the businessman's stare from across the aisle. He reddens and quickly turns away.

So does Mia, who tries to ignore a pang of regret as she glances out the window at the sun-splashed autumn morning. In the past, she'd have found herself fending off advances from a guy like that. Or encouraging them, if she were in the mood, as long as he wasn't married. Married men, of course, are strictly off-limits.

Mia still can't quite get used to men finding her attractive. She spent most of her adolescence and young adulthood overweight and mousy.

But those days are over, thanks to a complete makeover a few years back, after her grandfather won the lottery. As she likes to tell her friend Lenore, all it took to transform the ugly duckling into a beautiful swan was cash. Lots of it. All that money opened the doors to the finest salons and spas, to fabulous shops that carry the best couture. It allowed her to hire the famed celebrity nutritionist and trainer Fuji as her own personal diet guru.

Old habits died easily in Mia's case. Suddenly, there was so much more to do than lounge around in sweats every weekend tending to her small collection of windowsill orchids and eating Nana Mona's homemade lasagna. So much more to do, *and* wear, *and* eat. So many men to date . . .

Too bad her license to flirt is about to be exchanged for a license to wed.

Too bad? she asks herself, surprised. *Why are you suddenly thinking it's too bad?*

It isn't that she doesn't *want* to get married, because she does.

Never mind that she is *about to* get married, that in fact she *has to* get married . . .

She *wants to* get married. Really.

It's just that she can't help feeling a little sad about all she's leaving behind.

All?

Come on, Mia. You'll still get to enjoy all those other perks. In fact, this is the only way to ensure that you will. The only thing you're giving up is dating.

Well, okay, then it's just that she can't

quite quell the age-old instinct to engage in a little benign flirtation with every red-blooded male who crosses her path.

But she's quickly discovering that this wedding gown is to red-blooded men as a cross-shaped garlic necklace is to vampires.

So it's probably a good thing she overcame her initial reluctance and opted to wear it on the flight after all. It was Derek's idea. He's meeting her at the airport.

"I'll be the one in the white tuxedo with the yellow phalaenopsis orchid boutonniere," he said, giving her pause.

Pause because white tuxedos can be tacky, in Mia's opinion, and because yellow flowers are bad luck, according to Nana Mona.

But Mia quickly pushes her doubts aside.

Orchids are her favorite flower, and Derek's, as well. Orchids are the reason that they met.

And anyway, if she believed all of Nana's crazy Sicilian superstitions, she wouldn't be on this plane in the first place. Friday, according to Nana, is an unlucky day to begin a voyage. Nana would never consider leaving Astoria on a Friday if she couldn't be back well before nightfall, much less embark on a cross-country journey and married life all in one shot.

But you don't believe that stuff . . .

Do you?

Of course not, Mia retorts to her wishy-washy inner self, lifting her chin stubbornly.

Yellow flowers are *not* bad luck. And on the right person, a white tuxedo might be downright elegant.

Derek Jenkins is most definitely the right person. As in *Mr. Right* person.

Didn't Madame Tamar tell Mia that one day she would marry a man whose name started with a *D* and ended with a *k* sound?

Mia forgot all about the prophecy, not even remembering it when Derek popped into her life a week later, quite literally, via the Internet.

Who would have thought that spending her afternoons idly surfing orchid growers' sites on the Web while Nana Mona naps would have led to this?

Now here she is, going to the chapel . . .

More specifically, the Chapel of Luv.

The unorthodox spelling probably shouldn't bother her. And it doesn't. Not really. It's just that . . .

Well, she can't help wondering whether this whole thing wouldn't feel a lot more official if she were going to the Chapel of *Love.*

But Derek made all the arrangements, and she trusts him implicitly. As implicitly as one can trust a future husband whom one has never met.

Yes, Mia trusts Derek, and she trusts her instincts.

This is the right choice.

Never mind that it's her *only* choice.

She's goin' to the chapel, and she's gonna get mah-hah-harried . . .

Yes, and just in the nick of time, Mia thinks, smoothing the folds of her long white silk skirt before fastening her seat belt across her lap.

"Here you go, Mr. Chickalini," the pretty blonde gate attendant drawls, stapling something to his ticket and handing it across the counter. "We're boarding now. In fact, you might want to hurry on over. Takeoff is in a few minutes."

"Too bad," Dom tells her, flashing a flirtatious smile. "If I weren't about to leave town for a few days, I'd ask you for your phone number."

She giggles, her cheeks tinting pink. "Really? Well, if I weren't happily married, I'd definitely give it to you."

Married? And *happily?* She isn't even wearing a ring. Dom checked, out of habit, when he stepped up to the counter.

"Oh, well. Can't win 'em all." With an arm-swinging, finger-snapping "Darn!" gesture, he hurries away from the counter, toward the statuesque, uniformed redhead waiting beside the open Jetway. She, too, is married, he notes, following a perfunctory glance at her left hand.

After checking his ticket, tearing off the stub, and handing it back to him, she says, "Have a nice flight, Mr. . . . Chickeno, is it?"

It isn't, but Dom nods, accustomed to the butchered pronunciation of his surname. The redhead pronounces the first syllable *sheik* and invokes poultry with the remainder; the blonde at the counter's southern accent made it even more unintelligible.

Oh, well. Attractive women can get away with a lot, as far as Dom is concerned. Even attractive *married* women.

Striding along the Jetway with his garment bag slung over his shoulder, he contemplates the fact that the world — at least, his little corner of it — is primarily populated by married women. And men. Married *couples*.

They're everywhere, lately, touting wedded bliss as though they're part of some pro bono campaign for the World Organization of Happily Ever After.

Everyone is living happily ever after, dammit. Dom's older sisters, Nina and Rosalie; his older brother, Pete; his best friend, Maggie; his cousins, his neighbors, his old college fraternity brothers . . . even his kid brother, Ralphie, is engaged.

Dom's prized summer weekends were mainly spent at weddings, engagement parties, bachelor parties, even that couples shower for Ralphie and Francesca, at which Dom was the only solo attendee. He'd have brought a date, but he was afraid the bridal theme might give an unattached woman ideas.

Hell, mere dinner and a movie tend to give unattached women ideas these days.

It's no wonder that Dom himself is almost tempted to start getting ideas.

But he's going to put a stop to that. Nothing like a decadent getaway to Sin City to remind a red-blooded guy that footloose and fancy-free is the way to go. All he needs now is a cold beer in his hand, a stack of poker chips on the table, and a Catherine Zeta-Jones or Angelina Jolie look-alike on his arm.

At the door of the plane, Dom comes to a halt as two male flight attendants attempt to wrestle a double baby stroller into submission.

"Press that latch," one is saying.

"No, first we have to turn it upside down," the other retorts.

"Not until after you press the latch."

"Are you sure?"

When neither pressing the latch nor turning the stroller upside down proves effective in collapsing it, both men glance up at Dom.

"Don't look at me," he says with a shrug. "I have no idea how to fold that thing."

Nor is he in any rush to board a flight that contains at least two babies.

Not that Dom has anything against babies.

His world isn't just teeming with married couples; it's crawling with children. He relishes being Uncle Dom, whose pockets are filled with bubble gum and quarters to pull out of tiny ears and who doesn't hesitate to get soaked in a squirt-gun fight or crawl around in the mud on all fours giving pony rides. His sisters call him an overgrown kid.

But this morning, he isn't Uncle Dom the Overgrown Kid.

He's a grown-up businessman en route to a convention in Sin City, and he wouldn't mind a little peace and quiet along the way.

"Try pressing the latch again," one flight attendant urges the other, who obliges.

Naturally, nothing happens.

"Let's leave it here," the latch-happy attendant whispers conspiratorially.

"You're *evil!*" Deliciously evil, judging by the other attendant's expression. "What about the poor passenger?"

"What about her? She can buy another one in Vegas."

Dom, who has been to Vegas enough times to realize it isn't the most kid-friendly destination, can't help intervening on behalf of the hapless parent who will be forced to manhandle two kids and a mountain of luggage to the hotel after an exhausting cross-country flight.

He steps forward with a gruff, "Here, let me take a look," and in two seconds flat has the stroller folded and ready to stow.

"How'd you do that?" asks one of the dumbfounded stewards.

Dom, who isn't quite certain how he did that, shrugs.

"You must have one at home."

"A stroller? Me?" Dom laughs. "Nope."

"You're not a daddy?"

"Nope. I'm not even a hubby . . . and I don't plan to be any time soon." Dom wonders why he finds it necessary to make that clear to everyone he ever meets, including these two men, whom he suspects aren't in the market for wives, either . . . but for reasons vastly different from his.

Lest they have the wrong idea about him, he adopts his most heterosexual stride as he steps at last over the threshold onto the plane.

To the right is coach class, where passengers are jamming themselves into center seats, or struggling to load baggage into overhead bins, or casting wary glances toward the crying babies that seem to be everywhere.

To his left is first class, cordoned off by another flight attendant and a thick set of drawn curtains.

Dom goes left, grateful for the frequent-flier-mileage upgrade in his hand.

He moves past the curtains and is greeted by a welcome hush and the pretty female flight attendant, who pauses with an open bottle of champagne poised in her hand and asks to see his ticket.

"You're right up there in the second row by the window, Mr. Chickalini," she informs him with a blue-eyed gaze that's somehow both sultry and cheerful.

She even comes fairly close to pronouncing his name correctly.

"Perfect. Thank you."

She turns back to the seated couple in front of him, saying over her shoulder, "I'll be out of your way in just a moment so that you can get to your seat."

"Take your time."

He admires the view of her curvy posterior until a glance at her left hand reveals a diamond engagement ring.

Why is he surprised?

And why is he disappointed?

There are plenty of single women in the world. Certainly, there are in Las Vegas. After he checks into the hotel, he'll head right down to the pool and check them out.

Babes in bikinis. Yes, he tells himself firmly, that's just what the doctor ordered after what he's been through lately.

He spent last weekend babysitting his friend Maggie's children so that she and Charlie could get away together one last time before their new baby comes. He took Julia and Katie to Playland as promised, and they rode their beloved bumper cars over and over again. The chaotic weekend was followed by a whirlwind of a wining, dining workweek, capped off by a traffic-clogged cab ride to insanely busy LaGuardia Airport.

Babes in bikinis?

Sure as hell beats babies in diapers —
not that he doesn't adore Maggie's daughters.

The thing is . . .

Dom is tired.

Not just from babysitting and work and
traffic and endless lines, lines, lines. No, it
goes deeper than that.

Bone tired.

No, deeper still.

Soul tired.

Try as he might to conjure enthusiasm
for the long-awaited trip to Sin City, Dom
suddenly isn't entirely certain he has the
energy to . . . sin.

He wonders, as he watches the flight
attendant's diamond engagement ring
twinkling like a beacon in the sunlight,
whether maybe it's a sign.

Maybe all of this — the married women,
the seeming abundance of gold bands and
diamond rings, even the baby stroller — is
a sign that it's time for Dom to settle
down.

After all, he's pushing thirty.

No Chickalini man has ever retained his
bachelorhood past his thirtieth birthday.
A scant few, like his uncle Cheech, have
reclaimed it after failed marriages, but nobody in the family has ever successfully
avoided the altar for a full three decades.

Dom, whose birthday is next week, always intended to be the first.

Especially considering the fact that he's never found anybody he can even remotely conceive of spending the rest of his life with.

But now . . .

Now, he can't help wondering whether somebody's trying to tell him something. Somebody upstairs. Somebody with a divine plan.

The Chickalini family is very big on divine plans. And on signs. Especially the women — namely, Dom's sisters, his grandmother, and his aunt Carm.

A dream about somebody you haven't seen in a while is a sign that you should call that person right away because something — good or bad — is going on with him or her.

An ATM machine that isn't working properly is a sign that you shouldn't be spending the cash you intended to get.

A rained-out baseball game is a sign that your team would have lost if they had played.

"But the other team is rained out, too," Dom always pointed out. "And somebody has to win."

Nobody ever had a satisfactory reply to

that, because signs, as Dominic's family tends to believe, aren't meant to be questioned. They're meant to be noted, and perhaps heeded as advice or warnings, as the case might be. Signs mean somebody upstairs is trying to tell you something, and you'd better listen.

Dom watches the flight attendant pouring champagne for a pair of cooing, cuddling newlyweds.

How does he know they're newlyweds?

For one thing, they're wearing matching rings and gazing into each other's eyes, something long-married couples rarely do, as far as Dom can tell. For another thing, the flight attendant tells them to enjoy their honeymoon.

Honeymoons, newlyweds, rings . . .

All signs?

You've got marriage on the brain, and you're being ridiculous, Dom scolds himself. *You're getting all worked up over nothing.*

He's going to stop looking for meaning in every little coincidence. After all, it's not as though there's a neon billboard flashing *Get Married* in his face, or his dream woman popping up in a wedding gown begging him to say *I do.*

Now *that* would be a sign.

Anything short of it is mere coincidence and not the slightest threat to the unprecedented achievement in Chickalini bachelorhood.

"All set, sir."

"Thank you." Eager to sit back and relax for the next five hours, Dom at last stashes his bag, steps around the flight attendant, and down the aisle . . .

Then stops short in front of his designated row.

There, in all her silken white glory, a halo of sunlight beaming through the window to cast her in an actual glow, is the most beautiful Catherine Zeta-Jones/ Angelina Jolie hybrid — and the most beautiful *bride* — he's ever seen.

Chapter Two

"What's the matter? Haven't you ever seen a bride before?"

There. It's out there. Mia couldn't help blurting the thought aloud at last — not to the staring businessman across the aisle, but to the newcomer who is standing over her, gaping, undoubtedly waiting for her to gather up her billowing skirt, her champagne on the tray table, and the contents of her bag, which are currently strewn all over the seat he's about to claim.

What's the matter? Haven't you ever seen a bride before?

It's such a great line. She just knew she'd get to blurt it out sooner or later.

The stranger seems to recover quickly from his shock or dismay or fear or whatever you'd call the strange look that came over his face when he saw her.

He snorts and retorts, "I've seen plenty of brides, but they're usually on cakes, not airplanes."

Mia's heart promptly skips a beat.

Why, she has no idea. There's just some-

45

thing about the guy's attitude . . . and the unflappable manner in which he responded to *her* attitude.

Major *'tude* is a fine, upstanding characteristic, in Mia's opinion.

So is sexiness.

No, she can't deny that the hottie factor is a biggie. And this guy's hottie factor is elevated. Mia's always been attracted to guys like him. Guys who look . . .

Well, like *her*.

His hair, like her own, is so dark it's virtually black. So are his exotic almond-shaped eyes — again, like her own. And his complexion has the same burnished olive glow as hers, deepened by the fleeting rays of July and August.

Mia can't help but think that if she were a man, this is what she might look like. If she were lucky.

Furthermore, he's as well dressed as . . . well, not as *she* is, naturally. Not at the moment. In fact, he's wearing jeans. But a quick evaluation of his black linen dress shirt, shoes, and carry-on briefcase tells Mia that he's fond of designer labels. Being no stranger to Prada or Dolce & Gabbana, she can relate.

He smells good, too.

Why don't more men wear cologne?

Mia finds herself wondering as she some-what grudgingly begins to toss everything on the adjacent seat back into her carry-on. *She* would never leave the house without spritzing her favorite perfume be-hind each ear, but most men don't bother. Or if they do, it's the cheap stuff you buy in a drugstore.

It strikes her that for everything she's found out about Derek in all the weeks they've been online buddies — his likes and dislikes, his quirks and hobbies, what he looks like, what he sounds like — she doesn't know what he smells like.

How could she never have realized that before?

How could she have promised to marry a man who for all she knows might have some kind of . . . scent?

What if Derek is partial to some god-awful cologne, or perpetually reeks of garlic, or —

"Ladies and gentlemen, we're ready to push back from the gate," a disembodied flight attendant's voice cuts into her thoughts. "In preparation for taxi and takeoff, please take your seats with seat belts securely fastened and make sure all of your belongings are stowed safely in the overhead bins or underneath the seat in front of you."

Mia, whose belongings somehow don't seem to fit back into the bag, hurriedly shoves a stray bottle of hair spray, a few rolls of Mentos, her hastily prepared prenup, the new issue of *People* magazine, and her reading glasses into the seat pocket.

The man standing in the aisle clears his throat loudly.

Irritated, Mia looks up to find him somehow looking put out, yet good-natured — as though he isn't accustomed to expressing dissatisfaction to people who are in his space. He must not be a New Yorker, she concludes, softening.

Well, we can't have everything in common, can we? Looks, attitude, great taste in clothes and fragrance . . . they were three for three until now.

"I'm sorry," she says, scooping up loose change, a pad of yellow Post-its, and her cell phone from his seat. "I didn't know anybody was going to sit there. In fact, there's an empty seat right up there . . ." She gestures at the row ahead. Hint, hint.

"I see it, but that's an aisle. I like the window."

"You're kidding."

"Would I kid a bride?"

She smirks, then points out helpfully,

"But in the window seat you have to make somebody — namely, said *bride* — move every time you need to get up. If you're on the aisle, you can just come and go whenever you want. I like the aisle."

"Then why don't you move up to that seat?"

"Because I already have an aisle right here. And all my stuff is here."

"Yeah, I can see that. Although something seems to be missing . . ."

"What?" She peers into her crammed bag, wondering how he can possibly know about her emery board.

"The groom."

"Oh, him!" She reluctantly stands to give him access to the row. "He's in Vegas."

All at once, she realizes that she's face-to-face — and practically hip-to-hip — with her seatmate. Face-to-face, hip-to-hip, and fully aware that he's all male. All dark, handsome, delectably scented male.

"The groom's starting the honeymoon without you?"

"No." Mia gulps. "Um, that's where we're getting married. In Vegas. As soon as I get there."

"So you aren't married yet?"

She swallows hard. "Nope."

49

Either she's imagining things, or his eyes are gleaming as he looks into hers with a provocative "Really."

Not *Really?* as in the polite nonquestion one poses when casually conversing, with the emphasis on the second syllable.

No, his *Really* is a statement, a somehow intimate expression of intrigue. Emphasis on the first syllable.

How can one insignificant little word sound so darned sexy?

And why is Mia, an imminent wife, finding a man who isn't her imminent husband sexy?

"No, Dominic, you need to put on more cheese. See? Like this."

Standing on a chair in the kitchen of his father's restaurant, soon-to-be-eight-year-old Dominic watched as Pop tossed several added handfuls of shredded mozzarella over the pie in progress.

"What next?" Dom asked, trying to sound interested. On this sweltering August day, he would much rather be out playing stickball or running through the stream of water from the open hydrant with his friends Eddie and Ricky from down the block.

But Pop had traditionally taken each of

his Chickalini offspring into the pizzeria kitchen at this age to learn the family business. Dom, the second-to-last of five children, should probably have been thrilled that it was finally his turn. But all he could think was that it was too bad the family business didn't involve running Yankee Stadium, or something more exciting than pizza.

"Now we bake it," Pop said, shoveling the finished pizza into the enormous brick oven on a long-handled paddle. "And we start the next one. You can do this one yourself. Do you think you know how?"

"I think." He eagerly accepted the ball of soft white dough. This — the kneading and stretching — was the fun part.

"Good," Pop said, taking a break to wipe the sweat from his receding hairline with a floury hand that still wore a gold wedding band, even after all these years as a widower.

Watching Dominic slap the dough out on the wooden board, Pop gulped some Pepsi straight from the can. He was wearing a white tank-style undershirt beneath his sauce-splattered apron, and his bare arms bulged impressively.

"Pop, how did you get all those muscles?" Dominic asked, thinking his father

51

looked almost like a superhero. "Do you have barbells?"

His father laughed. "I have this," he said, and gestured at the wooden paddle. "If you want to have big muscles like me, all you have to do is take over the business someday."

Dominic, who quickly decided he would much rather achieve big muscles the old-fashioned, superhero way, asked, "What about Pete?"

"Pete's in the army," Pop told him — as if he didn't know. Pop talked about it all the time. He was so proud of Pete that he even pinned a picture of him wearing his military uniform right above the cash register out front, for all his customers to see.

Dominic secretly liked to think that someday, Pop would gladly take down Pete's picture and replace it with one of Dominic, posing in his own uniform — the famous New York Yankee pinstripes. Yup, he was going to be the best third baseman the Yankees had ever had. Better, even, than Graig Nettles and Clete Boyer combined.

"When Pete gets out of the army, he'll come back home and take over the business for you, Pop. Right? That's what he always said."

His father shook his head. "I don't know about that anymore, Dom. He sounds pretty serious with his new girlfriend. I wouldn't be surprised if he married Debbi and didn't come back."

"Ever?" Horrified, Dominic stopped kneading the dough.

"Probably not if he's married."

"Married? Pete? To a girl? Forever?"

Pop burst out laughing. "What's wrong with married?"

"Pete's not like that," Dominic said, thinking of his beloved big brother, who shared his passion for baseball. Back when he was at Most Precious Mother High, he spent every waking moment playing on the school team, talking about baseball, practicing, or sitting in the Yankees' bleacher seats eating hot dogs and Cracker Jack with his kid brother Dominic.

It was always just the two of them. Heck, Pete never even had a girlfriend until now.

But what if Pop was right? Lately all Pete's letters home, which used to be full of interesting details about Germany, where he was stationed, seemed to mention this girl Debbi an awful lot.

She was a soldier, too. Dominic couldn't help but wonder what kind of a girl would be a soldier. He couldn't imagine either of his big sisters shaving their heads and wearing ugly uniforms. Nor could he imagine why Pete would want to be with a girl who would do that.

"It happens to the best of us sooner or later, you know," Pop said, nudging him and nodding toward the dough.

Obediently kneading again, Dominic asked, "What happens to the best of us?"

"Sooner or later we fall in love and get married. It happened to me, it's happening to Pete, and someday, it's going to happen to you."

"Huh-uh."

"Sure. You'll meet somebody who will take your breath away and make you wonder how you ever got along without her."

Startled by an odd choking sound, Dominic looked up.

He was horrified to see that Pop was crying.

He didn't know what to do. Pop never cried. Or maybe he did, but not when Dominic was around.

He knew that Pop had to be crying about Mommy, who had died a few years ago when she was giving birth to Ralphie.

What upset Dom more than anything

else was that he had been too little to remember her. He always felt left out whenever his older siblings talked about her. So he pretended to have his own memories, just so that he could participate in those emotional conversations.

Pop never did, though. Nobody talked about Mommy when he was around. Grandma Valerio and Aunt Carm forbade it. They said it was too hard on Pop. In fact, nobody talked about Mommy when they were around, either. They were Mom's mother and sister, and they would start crying hysterically if you even mentioned her name.

"Pop," Dominic said, awkwardly touching his father's bare forearm. His fingers left flour-dusted fingerprints on Pop's skin. "What's wrong?"

Pop shook his head and cried some more. Dominic was alarmed. Should he run home and get Nina? She would know what to do. Nina always knew what to do, about everything.

"It's just . . ." Pop made another choking sound. "She would have been so proud of you, Dominic. Look how you're almost eight years old now. She called you her little imp."

Dom nodded. He'd heard that before, lots of times.

Pop sniffled. "She always wondered what kind of mischief you were going to get yourself into when you grew up, at the rate you were going back then."

Dom smiled. His toddler antics were legendary in the Chickalini family. His older siblings said that no matter how naughty he was, Mommy just couldn't bring herself to punish him. She would try her hardest to remain stern, but somehow, Dominic managed to charm her right into a smile and a hug.

He could still work that magic with just about everybody. Every female in the family, anyway. Pop had no problem being stern or doling out punishment when it was deserved.

"Maybe she knows, Pop," he said now, wishing he could stop his father's tears. "Nina always says she's looking down on us from heaven. Nina says she sees everything."

Yes, Nina said that was why Dominic had better behave even when he thought nobody was going to catch him.

To his alarm, his father cried even harder. Dom moved the pizza dough out of the way so that the tears wouldn't plop into it and make it all soggy and salty.

He wondered what else he should do,

and could think of nothing but to pat his father's arm again.

"I'm sorry," Pop said, finally. "I just don't think I'll ever get over it."

"Over what?"

"Losing her. She was the love of my life, Dominic. There will never be anyone like her again."

"Sometimes people get married twice," Dominic said, thinking of his father's brother, Uncle Cheech. "Sometimes even three times."

"I'll never get married again," Pop said firmly, taking a handkerchief out of his back pocket and blowing his nose loudly. "I'll never take a risk like that again. Never."

"What risk?"

"Falling in love and then —" He broke off, shaking his head, wiping a fresh flood of tears.

"But . . . Pop, I thought you just said it happens to the best of us."

Suddenly, his father seemed to snap out of it. He took a deep breath, let it out, and straightened his shoulders. "It does happen to the best of us, Dom. That's not what I meant. I just meant . . . it already happened to me. With your mother. She was my one and only true love. Somebody like her doesn't come along more than once in a lifetime."

"Oh." Dominic was still a bit confused.

And anyway, he would much rather talk about baseball. He tried to think of the best way to change the subject.

"When your true love comes along, you'll know it," Pop was telling him.

I might know it, Dom thought, but no way am I going to do anything about it.

No way, no how. He didn't want to turn into a sad, lonely old guy crying in a pizzeria. He wanted to be a New York Yankee, a superhero . . . the kind of man who would never, ever cry in front of his son, or anybody else.

"Pop?" he asked, watching his father rub his red eyes with a handkerchief again.

"Yeah?"

"Who do you think was the best Yankees third baseman? Graig Nettles, or Clete Boyer?"

"How are we doing here?" the first-class flight attendant asks hurriedly, appearing in the aisle wearing an efficient expression. "Is there any trouble with the seating arrangement?"

"No," Mia and her aisle companion say

in unison as he slides past her into the window seat at last.

"Good. We're hoping for an on-time takeoff so every second counts."

As soon as the flight attendant steps away, Mia shakes her head and mutters, "I'll believe that when I see it."

"You'll believe what when you see it?"

There he goes again, engaging her in conversation when she'd just as soon mind her own business.

Mia has no choice but to turn toward him and explain, "I fly this airline a lot, and they're never on time. Not out of New York. Watch, we'll be fortieth in line for takeoff."

Fastening his seat belt, her seatmate says, "They can't help it. The air traffic here is insane."

"You fly here a lot?"

"I live here."

"You live here?" A New Yorker. She should have known. Everything about him is urbane.

"All my life. You?"

"All my life."

"Let me guess. Manhattan? Upper East Side?"

Flattered, not to mention reassured that her efforts to shed her borough accent have paid off, Mia admits, "Queens."

"Queens?" he echoes as the plane lurches into motion, backing away from the gate. "Which part?"

"Astoria."

"Astoria! You're kidding!"

"Would I kid a nonbride?"

He laughs.

So does she, noticing that the cleft in his chin deepens when he smiles, and that his teeth are white and even, and that his breath smells like spearmint. His mouth couldn't be more kissably fresh if he were in a toothpaste commercial.

Not that she has any intention of *kissing* him.

No, it's just an expression. Kissably fresh.

Like squeezably soft.

Mia wonders why on earth she's sitting here pondering toilet paper slogans, until it occurs to her that she should probably be wondering why on earth she's sitting here pondering kissing a total stranger.

But you weren't pondering kissing him, she reminds herself. *You were thinking about how you have no intention whatsoever of kissing him.*

"Why are you looking at me like that?" she asks him, before he can pose the same question to her. Only he's looking at her in stunned disbelief, while she's undoubtedly looking at him with blatant lust, darn it all.

"Because I've lived in Astoria all my life."

She can feel her blatant lust giving way to stunned disbelief. Yet another thing they have in common.

Just to be sure she heard him right, she asks, "You're from Astoria?"

He nods. "Just off Ditmars, on Thirty-third Street."

She knows exactly where that is — practically in the shadow of the elevated subway line that bisects Astoria.

She informs him, "I live just off Thirty-fourth Avenue." Which is on the opposite end of the neighborhood. And, quite literally, on the other side of the tracks.

But not figuratively.

Figuratively speaking, most of Astoria is on the right side of the tracks these days. In Mia's lifetime, sections of it have gone from being primarily industrial to immigrant-populated to ethnic/family-friendly to café-trendy. In fact, now it's all of the above.

That's why it made perfect sense when, rather than pick up and move to Manhattan after becoming an overnight multimillion-aire, Grandpa Junie simply bought the four-story building he'd lived in all his married life. It was a great investment. And, as Grandpa put it, he'd already pulled up his roots once in his life, when he left Sicily for America. He didn't want to go through that ever again. And for him and Nana Mona, Queens and Manhattan might just as well be on different continents.

So he bought the building, then hired a contractor to gut and renovate the whole place. In the end, Grandpa Junie and Nana Mona transformed their tiny two-bedroom top-floor apartment into a glorious duplex penthouse, with Mia occupying equally swanky quarters on the second floor.

Sometimes she thinks she would rather have moved into a place entirely her own on the other side of the Queensboro Bridge, but Grandpa Junie wouldn't hear of her being "that far away from home."

Nor would he pay for it.

"A respectable woman should live at home until she's married," he insisted, and what choice did Mia have but to acquiesce?

Okay, she could have moved out on her own anyway. But she keeps telling herself that would break Grandpa Junie and Nana Mona's hearts . . . not to mention her meager pocketbook. Without her grandfather's money, she has nothing.

And whose fault is that?

Yours, because you spend every penny you get, and then some.

Maybe, if she were to crack down, start saving, and cancel all her department store credit cards, she'd save enough money for an apartment across the bridge in Manhattan.

Well, someday, she'll do that. For now, her grandparents' place isn't half bad.

Anyway, she likes living near them, and she likes Queens. For her, it's home, after having spent the first part of her life roaming the country aimlessly with her footloose, quarreling parents.

"I've never seen you around the neighborhood before," her newly discovered almost-neighbor says, almost accusingly.

"I've never seen you, either." She frowns. "Then again, it's not like Astoria's a small town."

"Sure it is. It's exactly like a small town."

"There must be at least a hundred thousand people there."

"Probably, but I meant that it feels like a small town," Dom says, and she has to admit he has a point. "Hey, where did you go to elementary school?"

"All over the country until I moved to Astoria." That, of course, was when her parents split. Not just with each other, but with their only child. She pushes aside the painful memory, telling Dom, "From that point on, it was Saint Theresa's, all the way through high school. What about you?"

"Most Precious Mother."

So he's a fellow Catholic school kid. One more thing they have in common. Not that anyone's counting.

Five for five.

"I'm Dom Chickalini," he says, sticking out his hand.

"Mia Calogera." Her hand seems to tingle as his warm fingers wrap around her knuckles and squeeze briefly, then let go all too soon.

"Mamma Mia, a nice Italian girl," he says in an exaggerated accent.

"You sound like my grandfather."

"And my grandmother and my aunt Carm. They've been telling me to bring home a nice Italian girl for years now."

Her heart leaps. God knows why, but it does. "So why haven't you?"

"Because I never found anyone who was permanently captivated by the famous Chickalini charm."

"You're not married?"

He shakes his head.

"Engaged?"

"Nope."

Mia can feel an elated smile threatening to burst forth.

Wait a minute. Why is she getting all excited about his marital status . . . or the lack thereof?

Because *some* old habits — even relatively new old habits — die hard. That's why.

Well, you've already landed a husband, Mia. Remember?

Of course she remembers. Who could forget . . .

Derek. His name is Derek. Remember?

Of course she remembers.

She just forgot for a split second.

The split second when she happened to be staring, yet again, at Dom Chickalini's kissably fresh lips.

"Ladies and gentlemen, we are currently twenty-fourth in line for takeoff."

At the announcement, Mia shakes her head and looks at Dom. "What did I tell you?"

"You said we'd be fortieth. We're only twenty-fourth."

She sighs and leans back in her seat, reaching up to twist the knob that controls the air flow for her seat. "Twenty-fourth is bad enough. It's going to be forever before we take off."

"I guess it'll seem that way for you. When was the last time you saw your fiancé?"

Mia frowns, pretending there's a malfunction with the knob, hoping that if she doesn't answer, he'll forget he asked.

"Um, hello?" he says after a minute, waving a hand in her face.

"Hmm?"

"I asked when was the last time you saw your fiancé."

"Oh! I'm sorry, I guess I didn't hear you. The air is blasting." She indicates the overhead valve.

He nods. Waits. Then asks, "Aren't you going to answer my question?"

She debates the wisdom of asking, *What question?* There's evasive, and then there's half-witted. She doesn't want him to think she's the latter — not that it matters what he thinks of her.

Except that it does.

"I'm sorry," she says. "Of course I'm going to answer your question."

Pause.

"What was the question again?"

"When was the last time you saw your fiancé?" he asks with extraordinary patience.

That's it. He's got her trapped. There's nothing to tell him but the truth. Which she mutters into her cleavage. Which, come to think of it, is looking quite *va-va-voom* from this vantage point.

Wow. Carlotta at the bridal salon was right. This undergarment really does make her look voluptuous.

"You've got to be kidding!" Dom exclaims, and for a moment Mia assumes he's referring to her impressive cleavage. Then she remembers. And squirms.

"Kidding about what?"

"You've never met him before, have you?"

"Technically . . . no."

"Technically? What does that mean?"

"I've seen pictures and videos. And we've called and e-mailed and IM'd and text-messaged and video-phoned. So it's really like we've met hundreds of times."

"I don't think so."

Mia scowls, fighting back a disproportionate wave of anger. "What do you mean, you don't think so?"

"I mean, either you've met the guy you're going to marry, or you haven't. And if you haven't, then . . ."

"Then what?" she demands, embracing her inner shrew. "Then you think I'm some kind of . . . half-wit?"

"Half-wit?" he echoes with a grin.

There's nothing worse than somebody smiling in the face of Mia's disproportionate anger to really get her worked up.

"Why is that funny? This is serious."

"I know, but . . . half-wit." He laughs.

Okay, the only thing worse than somebody *smiling* in the face of Mia's disproportionate anger is somebody *laughing* in the face of Mia's disproportionate anger.

"Who says half-wit these days?" Dom wants to know.

"I guess only a half-wit," Mia says icily, turning away.

"Hey, wait." He puts a hand on her arm. "I'm sorry. I didn't mean to be rude."

The ice maiden melts.

"I was just . . . shocked, I guess. You know, that somebody like you would marry a total stranger."

"Somebody like me?"

He shrugs. "Yeah. You know . . ."

She's silent. Waiting. Wanting to watch him squirm.

Except that he doesn't squirm. He just says, "Someone who isn't hard up for a guy."

"What do you mean by that?"

"Look, you've obviously got a lot to offer . . . it's Mia, right?"

Both the compliment and the sound of

her name on his lip send an odd little *zing* through her.

But *zings* are forbidden for soon-to-be-married women.

Aren't they?

"I definitely have a lot to offer," she confirms, because Dom is waiting.

"So why aren't you marrying some guy you've already met?"

"It's complicated," she admits, wishing she could spill the whole story. But if he thinks she's crazy now, he'll really think so if she tells him what's really going on.

Better to change the subject to something safe.

Like . . .

"So what do you think they'll be serving us for lunch?"

Airline food? That's the best you can do, Mia?

But like any masculine man Mia has ever known, Dom lights up at the mention of a meal. "Steak, I hope. Even though it will probably be the size of a brussels sprout."

"Huh?"

"The portion. You know, they always serve such tiny portions of food on planes, and I'm beyond hungry."

"Yeah, me, too."

"For what?"

"Steak would be good."

He laughs.

"What's so funny?"

"I once got into a fight over red meat with a woman I was dating."

Mia can't help asking, "What happened?"

"Long story."

She gestures out the window at the stationary backdrop featuring the distant runway. "I'm not going anywhere for the next seven or eight hours."

"In that case . . . it's funny now, but it was brutal at the time. I had this nice dinner date planned . . ." He shakes his head. "My friend Maggie was beside herself. How was I supposed to know Julie was a vegetarian?"

Maggie? Julie?

"Is one of them your girlfriend?" Mia asks casually. At least, she hopes she sounds casual. Her inner shrew is writhing with illogical jealousy.

He laughs. "No, Maggie's my friend — married with two kids now and a third on the way, thanks to me. And it had better be a boy."

"She's expecting your baby?"

"No!" He laughs. Hard. "I meant, she's married thanks to me. She only met her husband because she was trying to fix up

70

his friend Julie with me. Maggie thinks she knows everything, and she was convinced she'd found my perfect match."

"But she was wrong?"

"Big-time wrong. Julie and I couldn't have been more opposite. We both knew it the second we met. But something good came out of that whole disaster."

"What?"

"Maggie married Charlie," he says in a *but of course* tone.

"Oh, right! And Charlie is . . ."

"Julie's friend who thought I was right for Julie. They hooked us up at *Matchmocha, Matchmocha,* and —"

"You mean the computer dating café in Manhattan?"

He nods. "You've heard of it?"

"Hasn't everyone?" A few years ago, *Matchmocha, Matchmocha* was right up there on the local trend-o-meter with no-carb bread and the Kabbalah. But Mia hasn't heard any of her friends mention it lately.

"Yeah, well, I'll never be setting foot in that place again," Dom says with the conviction of one whose *matchmocha* has left behind a sour taste.

"Wait a minute, *you* tried computer dating? *Mr. Who on Earth Would Marry a Total Stranger?*"

"That was over five years ago. And I *dated* a complete stranger. I didn't *marry* her."

"But you can see why somebody might?"

"Not really," he says cheerfully. "So that's how you found your fiancé? On the Internet?"

"No!" Mia says, as though he's suggested that she was trolling the Lincoln Tunnel traffic for johns.

"Then how did you two *meet?*" Judging from his tone, he uses the last word loosely.

"Through a mutual, um . . ."

"Friend?"

"Yes," she lies, thinking there are some things Dom doesn't need to know. Including the fact that she met Derek on the Internet via a mutual interest in growing epiphytic orchids.

In fact, there are many things Dom just doesn't need to know.

What is she doing sitting here spilling her life story to someone she's never seen before and will never see again?

Maybe, Mia concludes, looking into Dom's dark gaze, that's just the point. Maybe she just needs to confide in somebody about the enormous step she's about to take.

And maybe there are some things you can share with a total stranger far more comfortably than with those who know you best. Or those who have other plans for you.

"Hey, we're moving," Dom exclaims as the plane jolts into motion.

It rolls all of a few yards forward and stops again.

"It's going to be an hour," Mia tells him, watching a distant jet career past the window en route to the sky.

"Then I'm all ears," Dom returns with an easy grin. "Why are you getting married in Vegas to a man you've never met?"

Why, indeed?

With a sigh, Mia says, "It's a long story . . ."

Chapter Three

"You're not saying anything."

"That's because I'm speechless," Dom informs his seatmate, and watches her pop a forkful of steamed, glazed baby carrots into her mouth as though she hasn't a care in the world. "Is there any more to the story or is that it?"

She chews, swallows, looks as though she's going to add a couple of twists, then shrugs and says glibly, "That's it."

"That's one hell of a story."

Long, too. Just like she said. Long enough to take up the near-hour they waited on the runway, continuing right on through taxi, takeoff, beverage service, and most of the meal.

It wouldn't have been so lengthy if she hadn't started way back at the beginning — as in, with her birth.

But Mia Calogera obviously likes to talk. About herself, at least. Whether she likes to talk about other things remains to be seen. She doesn't strike Dom as being particularly self-centered, but you never know.

"So in a nutshell, what you're telling me is that if you're not married before your grandfather's eighty-fifth birthday in October, you'll be cut out of his will completely."

"Right," she says with a firm nod.

She'll be disinherited from the vast fortune her grandfather won a few years back. At the time, he was the single biggest lottery winner in New York history.

Dom is pretty sure he vaguely remembers reading about that in the *Post*, possibly because the old guy was from his neighborhood. He recalls the stock lottery winner photo — beaming winner flanked by his beaming wife, smiling lottery officials in suits, everyone posing behind an oversized check.

At least, he thinks he remembers it. All lottery stories are more or less the same, aren't they? Your classic rags-to-riches, only-in-America tale. Maybe he remembers her grandfather's story; or maybe it was some other overnight millionaire's.

Whatever. The bottom line is that the overnight millionaire's granddaughter has somehow worked her way under his skin. He feels something for Mia, and he isn't entirely certain it's just pity — although pity is certainly at least part of it.

He can't help but feel sorry for the classic poor little rich girl, who actually started out as a poor little poor girl.

She grew up in her grandparents' blue-collar household after becoming a temporary spoil of her parents' bitter divorce. She laughed when she described how they fought a bitter custody battle more out of a desire to beat each other than out of parental love, but Dominic didn't miss the pain that overshadowed the irony in her dark eyes. Especially when she described how her mother handed Mia over to her grandparents to raise, then left town . . . and how her father didn't bother to come find her. He was too busy setting up a new life on the West Coast with a new wife who had three daughters of her own and didn't want a fourth.

"My mom said she just needed a break," Mia told Dom with an unmistakable catch in her voice.

The motherless little boy in him wanted to tell her he knows what it was like for her.

But then, he doesn't know. Not really. His own mother didn't willingly leave him behind. His vague memories of her loving presence are enough to assure him that she would never in a million years have done that.

"I figured a 'break' would take maybe a few days," Mia told him. "Or even a week. I didn't expect it to outlive my entire childhood."

But the *woe-is-me* tone and expression didn't last long. As far as Dom can see, she's right back to her buoyant self.

At least, he assumes she's typically buoyant. Maybe that's just today, which is, after all, her wedding day. All brides are buoyant on their wedding days. He's certainly seen enough of them lately to know.

Yes, and of all the showers, engagements, and weddings he attended these last few months, none of the couples were getting married for any reason other than good old-fashioned love. In Dominic's world — which is almost literally right around the corner from Mia's world — people meet, fall in love, and after a year or two, get married.

He can't help but feel incredulous at her boldly shallow deviation. Incredulous, and inexplicably annoyed.

"So what you're saying is that this came out of the clear blue sky?"

"More or less."

"You had no idea what your grandfather wanted you to do until now?"

"Well, he's been saying it for a few years,

but I never really realized he was serious until now. I never thought he was going to take matters into his own hands if I didn't land a husband on my own. I figured he might let me slide."

"But he won't?"

"No way."

"But I still can't believe you're going to marry a total stranger just for money," he tells her, finally cutting into his untouched steak, which, as he predicted, isn't much larger than a brussels sprout and will barely take the edge off his raging appetite.

"It isn't like that," she protests, reaching for her water glass.

"What do you mean? What is it like? You said it yourself. You said your grandfather is going to disinherit you if you don't —"

"I know what I said. But that wasn't what I meant, entirely." She drinks some water.

He waits for her to finish — the water, and her explanation.

But when she sets the glass down, she's apparently finished. With everything. Her half-eaten meal, which she pushes away, and the conversation.

He's forced to ask, "What did you mean? Is this guy or is he not a total stranger? More or less," he adds, acknowledging their different definitions of the phrase *total stranger.*

"Maybe I've never met him, but he isn't a total stranger," she insists. "I probably know more about him than most brides know about their grooms."

He quirks an eyebrow at her.

"All right, well, more than *some* brides know. And the thing is, this is the least complicated solution to the problem. Because if I weren't marrying Derek today, I'd be marrying somebody else very soon anyway. Somebody . . . scary."

"Who?"

"Some guy my grandfather is planning to find in Sicily."

"And I thought my family was wacky," Dom mutters. "Who is this guy?"

"Who knows? Whoever he can find, I guess, who happens to be single and willing. I just found out that's why he's over there."

"To scope out single guys?" He shakes his head, grinning at the image of a little old Italian man not unlike Uncle Cheech, cruising the Italian singles bars in search of eligible bachelors.

"Hey, don't laugh. I'm totally serious. He left last week. I thought he was on vacation, visiting his brothers. But then the other day my grandmother slipped and told me that he's setting up a match for me."

Dom, no stranger to being set up on disastrous dates by well-meaning loved ones, can certainly relate to her dismay. "Can't you just say thanks but no thanks, you'll find your own dates?"

"He's not arranging a date. He's arranging a *marriage*. That's how it's done in the old country."

"Maybe a hundred years ago . . ."

"My grandparents met that way. Their parents arranged the marriage. And that wasn't a hundred years ago. And my second and third cousins back in Sicily, that's how they all get married."

"Well, you're not in Sicily."

"It doesn't matter where I am, it's how my grandfather thinks."

"You can still just say no."

"You don't know Grandpa Junie."

"Grandpa *Junie?*" he cuts in.

"For Junior. His real name's Carmine. Anyway, he's very old-fashioned Italian." She sighs. "You just don't get it. I wouldn't expect you to."

Dominic, who is also no stranger to old-fashioned Italian relatives — some of them also named Carmine or Junior — gets it.

At least, that part. "Hey, I totally under-stand. Your grandfather's a stubborn con-trol freak."

She snorts. "That's like saying Bill Gates is comfortable."

Dom persists, "So he wants you to get married to some guy you've never met be-fore, right?"

"Right."

"And you don't want to?"

"Not —"

"Tell me if I'm wrong here, but . . . aren't you, in fact, getting married to some guy you've never met before?" He feels — and sounds — like a smug prosecutor badgering a hapless defendant on the stand.

"Yes," she says firmly, sounding not the least bit defensive, much less hapless, "but *I* chose him."

Ah.

There's the difference. She's marrying *her* stranger, not Grandpa Junie's stranger.

Dom can't help but note that the apple didn't fall far from the control freak tree.

She smiles and tilts her head at him. "You think I'm crazy, don't you?"

Yes. I think you're stark, raving mad. But that's your business. I'm just a captive audience from here to Vegas.

81

"Nah, I don't think you're crazy," he lies, poised to bite into his steak at last. "Who am I to judge what a person does for love? I mean, cold hard cash?"

She smirks. "It's a *lot* of money, Dom."

For a moment, he's too struck by her use of his name to hear the actual words that come before it.

Nothing about this — not the setting, not the conversational topic, not her tone — is the least bit romantic.

Yet her calling him Dom somehow signals a new note of — well, not intimacy, exactly. More like . . . casual familiarity. As though they've known each other for much longer than a scant hour or so.

Then the rest of what she's saying sinks in. The part before the almost-intimate, casually familiar *Dom*. The part that tells him he doesn't really know her at all . . . and probably wouldn't want to.

He sets down his fork, having momentarily lost his appetite. She doesn't strike him as a coldhearted, money-hungry manipulator, but she sure as hell sounds like one.

It angers him. It shouldn't, because why should he care what motivates an utterly frivolous stranger to get married?

And she is utterly frivolous, and she is a

stranger, and you'd do well to remember that.

"I'm sure it is a lot of money," he says curtly.

She looks a little taken aback by his tone. "Look, it isn't just that he'd be cutting off my inheritance. He'd be cutting off my salary, too."

"Your salary? You work for him?"

She nods.

"What do you do?" he asks, wondering if there's some kind of family business she failed to mention. He could have sworn she said her grandfather was a retired subway conductor before he won the lottery.

While quenching an apparently urgent thirst, she mumbles something into her glass.

"What? I can't hear you when you're underwater."

She lifts her head. "I said, I'm a personal assistant."

"For who?"

"My grandmother."

His irritation promptly gives way to amusement. He can't help but picture a little old Italian lady not unlike his own grandmother lounging poolside in sunglasses with a martini in one hand and a cell phone clasped to her ear.

"What's so funny?"

"Is your grandmother that big a lottery celebrity that she needs a personal assistant?"

"It isn't like that. Nana Mona needs me."

"She needs you to — what? Keep the paparazzi at bay? Schedule photo shoots and lunches at Sardi's?"

"Very funny."

"*I* think so." Still chuckling, he realizes she hasn't even cracked a smile. His own fades. "Look, I'm sorry. I just don't see you as the personal assistant type."

"Is that a compliment?"

"Definitely."

"In that case, thank you. I guess."

"You're welcome."

"If I'm not the personal assistant type, what am I?"

The control freak type. The crazy lunatic bride type. The not-my-type type, that's for sure.

He just shrugs, and finally takes a bite of his steak, saying around a mouthful, "I don't know. I'm not very good at figuring people out."

People meaning *women.*

If he could figure them out, he'd probably be married by now. Or at least have sustained a monogamous adult relationship for more

84

than a couple of months.

And yet back there in the airport, you were telling yourself it might be time to settle down?

Dom shakes his head vigorously, as if to rid his brain of that notion.

"What's wrong?" Mia asks, clutching his sleeve. "Is your steak rancid?"

"What?"

"You look like you just had a taste of something really awful."

He can't help but laugh at that. "No, the steak is great. All three milligrams of it."

"Then what . . . ?"

"Never mind."

Staring up at the four-story brick apart- ment building, eleven-year-old Mia thought wistfully of the ramshackle little house on the Gulf of Mexico that she had called home for the last year of her life.

This place was somewhat nicer and much, much larger, but she missed the beach already.

Mom said there was a beach here in New York City, too, but she must be lying.

It wouldn't be the first time.

She lied for years when she promised Mia that the terrible screaming fights she and Daddy had every single day were normal. That they didn't mean Mia's parents were going to get divorced.

Yeah, right.

Mia shivered in her thin blue windbreaker, the warmest jacket she had. Daddy had bought it for a dime at a church rummage sale when they were living in West Virginia. Now the sleeve cuffs were well above her wrists, but there was no money for new clothes. Not even new used clothes. What money they had saved had been spent on the divorce lawyers.

"Mia, brush your hair out of your eyes," Mom told her, reaching for what looked like a row of doorbells beside the door. "And remember, if Grandpa and Nana ask where Daddy is, just say he's away on business."

"What kind of business?" Mia asked. Her father didn't even have a job, unless you counted fishing.

"It doesn't matter. Just go along with whatever I say, Mia. Got it?"

"Got it." Mia didn't know where her father was, exactly, and she had a feeling he didn't know where they were, either. He hadn't slept at home in several months. Mia had seen him only in court, as he and her mother fought bitterly over her.

Her mother had won, finally. But she

didn't seem very happy about it for very long. The next thing Mia knew, they were packing their meager belongings into duffel bags and leaving town.

"What about Daddy?" Mia protested. "I'm supposed to spend Saturdays with him. He'll worry when I'm not here."

"If he even notices, he'll get over it," was her mother's disconcerting reply.

"Well, when will we be back?"

"Soon," Mom said vaguely.

Now, watching her mother press the button marked 4G, Mia reached into her pocket and felt around for the last morsel of cheese from the free samples she and Mom scrounged at a deli after they got off the bus at the Port Authority this morning. The endless, exhausting trip from Alabama had taken two days, and every penny they had.

Not that they'd ever had much money. Nor had Mia's vagabond life ever been settled, as her parents worked odd jobs to support them for a while before moving on.

Still, this latest move was different for two reasons.

One was that Daddy wasn't with them.

The other was that Mia was about to meet her mother's parents for the very first time.

Nibbling the cheese, Mia wondered what they'd be like, and what they'd think of her.

She hadn't even known she had grandparents until a few years ago, when Mom got mad at Daddy and dragged Mia to a phone booth, where she made a collect call to Queens, New York.

From her mother's end of the conversation, Mia pieced together that she wanted her father to send her enough money to live on. But he didn't want to send the money; he wanted to send bus tickets to Queens. Mia's mother slammed down the phone, and never mentioned calling her parents again.

She didn't even call before they got on the bus yesterday. Mia thought she probably should have. But her mother had been in such a bad mood lately, crying and ranting about Daddy, that she didn't dare say much of anything.

"Who is it?" a man's voice crackled abruptly, and Mia was startled until she realized the row of doorbells contained an intercom.

"It's me. Terry. And I've got Mia with me."

For a long time, there was silence.

Mia shifted her weight from one tattered sneaker to the other, shivered in the chilly

November dusk, and wished she had something to eat.

Then the door buzzed and made a clicking sound.

Mom reached out and opened it. "Come on," she said, ushering Mia into the drafty vestibule. "Let's go."

They rode a rickety elevator up to the fourth floor. Mia hadn't been in an elevator since they lived in a high-rise building in the Chicago projects back when she was in kindergarten.

When the doors opened, Mom led the way down the dimly lit hall lined with doors. She had grown up here, Mia knew, and she tried to picture her mother as a little girl in this place. She couldn't do it. Her mother had wrinkles, a smoker's cough, and straggly gray hair. It was impossible to imagine that she had ever been young.

When they reached the door marked 4G, it was closed.

"You'd think he'd be waiting," Mom muttered. "He knew we were on our way up."

She knocked.

After a few moments, the door opened. An elderly man stood there in a worn sweater and baggy trousers.

He reached out awkwardly, and Mia

watched her mother step into his brief embrace.

"Where's Ma?" she asked, her voice sounding oddly hoarse.

"She's at novena. Is this Mia?"

He knew her name! She was surprised.

"It's nice to meet you, sir," she said meekly.

"Sir? You can call me Grandpa." His tone was gruff, but Mia noticed that his eyes were kind. At least, when they were looking at her.

He turned back to her mother. "I have two questions for you, Terry, before this goes any further."

Her mother shrugged. "Go ahead."

"Where's Frank?"

"He's away on business."

"What kind of business?" her father asked dubiously, and Mia wondered why her mother hadn't mentioned the divorce.

"Is that your second question?" Mom asked. "Because you only get two."

"No. My second question is, are you planning on staying this time? Because if you're here for help, I'll help you on one condition. That you stay. At least until you get your life together."

Mia held her breath, waiting for her mother's reply.

"She's *staying*," her mother said, and Mia found herself being propelled forward, over the threshold into a tiny, unfamiliar apartment that smelled of something delicious. Something that made her all too aware that she hadn't eaten a regular meal in days. She felt faint with hunger, and it was difficult to focus on what her mother and grandfather were saying.

"What? where are you going, Terry?"

"I'll be back for her," Mom said, already putting down one of the duffel bags and giving her a big hug. A fierce hug. A hug that scared her.

Mia hugged back, her heart pounding, until her mother slipped out of her grasp.

"Mom," she protested, "where are you going?"

"I'll be back," her mother said, backing away. "I have to go deal with something, and then I'll be back."

"Terry! What are you doing? You're leaving her here?"

"I'll be back," Mia's mother promised over her shoulder, almost running down the corridor. "I just need a break."

And then she was gone.

Dominic Chickalini loves women as much as the next red-blooded man. He just doesn't understand them.

Especially this one.

And he doesn't want to marry one any time in the near future.

He'd think "especially this one" again, but luckily, Mia Calogera is decidedly off the market.

If she weren't, he can almost see how he might find himself tempted to date her. She isn't just gorgeous, she's fascinating. Far more so than your run-of-the-mill ravishing beauty. Your run-of-the-mill ravishing, *greedy* beauty.

Yes, if Mia were single —

She's still single, he reminds himself.

Well, if she were planning to *stay* single for longer than the next few hours, Dom would probably be asking her for her cell phone number.

And then what?

You'd be asking for trouble, that's what.

"You still haven't told me what type I am," Mia informs him. "What would you think I did for a living if I hadn't just told you?"

"I don't know, actress? Fashion magazine editor? Sales rep, like me?"

"You think we're the same type?"

"I think you're good at charming people."

"Which means you must be good at that, too."

"Oh, I am. Or so I hear." He takes a bite of his twice-baked sour cream and chive potato, which constitutes more than half the portion, and asks, "What about love?"

"Huh? Where did that come from?" She's looking at him as though he just pulled a rabbit out of his seat pocket.

"The question?"

When she nods, he shrugs and admits, "I'm just curious. I know it's none of my business, but I can't help wondering. Do you love this total stranger you're marrying?"

"No. But that doesn't matter," she adds before he can pounce. "It's not like this is happily ever after or anything. It's most likely just going to be a temporary marriage."

"Temporary?"

"After a few years, we'll probably just get divorced and go our separate ways."

"How can you be so casual about marriage and divorce?"

"Because I figure this is going to be pretty much platonic."

"Pretty much platonic?" Dominic echoes. "Either it's platonic, or it isn't. No middle ground there."

"What I mean is, I'm going into it

thinking it's platonic, but someday I might fall in love with him and we might want to stay married. Which would be great."

"Well," he says, fighting a wave of insane, irrational jealousy, "isn't that a big chance to take?"

"It's not taking a chance at all," she says with an enigmatic smile, toying with her empty fork. "I'm going into this in a very levelheaded way."

Dom, while he would most definitely beg to differ, manages to remain silent.

"My grandparents didn't marry for love, and look at them now. Fifty years later, they're still married."

"That's great," Dom says sincerely, having attended almost as many family golden anniversary celebrations as he has weddings.

"Meanwhile, my parents were crazy about each other from the second they met. It was love at first sight. Head over heels. And look at them now. They hate each other's guts."

"I'm sorry."

"Me, too."

"But it isn't always that way. My parents were crazy about each other from the second they met, too."

"And they're still together?"

They would be, Dominic thinks. He might not cry about her anymore — not that Dom knows of, anyway — but Pop still misses his late wife every day of his life.

Before he can force an explanation past the painful lump in his throat, Mia is saying, "Look, maybe your experience has been different, but watching my parents' marriage fall apart was enough to convince me that I was never going to do what they did. You know," she says in response to his quizzical look, "think I was madly in love, and get married. Doesn't it make more sense to find a potential mate and evaluate their qualities from afar, on paper, as opposed to in person? That way, feelings can't get things all mucked up."

Dominic can't help but admire her skewed logic. Feelings certainly can get things all mucked up, as she so eloquently put it.

In fact, his dating philosophy has always been to keep feelings out of the mix. Deep feelings, that is. Friendly camaraderie is good; physical attraction is great. Anything more profound has always sent him running in the opposite direction.

"So you chose this guy because he seems right on paper?" he asks Mia.

95

"No! Well, kind of. I mean, we're friends. We e-mail all the time." Judging by her vaguely sheepish expression, even *she* seems to think that sounds lame.

"And you're marrying him because you need to preserve your inheritance — and your salary. With no expectations whatsoever of any emotion entering into it."

"Exactly." She nods so vigorously that her wedding veil just misses getting snagged on the tines of her fork.

"Does he know this?"

"Of course he knows this. What kind of a person do you think I am?"

He wishes she would stop tempting him with questions like that. He really does.

"Derek and I have *both* agreed to a platonic marriage, unless we decide otherwise after we meet."

"What does he get out of it, besides a cut of your money? I hope you've got a prenup."

She pats the seat pocket where she earlier stashed some of the contents of her bag. "Of course I've got a prenup. I had it drawn up yesterday."

"So he doesn't get a cut of your money?"

"He gets *some*. But he also gets to move to New York, which he's always wanted to do. He lives in the middle of nowhere."

Terrific. "Where in the middle of no-where?"

"Iowa?"

"You're asking *me?*"

"No, I just . . . it's either Iowa or Idaho, in a suburb of some semibig city that has an 'oi' in it. I've never been there."

"Is it Boise? Des Moines?"

"One of those." She shrugs. "I know it sounds crazy, but I've never visited him and I didn't pay much attention to his mailing address. We mostly e-mail and call each other."

"What does he do?"

"He's an actor."

"In *Boise?*"

"I know. That's why he wants to come to New York. But right now, he's flat broke. So this is definitely good for him."

"And you hooked up with this" — *opportunistic loser* — "guy, how?"

"Does it really matter to you?"

It does. It shouldn't, but it does.

Still, Dominic decides to leave well enough alone. Her marriage — and her mo-tives — are her business. He would be wise to keep his opinions to himself for the dura-tion of the flight, and stick with safe topics.

Like, say, religion, or politics. Or airline food.

"Did you ever see such a small cut of steak?" he asks, having polished off his and hopefully eyeing the remainder of hers. "The first thing I'm going to do when I get to Vegas is hit the buffet at my hotel."

"Yeah? Where are you staying?"

"Mandalay Bay. How about you?"

"I have no idea. Derek said he reserved a bridal suite somewhere."

"Bridal suite? I thought this marriage was going to be platonic."

Although "pretty much platonic" were her exact words, leaving the door open for all sorts of uninviting scenarios.

Mia shrugs. "Who knows? It's still my wedding night. I'm sure it'll be fabulous no matter what."

"I'm sure it will."

Yes. Because it's her wedding night, and wedding nights are always pretty much romantic . . . aren't they?

Having never experienced a wedding night of his own, Dom has no real frame of reference. But he'd be willing to bet that the best-laid platonic plans go awry when the groom whisks the bride off to a bridal suite in the world's most decadent city.

You met her, what — two hours ago? And you're all but cringing at the thought of her with another man? And not just any man . . . her husband?

Two hours?

Two hours is nothing.

Two hours is . . .

It's two hours longer than her groom-to-be has had with her, that's what it is.

This is ridiculous. You're trying to one-up the guy she's about to marry? You feel like this is some kind of competition? Like you're in the running for something? For her heart?

She doesn't even believe in love, for Pete's sake. What kind of woman doesn't believe in love? Most single women, in Dom's experience, are desperate to fall in love and get married.

That's precisely what's wrong with all of the women he's ever dated, in his opinion.

Now along comes this breath of fresh air, this woman who's not only off-limits to him, but who is the total opposite of every female he's ever met . . . no wonder he's smitten.

Safely smitten.

That's the beauty of it. He can sit here and flirt and fantasize all he wants, but when the plane lands in Vegas, they're going to go their separate ways no matter what.

He'll head off in search of buffets, beers,

and babes in bikinis, and she'll march down the aisle with some undeserving starving actor who's about to hit the Vegas jackpot of a lifetime.

Chapter Four

"Thanks for helping me with my stuff," Mia tells Dom as they emerge from the Jetway into the airport gate area.

"No problem."

Funny how abruptly the intimacy they shared back there on board the plane has evaporated. It's like coming out of a cozy movie theater after a great, romantic movie date into the glaring lights of a crowded lobby. The mood is irrevocably shattered; the man beside Mia might just as well be a . . . okay, a total stranger.

Mia finds herself looking around the airport; looking anywhere other than up at him. The place is an absolute zoo.

There are rows of slot machines everywhere she looks, and the people here are a more eclectic bunch than one might find anywhere, even in New York. There are middle-aged women in polyester, redneck trucker types, glamorous movie star types, families with young children, senior citizens traveling in packs, obvious newlyweds, clergymen. She isn't even the only one here wearing full wedding attire, although the others are accompanied by grooms in tuxedos.

"Do you want me to carry this down to the baggage claim for you?" Dom is asking at her side.

She eyes his own fairly large garment bag, which he had stowed on board. "Did you check any luggage yourself?"

"No, but I can go with you if you —"

"No, you don't have to go out of your way. I'm fine," she assures him quickly, reaching for her carry-on bag. After all, Derek will be meeting her by the baggage claim. Derek in his white tuxedo with his bad-luck yellow orchid.

"Well, at least let me —"

"No, really, I've got it." She wrestles the bag from his grasp and attempts to sling it effortlessly over her shoulder.

That feat might be easily accomplished if she were wearing street clothes, and if the bag weren't bulging with items from the seat pocket and so heavy she can't help but wonder if somebody stashed a pile of books — or a barbell — in it when she wasn't looking.

"Look, just let me help you," Dom says, uneasily watching her struggle.

"I'm fine," she repeats through clenched

teeth. "You go ahead. Have a great time in Vegas."

He hesitates. "Are you sure?"

"Positive." She smiles cheerfully at the man with whom she just shared her deepest, darkest secrets, along with a lot of other miscellaneous information. She couldn't help it. It was a long flight, and he was surprisingly easy to talk to, when he wasn't interrogating her about her upcoming nuptials.

They spent the remainder of the flight discussing their families — well, her grandparents, and so many relatives of his that Mia can't help but wonder if he's related to half of Astoria. It really is a small world. As it turns out, his father owns Big Pizza Pie, a pizzeria just off Ditmars Boulevard. She used to go there when she was drowning her postdivorce sorrows in triple-cheese sausage pies. Whole pies.

"I wonder if I ever waited on you," Dom said when she told him she'd been there.

She didn't tell him that her pizza days are long over. If he had ever waited on her, he wouldn't remember, because he wouldn't recognize her.

And if he had ever waited on her, she would most definitely remember, because he's possibly the best-looking man she's ever seen.

Instead, she asked why a big-shot businessman like him ever rolled up his sleeves in a pizzeria.

"Sometimes I have no choice. It's a family place . . . Pop still owns it, my sister Nina's husband, Joey, runs it, and we all have to help out when it gets busy," he explained, and she found herself envying him.

It sounded like he had the kind of big happy family she'd always dreamed about. He was full of anecdotes about his siblings and nieces and nephews, and his friends and their children, which led her to ask him if he planned on having a wife and children of his own someday.

"Me? Nah. Not any time soon, anyway," was the disappointing reply.

Disappointing merely because he would make a great father. A terrific husband, too, she thought illogically . . . as if she had any way of knowing that. Or any business even thinking about it, for that matter.

When you come right down to it, she and Dom Chickalini were merely strangers getting to know each other on a plane, and now they're strangers *off* a plane, which makes a farewell necessary, imminent — and permanent.

Might as well just get it over with, Mia

tells herself, feeling oddly reluctant to say good-bye.

If she weren't about to get married, she would be all-out attracted to a man like Dom.

And she has a feeling that he might be attracted to her, as well. Unless it was her imagination, some major chemistry was on the verge of bubbling up between them back there on the plane.

Now here she is, feeling quite unsuitably wistful.

She should be eager to go meet Derek and get the next chapter of her life under way.

Yet all she can think is that she'll never know whether Dom's neighborhood basketball team wins their big game next weekend, and whether Dom's pregnant-again friend Maggie has another girl or the boy her husband is hoping for, and whether Dom loses his shirt at the craps table, as he claims to have done in the past.

None of it matters, really. At least, none of it *should* matter to a woman who's about to marry another man.

But Maggie had been caught up in Dom's world for a little while there, almost feeling as though she were a part of it.

Or at least, as though she *wanted* to be a part of it. Or something like it.

That's not about to happen. She knows Derek doesn't have much family. Just a mother who doesn't have much to do with him, and a much-older half sister who lives somewhere in the South.

Mia tells herself she should be grateful there are no meddling in-laws in her immediate future, but she can't help feeling a little wistful. She does have her grandparents . . . but no siblings. And her parents might as well be casual acquaintances for all she sees of them.

So what else is new? Come on, snap out of it, Mia.

She needs to get Dom out of her system fast if she's going to go to her wedding with a clear, level head.

Right. The quicker you get away from him, the better.

She wonders if simply walking away will really do the trick. If she walks away, she might start focusing on what she might be missing.

It's almost like spotting a delicious raspberry turnover — Mia's all-time favorite dessert — in a bakery case when she hasn't had a treat in ages and is trying to lose the few pounds that occasionally creep back on.

If she summons her willpower and walks away from the bakery, she invariably starts to dwell on the turnover. She thinks about it all day, all night, the next morning . . .

At the oddest times, she finds herself dreaming about biting into triangular layers of flaky pastry, a sprinkling of crunchy golden sugar on top, luscious fresh fruit filling . . .

The turnover comes to symbolize the ultimate golden prize, and she obsesses about it until she can no longer live with such cruel deprivation.

The next thing she knows, she's wolfing down an entire boxful of bakery raspberry turnovers. Or worse yet, substituting an entire boxful of cheap cellophane-packaged snacks because the bakery is closed or the turnovers are sold out.

The last thing Mia wants to do is go into her marriage feeling deprived of anything.

No, actually, the *last last* thing she wants to do is to find herself satisfying an insatiable carnal craving with the male human equivalent to cheap cellophane-packaged snacks.

So what's the solution?

Fuji, her diet guru, taught her to allow herself a little taste of a treat once in a while, just to curb her craving. He told her to go ahead and buy a turnover, take a big bite, savor it . . . and then toss the remainder into the nearest garbage can.

It isn't easy, but it somehow does the trick.

"Uh . . . are you okay?" Dom asks, and she realizes she's standing absolutely still amid the airport bustle, staring off into space.

"Oh! I'm fine!"

"Are you sure?"

"Positive!" she says brightly, noting that his lips are precisely the color of luscious raspberry filling.

"Well . . . okay. I guess I'll see you, then."

"Right. I'll see you. It was nice talking to you."

"You, too."

"No," Nina said, shaking her head adamantly. "Absolutely no way."

"Nina, come on," fourteen-year-old Dominic protested. "Don't be such a meanie."

"A meanie?" His older sister raised her eyebrows in disbelief. "You think I'm a meanie because I won't let you go to the senior prom with a girl who drives her own car?"

"Donna doesn't have her own car. It's her brother's car," he pointed out logically, wishing these decisions were up to Pop, and not Nina. But in the Chickalini household, it was Nina who doled out permission for everything from school field trips to Ralphie's playdates.

"I don't care whose car it is," she said with a maddening toss of her head. "You're not riding in it."

"But —"

"Case closed, Dom."

Wow. She actually sounded like she really meant it. He couldn't think of a time when Nina couldn't be talked into bending the rules. And anyway, there was no rule in the Chickalini household, as far as he knew, about the high school senior prom.

He pointed that out to Nina, who just shrugged and said, "There is now."

"Come on, Nina. I bet you were so beautiful in high school that you got invited to the senior prom when you were a freshman."

That would get her. Nina always softened when he told her how pretty she was.

Nope, not this time.

"Nice try, Dom, but you're still not going."

He began again, "But —"

"No."

"That's not fair."

"Come talk to me when you're a senior."

Scowling, he stormed up to his room, where he found his kid brother, Ralphie, sorting his baseball cards all over the floor.

"Hey, Dom, want to help me?" Ralphie asked, snapping his bubble gum.

"Nope." Dominic flopped moodily onto his bed and stared up at the picture of Donna DiLorenzo wearing her skimpy basketball cheerleading uniform. He'd taped it up on the wall beside his pillow just a few weeks ago, tossing into the garbage the Bucky Dent poster that used to hang there.

"Hey, what the heck are you doing with that?" Ralphie had protested, promptly fishing it out.

A very wrinkled Bucky Dent now hung above Ralphie's bed.

"What's wrong with you?" he asked now, glancing up at his brother.

"Nina's ruining my life," Dom replied.

How was he supposed to tell Donna that his big sister vetoed the prom? Didn't Nina realize that it was an honor to be asked? That not just any old freshman boy got invited?

In fact, he was willing to bet that no freshman boy in the history of Most Precious Mother High School had ever been invited to the senior prom. Certainly not by the head cheerleader and prettiest girl in the senior class.

Maybe, Dom thought, he could sneak out to the prom anyway. Nina wouldn't even have to know about it. She always worked at the pizza parlor with Pop on Friday nights anyway.

Rosalie would be home, but she'd probably be busy with her friend Bebe and their usual weekend ritual: watching movies, fixing each other's hair, eating a whole batch of fudge, and moaning about their lousy love lives. Rosalie would never even notice Dom was missing.

He'd have to secretly rent a tuxedo. And buy a corsage. But that was doable. He just had to figure out whether he'd be committing an all-out sin, or a minor indiscretion. For all his faults, he wasn't a sinner. Not on purpose, anyway.

There was a knock on the bedroom door. It opened a crack, and Pop peered in. "Dominic, I'm going to the store. Tomorrow is trash day. Everything had better be out by the curb by the time I get back."

"It will be," Dom promised.

As soon as his father closed the door, he sat up and looked at his brother.

"Oh, no," Ralphie said, shaking his head. "No way. Not again. I took the trash out for you last week, Dom. And I walked the dog for you every day this week."

"Come on, Ralphie."

"No. I'm busy."

"I'll give you one of my baseball cards if you do it."

Ralphie looked up with interest. "Which card? Wait — I want Dave Winfield."

"Are you crazy? No way. I'll give you Gossage."

"I already have two."

"So? Trade them with one of your friends."

"Nope."

"I'll throw in a Righetti, too. But you have to walk the dog for me tonight, too."

"Deal," Ralphie said reluctantly. "Hand them over."

"I will. Later."

"Now."

"I said, later. What . . . you don't trust me?"

"Sometimes you forget stuff, Dom."

Ralphie had a point there. "Well, I won't forget this. I promise."

Feeling smug, Dominic watched his

brother put aside his own cards and carry their wastebasket out into the hall.

What a deal! He wasn't about to admit to Ralphie that he'd lost interest in baseball cards the moment Donna DiLorenzo kissed him for the first time, behind the bleachers right before his baseball tryouts last month.

Heck, after that, he pretty much lost interest in a lot of things he'd been passionate about, including skateboarding, playing video games at the arcade, even baseball itself.

But somehow, he managed to make the team. Good thing, because now Donna kept telling him how cute he looked in his uniform.

Dom had no idea what he had done to deserve all this attention from a girl like Donna, but he did know one thing for sure: He wasn't going back to skateboards and baseball cards any time soon.

"Hey, good luck at the craps table this time," Mia calls before Dominic can disappear into the crowded airport terminal.

She can't let him go just yet. She doesn't quite understand why, but she can't.

He stops, turns, grins. "Yeah, you, too.

Good luck . . . with your wedding and everything."

She smiles. At least, she tries to. "Thanks."

He's about to leave again. Forever.

She has to stop him.

No, you don't. You have to let him go.

No, she doesn't. She has to stop him.

"Hey," she calls, much louder than she intended.

He turns back. "Yeah?"

He isn't a raspberry turnover, Mia. He's a human being. You can't go take a nibble of him and toss him into the nearest garbage can.

Yeah, well, the human being is waiting with an expectant look on his beautiful face.

She has no idea what to say.

She only knows that she can't nibble, yet she also can't let him walk away.

Nor can she continue to just stand here, mute, wearing a wedding gown and what must be a flimsy, helpless expression.

So she forces herself to say the first thing that comes to mind.

Unfortunately, the first thing that comes to mind is, "You forgot to kiss the bride."

Dom just blinks.

Somewhere nearby, a slot machine rains

down coins and a joyous crowd whoops and hollers.

Mia swallows hard.

What are you saying? What are you doing, Mia?

You're tempting fate, that's what you're doing. You don't invite the best-looking man you've ever seen to kiss you. Not even in the middle of a public place. Not even on your wedding day to someone else.

But it wasn't an invitation. It was merely an observation. He forgot to kiss the bride.

Oh, please. You might as well close your eyes and pucker up.

Okay. So it was an invitation.

But it's the right thing to do, she reminds herself. *Fuji said so. One kiss is the nonfood equivalent of one taste of a raspberry turnover. Forbidden pastry, forbidden kiss. What's the difference?*

Okay, big, big difference.

Well, the point is, it'll get him out of your system so you can go off and get married without a backward glance.

"Do you *want* me to kiss the bride?" Dom asks at last, looking hesitant . . . but not entirely opposed to the idea.

"Sure. Isn't that what people do? You know, a kiss for luck and I'm on my way . . ."

He takes a step closer to her and says,

low, in her ear, "I think we both know that if I kiss you the way I want to kiss you, it won't be a pleasant little good luck peck on the cheek."

Yes, and she won't want to be on her way, either. She looks into his eyes, and her heart races beneath her cleavage-baring bodice.

Wow.

So she wasn't imagining it.

The chemistry. It was definitely there, on both their parts.

"Why don't you go ahead anyway?" she hears herself ask him.

She drops her bag at her feet without looking down, not even flinching when she hears things dropping out of the open top and rolling away.

"Go ahead and kiss you?"

She nods, her gaze dropping from his inquisitive dark eyes to those full lips that she has to feel against hers. Just once. Just once, and it will be enough to last a lifetime.

"Are you sure?" he asks, dropping his own bag and leaning closer still. "You're about to get married."

"Just think of it as my last hurrah," she tells him, and, closing her eyes, tilts her face up to his in anticipation.

She expects his mouth to seize hers hungrily in one of those fervent, old-movie, good-bye-forever kisses.

Instead, he pulls her close and his lips brush her lips tenderly, sweetly, lingering only a few seconds. It isn't a chaste kiss; far from it.

Nor is it an intensely satisfying kiss that sweeps the longing right out of her soul.

It's a fleeting kiss; one that ignites something far more powerful than carnal longing.

It takes her a moment to become aware of a smattering of applause and a female eyewitness drawling, "Aw, look, honey. Newlyweds!"

"Hey, congratulations!" somebody else calls, and Mia opens her eyes to see that she and Dom have somehow managed to attract more attention than the blinking, jangling slot machines and bizarre parade of characters.

The crowd of gaping onlookers is more than enough to jar her back to reality.

Reality being her imminent wedding to somebody other than the man who just swept her off her three-inch white satin pumps.

Maybe she should just say the hell with it — all of it. Derek, the Chapel of Luv, her grandfather's money, her financial future. Maybe she should just go with Dom, here and now, forever and always.

Go where? a skeptical inner voice asks.

A ridiculously hearty one answers, *Who cares? You'll be with this incredible guy. Does anything else really matter?*

She opens her mouth to tell the incredible guy of her momentous decision, but he's already started to speak.

And what he's saying is, "Well, see you."

See you?

See you?

After a kiss like that, all he has to say is *see you?*

For a moment, Mia is too stunned and dismayed to react.

Then, fuming, Mia glares at him, fully prepared to tell him off.

But she can't.

She can't, because he's already turning around and walking away.

Fine. The second he looks back, she'll gesture him over so she can give him a piece of her mind.

There's only one problem with that plan.

He never looks back.

Chapter Five

The desert heat hits Dom full force as he steps outside McCarran Airport's Terminal One. He fights the urge to turn on his heel and hightail it back inside.

All right, not just because it's hotter than a brick pizza oven out here.

But also — all right, *mostly* — because *she's* in there.

Mia.

The woman of his dreams.

Huh?

His sensible inner self begs to differ.

The woman of your dreams is a money-hungry, otherwise-engaged lunatic in a wedding gown?

Why, yes, Sensible Inner Self. Yes, she is.

If Dom had any doubts about Mia — and he most certainly did — they were erased the moment he took her into his arms and kissed her.

Kissing Mia was the most heartfelt, sensual, frightening experience of his life.

Which is precisely why he fled without a backward glance.

Out of fear. Sheer, blood-chilling terror.

In the space of a few hours, he was not only transported from one end of the country to the other; he also went from being a happy-go-lucky confirmed bachelor to a man with marriage on his mind and a bride in his arms.

Which might not be so scary, even, if it were his own bride.

Come on, who are you kidding? Your own bride? That's scary as sh—

"Hey, Chickalini! What are you doing here?"

Startled by the sound of his name — pronounced correctly, no less — he turns to see strapping Paulie Caviros, an old friend from the neighborhood.

All right, not *friend,* exactly. Paulie is a pal of Nina and Joey's; the kind of guy who has always treated Dom like somebody's pesky kid brother. Probably because he *was* somebody's pesky kid brother.

He still hasn't forgiven Paulie for a childhood's worth of atomic wedgies and noogies, nor for ratting him out to Sister Agnes when he prankishly stole every last eraser in her classroom after she made him write *I will not crack jokes in class* two hundred times on the board.

These days, whenever Dom runs into

Paulie — who can usually be found bench-pressing ridiculously oversized barbells at the neighborhood gym — things are at least more civil. The frequently-single-again Paulie seems to view Dom as a kindred bachelor spirit of sorts. He's always after Dom to hang out with him, which isn't the least bit appealing. Paulie is the kind of guy who calls women "chicks" or "skirts," and frequently talks about "scoring" in no relation to team sports.

"Hey, Paulie," he says, shaking hands. "I just got off a flight from New York."

"Me, too. Which flight?"

Dom tells him, and it turns out Paulie was on the same plane. "How come I didn't see you?"

"I was in first class."

Paulie whistles. "Look at you, Chickalini. First class, fancy vacation, fancy clothes . . ."

Dom wants to protest that he's wearing jeans, but then, next to Paulie's sleeveless tank, shorts, and sneakers, he supposes he *is* pretty fancy.

"It isn't a vacation, Paulie; I'm here on business. How about you? Another quickie wedding? Or maybe another quickie divorce?"

"Hey, quit bustin' my chops," says

Paulie, a veteran of three marriages in the last decade or so. "I'm here on business, too."

That's surprising, considering Paulie's a bartender back in Queens. Before Dom can ask what kind of business, or better yet, beat a hasty retreat, Paulie is telling him all about the amateur bodybuilders convention being held this week at Harrah's.

"As soon as you get a chance to take a break from your meetings or whatever you're doing, come check out the scenery, if you know what I mean," he invites Dom with a wink.

"I don't know . . . I'll be pretty busy."

"Come on, you gotta have some free time built in."

"Well, yeah, but I'm kind of thinking of lying low."

"You?" Paulie raises an eyebrow. "Since when does Dominic Chickalini turn down the chance to meet women?"

All right, in the past, he never has. So he can hardly blame Paulie for looking so shocked. Still, he can't help but bristle at the ladies' man image of himself.

"How do you know I don't have a girl-friend back home now, Paulie?"

Paulie snickers. "Who said you don't?"

Ouch. That stings. Paulie, who has known him his entire life, is obviously well aware of Dominic's track record in the monogamy department.

To be fair, it isn't as though he's cheated on any woman with whom he was the least bit serious . . . because unlike Paulie the Serial Groom, Dom has never been even the least bit serious with any woman.

He doesn't lead them on, or pretend to be anything more than what he is: a fun-loving, carefree guy. He's never promised any woman he wouldn't date others; thus, he's never technically cheated.

Then again, everyone has been warning him for as long as he can remember that sooner or later, he's going to grow up and realize it's time to settle down.

Is it finally happening?

Now? Here? In Vegas, of all places?

"Anyway, listen, I owe you."

"What do you owe me?"

"A big favor." At Dom's blank look, he says, "You know. For the tickets to that sold-out Jimmy Buffett concert a few weeks ago. Thanks, man. It was great."

Dominic, who reluctantly gave the prized tickets to Nina and Joey so that he could attend Carolyn's wedding, is aware that the Materis had to cancel at the last minute because the kids had a fever. But . . .

"I thought Joey gave the tickets to Danny and Barb," he says, wondering how on earth Paulie, of all people, ended up with them. Somehow, it adds insult to injury realizing that while he was hiding out in the catering hall's men's room as the wedding singer summoned all the single men to the dance floor for the garter toss, Paulie was listening to Jimmy Buffett's live version of "Let's Get Drunk and Screw."

"Yeah, but Danny forgot Danny Junior was invited to some sleepover that night, and Barb didn't want to be out at Jones Beach with the kid staying at a strange house."

"Oh, for the love of . . ." Dom trails off, shaking his head.

"Yeah, that's how Danny felt, too. But you know how Barb is about the kid."

Yes, he knows how Barb Andonelli is about her precious only child.

"You know, Barb used to be normal," Paulie comments. "Now she's a freakin' nut job. I swear, the kid sniffles and she's calling an ambulance."

"Yeah, I know." Quoting Nina, who frequently shakes her head over her friend's maternal frenzy, Dom adds, "I guess it just took her so many years of trying before she actually got pregnant that she goes a little overboard, even now that the kid's what, nine? Ten?"

"If you ask me, they all go overboard. Every normal babe goes freakin' insane the second you put a kid in her arms. Listen, if you want a normal babe, you've got to meet some of these bodybuilder chicks," Paulie informs him. "All oiled up in string bikinis . . . you never seen anything like it. I'll hook you up. Like I said, I owe you."

The old Dom — the Dom of a few hours ago — might have taken him up on it.

But the new Dom — the Dom who just kissed an amazing woman and barely escaped with his sanity — just shakes his head. "I don't know, Paulie. Maybe, but don't count on me. I'm kind of tired."

"You're getting old, Chickalini," Paulie says with a dismissive wave of his hand, which bears gold rings on just about every finger except the fourth one of his left hand. "You're starting to sound just like your sister and brother-in-law and Danny and Barb. All they want to do is sit around and talk about their kids."

"I don't have any kids."

"Damned right you don't. You and I are the only guys I know these days who know how to have a little fun. Thank God for

Vegas. You ever been here before?"

"A few times." Back in his overly indulgent Fun-Loving Carefree Guy era, which seems to have drawn to a rapid and unforeseen close.

"I've never been here. Isn't it the most beautiful thing you've ever seen?" Paulie gestures at the impressive skyline, complete with the Luxor's Egyptian pyramid, clearly visible in the distant, shimmering heat.

Still thinking about the most beautiful thing he's ever seen — and it wasn't the Las Vegas strip — Dom merely nods.

He glances at the glass doors, not even realizing he's hoping for a glimpse of Mia until he doesn't spot her and the overhead sun seems to dim a couple of thousand watts.

"Want to share a cab?" Paulie asks.

"Nah, I'm renting a car while I'm here. Come on, I'll give you a ride."

"Yeah? Where's the car?"

"I just got off the plane, Paulie. I've got to take the shuttle over to the —"

"Forget it. Too hot to wait around in this heat. I'm going to grab a cab and go hit the pool." Paulie lifts his bulging suitcases as though they're filled with marshmallows. "Catch you later, dude. I'll be hanging out

126

at Harrah's the next coupl'a days. Come find me."

Come find him? At Harrah's? What does he think it is, a small-town Holiday Inn with a one-couch lobby? Dom has been in enough Vegas strip superhotels to realize each one is a complete universe unto itself.

He supposes that if he actually does find himself wanting to locate Paulie, he can always call the desk at Harrah's and ask for him. Though the chances of finding anyone actually occupying his Vegas hotel room are slim, unless it's the middle of the night. Come to think of it, even then.

Dom waves at the departing Paulie, figuring he won't be seeing him again until next week back at the gym in Astoria. By then, he'll undoubtedly be full of stories about his wild Sin City adventures.

And so will you, Dom assures himself. *You're just jet-lagged and woozy from the heat. You'll be your old self again in no time and prove that Fun-Loving Carefree Guy is still alive and kicking.*

Mia has spent the last few days of her life thinking that life will be perfect if Derek turns out to be a wonderful guy in person.

Now, she can't help thinking that life will

be perfect if Derek turns out to be a first-class jerk.

As she lugs her heavy carry-on toward the Terminal One baggage claim area, she isn't at all opposed to prolonging their first meeting by stopping every few seconds to rest her aching arms and her aching feet. She can't help but wonder why the white satin pumps that seemed to fit her perfectly now seem several sizes too small . . .

Or why the quickie marriage that was the answer to her biggest problem now seems to be the problem itself.

Dom.

It's all because of Dom.

Well, not the shoes, but everything else.

The brief time she spent with him was life-altering.

But he didn't change your mind about love, Mia reminds herself sternly. *If anything, he's gone and proved your theory.*

Yes, because all it took was a dash of romance and one hot kiss to knock the logic right out of her. If he had asked, she probably would have called off the wedding. But of course he didn't ask.

Only because he probably didn't think of it, she tells herself. *He probably had no idea that you were* this close *to deciding to forget the whole thing. Maybe if he'd known there was a chance . . .*

She has half a mind to change into sneakers and run after Dom.

You have half a mind, all right. You do that, and you're going to find yourself living on the street without a job . . . and without Dom, because he has no interest in you. If he did, he wouldn't have kissed you and walked away.

She sets down her bag, peels off a white satin pump, and leans against a pillar, rubbing her aching toes and trying to think straight.

Will Grandpa Junie really kick her out of her apartment and cut her off financially if she refuses to marry his handpicked Sicilian?

Quite possibly.

Quite *probably.*

Nana Mona said so. She told Mia Grandpa Junie would definitely cut her out of the will if she didn't marry the man he'd chosen for her, and that he'd also stop paying her salary, and most likely stop speaking to her altogether.

That last part is the worst. She can't bear the thought of Grandpa Junie angry at her. She adores him. He'd do anything for her, and she'd do anything for him.

Except marry some imported Mr. Right

just because he says so.

Stubborn old guy. He's always been bull-headed, but much more so since the lottery. Sometimes it's almost as if his fortune has transformed him into a smug puppeteer, pulling all the strings in an infinite one-man show.

And what does that make you, Mia?

A puppet incapable of doing anything on her own? Look at her, rushing down the aisle just because he wants to see her married. It's blackmail, that's what it is.

But he doesn't mean any harm. Grandpa Junie just wants you to be settled before he dies, she reminds herself.

In his mind, a woman needs somebody to take care of her. He can't stand the thought of something happening to him, and Mia being left all alone.

That's what Nana Mona told her the other day, when Mia found out about the arranged-marriage scenario.

"He's worried about me, so he's going to cut me off without a penny? That doesn't make sense, Nana."

To Nana, and to Grandpa Junie, it apparently makes perfect sense.

"If your grandfather had handpicked a husband for your mother, everything would have turned out okay for her," Nana Mona

130

said with conviction. "Instead, we let her go off trotting all over the world, wasting all her best years. She didn't even meet your father until she was halfway through her thirties, and by then it was too late."

"Too late for what?" Mia asked.

"Too late for a family."

"She *had* a family. She had me."

Her grandmother shook her head sadly. "An only child is a terrible thing."

Gee, thanks a lot, Mia thought. "How can you say that, Nana? Look at me."

"Yes, look at you. Are you happy? Did you have a happy childhood?"

Well, all right, Mia had to admit that she didn't. Not until she came to live here with her grandparents, anyway. Even then, there was always the sense that something was missing.

Because something was *missing. Something huge. Both parents.*

"Your mother waited too long to settle down. And when she finally did, she married the wrong man. The one who made her heart go pitter-patter," Nana Mona said quaintly. "She made too many mistakes. You're not going to make the same mistakes, Mia. You need a husband now, while you're still young enough to have lots of babies."

That was the craziest thing she'd ever heard. It was sick, that's what it was. Sick, and twisted, and —

So why are you wearing a wedding gown?

Not so that she can live happily ever after and make lots of babies, that's for darned sure. But her grandparents don't need to know that.

Derek knows what this marriage of convenience is all about, and that's what counts. He doesn't expect anything more from her than she's already agreed to give.

Which includes not just a roof over his head and the best acting coach in New York, but also a hefty amount of cash up front. The certified check she promised him is in her bag.

Which begs the question . . .

Is Derek a gold digger?

Well, when you get right down to it, who isn't?

You're not, Mia tells herself . . . even as she realizes that's exactly what she is.

Look at you, rushing into marriage just so you can go on living in the decadent style to which you've become accustomed.

And whose fault is that?

Grandpa Junie's, that's whose. From the moment he won the lottery, it was as

132

though some invisible, bottomless bucket in the sky tipped and money began fluttering down all around Mia. Everything she ever wanted was suddenly hers for the taking . . . and she'd been taking, all right. Grabbing it all up in her greedy little fists. Designer clothes, expensive jewelry, the latest electronics, exotic vacations . . .

She, the girl who spent most of her life longing for all that was unattainable, hasn't wanted for anything in years. Anything material, that is.

So that's what counts? Material things?

All right, that's it. She's officially quite ashamed of herself.

Dom or no Dom, she's not going to go through with this wedding. No way. Not even if Derek turns out to be the greatest guy in the world . . . which he won't, because what kind of great guy agrees to marry somebody, sight unseen, for money?

You're going to march right down to the luggage claim and find the guy in the white tuxedo with the yellow boutonniere, Mia instructs herself. *And you're going to tell him you made a big mistake, and you can't go through with this marriage. You'll give him a little cash for his trouble, or even the whole damned certified check, and then you'll send him on his merry way. Then . . .*

What?

You'll go off in search of Dom from the plane?

The more time that passes since she saw him — since she *kissed* him — the more the whole thing seems surreal.

Maybe Dom wasn't even real. Maybe her imagination conjured him as part of this epiphany. Maybe she slept the whole flight, dreaming of a man who doesn't exist.

But what about that incredible kiss? She sure as heck didn't sleepwalk her way through that.

Anyway, real or not, she can't go off in search of Dom. That would be even crazier than all the crazy things she's done so far.

No, she'll just get on a New York–bound plane and she'll fly back home . . .

Where you'll find Grandpa Junie waiting for you with his handpicked groom.

The way Mia sees it, she's right back at square one, with two choices.

She can stick with Plan A and tell her grandfather she isn't getting married to anyone, because she's already married to Derek . . .

Or she can go to Plan B, tell him thanks but no thanks, and say farewell to life as she knows it.

Yes, those are her only two options. They've always been her only two options.

So which one will she choose?

Plan B?

She allows herself to imagine, for a moment, what it will be like to pack her bags and leave her comfortable, professionally decorated floor-through with its view of distant Manhattan across the sea of rooftops.

She's never lived alone before; where would she go? And how would she pay her rent? She'd need to find a job right away, but what is she qualified to do? She didn't even bother to finish college.

She was working her way through CCNY when the lottery hit, but she was goofing off in liberal arts, without a solid career plan. She hadn't yet figured out what she wanted to be when she grew up . . . and now here she is, all grown up, still without a clue.

How dare you look for the easy way out: somebody else's money.

Look at you. You can't even take care of yourself.

Shame continues to seep in, wrapping around her like cheap perfume.

But I can't help it. I just don't want to be poor again.

She can't help but remember the old threadbare days, when she was still under her parents' care and money was short. They lived in a plastic and polyester-draped world; they ate white bread and ramen noodles — when they ate at all.

Terrific. With that diet, you'll be overweight again in no time.

Come on, Mia. Get serious.

This isn't just about simple carbs or natural fiber thread counts. Far from it. This is about making levelheaded decisions; about taking advantage of the extraordinary financial opportunities that have been offered to her.

Who in their right mind would willingly choose poverty?

Mia Calogera won't. Absolutely not.

With a sigh, she wedges her throbbing foot back into her too-tight white satin pump, thinking the shoes will probably stretch out in no time. All she has to do is wear them for long enough, and they'll fit just right.

She picks up her bag and continues limping painfully on to the baggage claim, in accordance with Plan A.

At least, she tells herself wistfully, thinking of Dom, *we'll always have McCarran Airport.*

★ ★ ★

At long last, Dom climbs onto the air-conditioned rental car shuttle bus, sinks back into a seat, and allows his thoughts to wander back to Mia.

Back to how he kissed her.

Right.

He kissed her *good-bye,* that's what he did. Kissed her and ran away.

He can't believe he'll never see her again.

He can't believe that he *can't* see her again, even if he wanted to. Because even if he knew where she's staying . . .

What are you going to do? Camp out in some hotel lobby until you find her? You're not going to find any one-couch Holiday Inn here, remember?

Okay, so she's gone. For good.

It's time for a major attitude adjustment.

She's gone! For good! You're free!

Free? He's always been free.

But now, because of *her,* he feels anything but. He's going to drag that kiss around for days. He can already tell.

In no time, it seems, the shuttle bus is pulling up to the rental car terminal, cutting short Dominic's daydreams about the only woman who might have been able to convert him from confirmed bachelorhood.

137

"Good luck," the driver says as Dom reluctantly prepares to shuffle back out into the stifling heat.

Good luck.

It's the standard parting phrase here in Las Vegas, where people flock to make impossible dreams come true. Dom's been here often enough to pick up on that quirky local turn of phrase.

Good luck. Everybody says it, everywhere you go: drivers, store clerks, chambermaids, waiters . . .

Some of them probably even mean it.

But nobody means it the way Dom finds himself taking it now.

And anyway, it would take a whole lot more than a lucky crank of a slot machine handle or a roll of the dice to make this particular impossible dream come true.

"Thanks," he says halfheartedly and tips the driver before trudging out into the desert sun, the memory of Mia Calogera weighing on him like one of Paulie's barbells.

"Nana?"

"Yes, Mia?"

"Why don't any of the boys at school like me?"

Her grandmother stopped rolling out the piecrust and looked flustered. "Mia! You're too young for boys. Aren't you?" she added, as though she wasn't sure.

"I'm thirteen. That's old enough." She plucked a chunk of apple out of the bowl she was mixing. It was deliciously gritty with sugar and cinnamon. "Almost all the girls in my class have boyfriends."

"Oh. Well . . . give it time, Mia. You'll have a boyfriend one day."

"It's because I'm fat," she muttered, eating another chunk of apple. She didn't want to mention in front of her grandmother that it was also because she didn't have any nice clothes, other than her ill-fitting school uniform. Nana would feel bad. She couldn't help it that she and Grandpa couldn't afford to buy Mia fancy outfits.

At least I have a home, and enough food to eat, Mia told herself.

More than enough food to eat. She was starting to realize that was part of the problem.

But all that delicious food her grandmother made helped to erase the hollow feeling Mia carried inside. It made her feel better. Until she looked in the mirror, anyway.

"What did you say, Mia?" her grandmother was asking, looking surprised — and dismayed.

"I said I'm fat. That's why nobody likes me. No boys, anyway."

"You're not fat, Mia. You're healthy. When I think of how scrawny you were the first time I saw you . . ." Nana Mona shuddered and shook her head. "You needed to get some meat on your bones."

"Well, now I have too much meat on my bones. Nobody is ever going to fall in love with me if I look like this."

"Fall in love?" Nana Mona echoed, sounding alarmed. "Don't you go around worrying about falling in love. That's not all it's cracked up to be."

According to her friends at school, it sure was. But Mia decided Nana Mona might know a thing or two more than they did. "What's wrong with falling in love, Nana?"

"Did you ever hear the saying 'Love is blind'?" At her nod, Nana Mona said, "Well, it is. Love makes people see only what they want to see, and not what's real. That's dangerous. It gets people into all kinds of trouble. Especially women."

"What kinds of trouble?"

"You don't want to know." Nana just shook her head. "Just make sure you always do your thinking with that brain of yours, Mia. Not with your heart. And you'll be fine. I told your mother the same thing when she was your age . . . but she never listened to me."

"Why not?"

"She was too independent. She thought she should be able make up her own mind about things. About everything. And your grandfather and I . . . well, we made mistakes. We let her make her own decisions because she was so headstrong, it was just easier to let her go her own way than saying no all the time. And look what happened."

Mia nodded in silence, stirring the apples, thinking of her mother, whom she had seen only during a few fleeting hour-long visits since the day she left.

Mom said she was traveling, and working, and trying to save up enough money so that Mia could come live with her again. But Mia doubted that was going to happen.

And even if it could . . . she doubted that she'd want to leave Queens and her grandparents' home. They made her feel safe, and wanted, for the first time in her life.

She never wanted to leave them. Ever, ever, ever.

"Nana? Do you think my mother will

really be here tomorrow for Thanksgiving, like she promised when she called?"

"Do you think she will?" Nana Mona asked in return, focusing her attention on the piecrust again.

Mia wanted to say yes. She wanted to say it, and mean it, more than she had ever wanted anything in her life.

But Grandpa Junie and Nana Mona had taught her so many things these past few years. One of them was never to lie. Another was never to believe anything her mother told her. Not even promises.

They were probably right. She could still remember her father screaming at her mother in the throes of their divorce, "But you promised! You promised to love and honor and obey me until death do us part!"

"I didn't know what I was doing, making a vow like that," was her mother's reply. "I never should have done it in the first place, but you can't hold me to it now."

Mia thought about the wedding picture . . . the one that was probably never framed and on display. She had found it not long after she came to live here, tucked away in the back of the family Bible.

It was a snapshot — a candid, taken

very close up. At first, she didn't even recognize the bride and groom. She was just captivated by how beautiful they both were, and how in love. Everything about them — their expressions, their body language — betrayed that they were crazy about each other; madly in love, the way a bride and a groom should be.

Then she recognized the curve of her father's jaw, and her mother's familiar profile, and she was so startled she dropped the picture.

Had they ever been that young? Had they really loved each other that much?

She thought about what Grandma had said about love being blind. That must be why her mother got married to her father; why she made promises that were impossible to keep. She must have been thinking with her heart and not with her brain, like Grandma said.

Mia won't make that mistake. Not in the future, and not right now.

She thought with her brain and she told her grandmother in a small voice, "No, I don't think she'll come tomorrow, even though she promised."

"That's all right, Mia. We'll have a nice Thanksgiving anyway, just the three of us. And if Terry does happen to show up, it'll *be a wonderful surprise. Won't it?"*

"Yes," Mia said.

But she knew there would be no won-derful surprises.

And she was right.

The second she reaches the designated spot, Mia spots a man wearing a white tuxedo standing by the now-empty luggage carousel for her flight.

In that instant, she knows she can't do it.

She can't go through with it.

The hell with Plan A. The hell with the money. Her personal pride is worth more than any lottery fortune.

She's not going to marry Derek, and she's not going to marry her grandfather's Sicilian stranger, either.

She'll just have to work up all her nerve and tell Grandpa Junie, then hope for the best.

But first, she'll have to work up all her nerve and tell Derek, then hope for the best.

At least his back is to her, giving her a few moments to prepare herself to deliver the big bombshell.

Just tell him right away, and don't mince words. Tell him, pay him, and run.

Yes. That's the plan.

Plan C, if you will.

Some plan. She wonders, yet again, and without resolution, how on earth she managed to get herself into this situation.

Well, there's nothing to do now but get herself out of it. Only then can she even consider turning her attention to Plan D. The *D,* of course, stands for *Dom.*

She won't even hold a grudge that he kissed her senseless and then ran away.

All will be forgiven, if only she can find him. She'll go to Mandalay Bay and camp out in the lobby if she has to.

All she knows is that she can't let a man like him walk out of her life.

Right. But first things first.

"Derek?" she calls.

He obviously doesn't hear her above the cacophony in the airport — or maybe it's just that her voice didn't come out loudly enough. It was more of a strangled whisper.

She tries again. "Um, Derek?"

He still doesn't hear her.

Come on, Mia. Just do it.

She hobbles closer to him, wishing she had stopped to get her luggage first so that she could put on her sneakers. The most appealing part of Plan C — the "run" part — won't be easy in these torturous shoes. She hopes the spurned groom won't give chase.

"Hey, Derek!" She jabs him in the back,

then holds her breath as he turns around.

Good Lord!

He can't blame me if I call the whole thing off now, Mia thinks as a wave of relief sweeps over her.

How can he? He totally lied . . . at least, about his looks. And God knows what else.

Derek looks nothing whatsoever like his pictures. He has pockmarked skin and a bushy gray mustache, and is a good three decades older than she is. The orchid boutonniere on his lapel is as white as his tuxedo, but his teeth are definitely as yellow as the tobacco stains in his mustache.

"We have to talk," Mia says in a giddy rush.

Derek blinks. "We do?" He looks positively intrigued. And — eww — he's leering at her.

"Yes. I can't marry you."

"Marry him? Whoa, sister, he's mine." A towering woman materializes at his side, wearing a bridal gown, boots — *boots?* — and a menacing expression.

He's all yours, sister. Trust me.

But before Mia can say it, she hears a male voice calling her name.

She turns around . . .

And there, lo and behold, is another man in a white tuxedo.

Chapter Six

Mia's first thought is that the Vegas airport is positively crawling with grooms. Is this a typical day, or a cruel twist of fate?

Her next thought is that this groom is clean-shaven with white teeth and a yellow orchid pinned to his lapel.

This groom, she realizes in dismay, is definitely Derek. He looks just like his head shots. Better, even, in person, all tousled blond hair, and wide blue eyes, and strapping muscles he probably got hoisting hay bales or something.

He looks very *boy next door,* very *last person on earth who would be marrying a stranger for her money* . . . which, Mia reminds herself, is exactly what he is planning to do.

She wants to hate him on sight, but she can't, any more than she can truly hate herself for falling victim to her grandfather's grand plan. Human beings will behave oddly under stress, especially when millions of dollars are at stake.

"Well, hi there." Derek smiles at her, and

then he reaches out and hugs her.

"Um, hi." Mia stiffens in his embrace and wishes he would let go.

At last he does, but not before kissing her on the cheek. She fights the urge to glance around and see if any of the on-lookers who applauded her kissing Dom upstairs happen to be privy to this display. The last thing she needs at this point is a booing, hissing crowd.

Luckily, there is no audience this time. Even old Yellow Tooth and his hulking bride have lost interest in her.

Oozing farm-fresh sincerity, Derek thrusts a bouquet of yellow phalaenopsis orchids into her hands and gallantly takes her heavy carry-on bag from her without flinching. "It's great to finally meet you, Mia."

"You *are* Derek, right?" she asks, just to be sure, telling herself *you never know* even though she most certainly *does* know.

"Yup, I'm Derek. Where's the rest of your luggage?"

She gestures at the baggage carousel trundling along a few yards away. The *vacant* carousel. She double-checks to make sure her airline and flight number are posted above it. "I guess it's not out yet."

"I don't know . . . I think it's already come and gone. I saw a bunch of people grabbing bags from there up until a few minutes ago."

"Uh-oh. I guess I missed it. It took me awhile to get down here . . ." *Because I was in a passionate clinch with a stranger I met on the plane . . .* "But I'm sure they must have just set it aside or something."

"I'm sure they must have. Oh, Mia, can you believe we're really here?" He clasps her hands, both of them, in his own. The gesture, and his tone, are reminiscent of one of those vintage Rodgers and Hammerstein musicals Nana Mona likes to watch. She half expects him to swing her around dreamily and break into song after he says, "I've been waiting for this day my whole life."

His whole life? His whole life? Oh . . . *Please.*

"I know it sounds crazy," he goes on breathily, gazing at her with a winsome smile, "but I really believe in fate. Don't you?"

Pushing the memory of Madame Tamar's prediction to the farthest reaches of her mind, Mia protests, "But —"

"I know we just decided to do this, Mia," he cuts in. "But I swear I've always known you were out there somewhere."

Mia decides that if anybody's *out there,* it's Derek.

What the heck is he talking about? It's as though he's starring in a romantic production, and she's an extra who forgot her lines. Or worse yet, wandered onto the wrong stage.

"Yeah, I was . . . um, out there," she murmurs in agreement.

"I always knew I'd find that special someone, but I never dreamed I'd meet her because of a cattleya brassolaelia."

Okay, this is getting cornier by the second.

Determined to nip his rhapsodizing in the bud, so to speak, Mia points out, "It was actually an odontoglossum. Remember?"

He smiles vaguely. Does he even recall the circumstances of their meeting two months ago?

They were both on an orchid-growers' website, where Mia had posted a question for the site's official horticulturalist.

The next thing she knew, she was reading an e-mailed message from a total stranger and self-professed avid orchid grower who offered the information she was seeking.

"I remember thinking you and I had everything in common right from the start," Derek says fondly now.

What? Did she miss something? Does he think they fell in love somewhere between the odontoglossum and plotting Plan A? Because if he does, she'd better set him straight right from the start.

"Derek, you know we're probably going to keep this agreement totally platonic, right? And most likely temporary? I mean . . . that's what we agreed."

"I know what we agreed, Mia, but the truth is, I wouldn't mind if we took this marriage thing all the way."

All the way as in . . . *all the way?*

A lifetime of marital celibacy is suddenly looking mighty appealing.

"I've been thinking about it ever since you asked me to marry you, and I guess I'd like to try and make this work."

She asked *him* to marry her?

Nuh-uh!

He volunteered to marry her when she was lamenting her grandfather's scheme in a rambling e-mail.

In fact, when he first offered to help her out, *she* was the one who said they didn't even have to get married; that it would probably be enough if she had a supposedly serious relationship to head off the would-be arranged marriage. She said she would fly him to New York and he could pose as her boyfriend until the whole thing blew over.

It was Derek who pointed out that her grandfather wanted her *married,* not merely dating somebody. He offered to bail her out by putting a bona fide ring on her finger, no emotional strings attached.

She was tempted to turn him down until she remembered the psychic — and realized that the prophecy would make sense if she married Derek. Yes, because she wasn't about to marry anyone for love, but Madame Tamar *was* pretty adamant about her getting married before the year was out to somebody whose name starts with a *D* and ends in a *k* sound.

Maybe there's a tiny part of Mia that longs to believe.

In clairvoyance, that is. *Not* love.

"And now," Derek goes on, "seeing you here in person, Mia, I'm just . . . well, I'm just really, really, really happy."

Her heart sinks.

"Derek . . . I mean, I just want to make sure you're not thinking this is something more than it is."

"You mean, more than a one-way ticket

to New York?" He smiles. "I don't expect anything more. I just can't help being excited. I've been trying to get out of that town my whole life. And I really appreciate your giving me the chance."

And . . . cut! Mia thinks, as an imaginary director snaps an imaginary black-and-white clapboard in Derek's face.

She relaxes just a tad. He can't help it that he's an actor who sounds as though he's delivering canned lines whether he is or not. For all she knows, he might just be as sweet and genuine as he sounded on the phone.

It's just . . . well, maybe sweet and genuine isn't her cup of tea.

So what is? Rude and abrasive?

You're being awfully hard on Derek, Mia tells herself.

After all, he isn't a loser, per se. He's just theatrical and corny and a little too enthusiastic about her; perhaps, she suspects, about life in general.

But at least he doesn't have yellow teeth, and he doesn't stink, and besides, she isn't sure she has the heart to let him down.

When you get right down to it, there's nothing horrible about him that warrants her changing her mind at the last minute. Nothing at all.

Nothing other than the fact that he isn't . . .

"Dominic!"

A voice is calling his name from somewhere across the crowded, stunning marble lobby of Mandalay Bay.

The *wrong* voice, Dom can't help thinking.

The right voice would be female. And it would belong to Mia. But she's probably using hers to say *"I do"* right about now.

He turns away from the registration desk, and it takes a moment for him to recognize Jonathan Spencer striding past the tropical palm trees, exotic fish tanks, and squawking caged parrots. "There you are. I was wondering if you'd checked in yet."

Dom has never seen the head of advertising sales at MAN in anything other than a business suit. But Jonathan fits right into the island resort theme in chinos and a short-sleeved Hawaiian print shirt, and there's a beer in his hand. Ice cold and freshly opened, judging by the tendril of frost swirling from the brown bottle neck.

If Dom had any illusions about this trip being strictly about business, they've been shattered in an instant.

"My flight just landed," Dom tells him

as they shake hands.

"You've got some catching up to do. Things are hopping already."

"Don't worry. As soon as I check into my room I'm going to get caught up on all my accounts. Did the media buyer for Heineken get back to you yet?"

Jonathan laughs. "I didn't mean catching up on work, Chickalini. Didn't anyone ever tell you that all work and no play makes Dom a dull boy?"

With a slow grin, Dom says, "You know, I tell myself exactly that every day of my life."

"I knew you'd be a good hire." Jonathan claps him on the back.

Dom revels again in the good fortune that led him from the hectic Blair Barnett Advertising Agency to the laid-back ad sales department at the new MAN cable television network. The programming caters not to the family man, or the retiree, or the college student, or the homosexual, but to well-off men who enjoy women, sports, popular music, adventurous travel, high-performance cars, decadent indulgences, cutting-edge technology. In other words, men like Dom himself.

He can hardly believe he's getting paid for this — and paid very well, at that. He might even be able to afford a Manhattan apartment if he buckles down and socks away the promised bonuses and commissions. He's never been very disciplined with his finances, but now is definitely an opportune time to start saving. He's going to be thirty in no time, and a thirty-year-old man should own a home of his own.

Until now, the lack of a down payment or even the hefty Realtor's fee on a Manhattan rental hasn't been the only thing keeping Dom at home with his father. He has to admit — to himself, only — that life has been pretty cushy on the Chickalini homefront.

Between his sisters, who pop in at least once a day, and his aunt Carm, who long ago took the motherless Chickalinis under her ample wing, he's never lacked for hot meals or clean laundry.

Then again, on his new salary, if he buckles down and budgets his expenses, he might be able to afford not just a great apartment, but a housekeeper as well.

More money isn't the only perk his new position offers. The job revolves around wining and dining media buyers and potential advertising clients at the best Manhattan eateries and bars. Not only that, but many of the buyers and clients are attractive, successful, single females.

At this point in his life, with a bachelor pad on the horizon and a bevy of business-women to entertain, settling down with a spouse should be the last thing on his mind.

And it is, he reminds himself firmly, as the bride from the plane tries to work her way into his consciousness yet again.

The waiting desk clerk clears his throat. "Sir?"

"Oh, sorry." He hands over his new gold corporate credit card.

"I called your room a while ago to tell you to meet me in the casino," Jonathan informs him, and pauses to sip his beer. "I thought you might be up for some poker."

"I would have been. The flight was late and it took me forever to get over here from the airport. There's more traffic on the strip than I remember from my last trip. Is it really bad all the time, or just right now?"

"Traffic? Yeah, I wouldn't really know about that. This hotel is amazing. I haven't left the place once since I got here."

"When was that?"

"Yesterday. Like I said, you've got a lot of catching up to do, my friend. Why don't you go get rid of your bag and meet me in the casino?"

"Now? Are you serious?"

"Yeah-ah."

"I knew this was my kind of job," Dom says with a grin, relieved to feel almost like Fun-Loving Carefree Guy again.

He was temporarily insane back there on the plane, obsessing about Mia. It must have been the altitude.

Okay, you were still obsessing about her long after you landed, he reminds himself. You were still obsessing about her until . . .

Well, until right about now.

Well, that must have been the heat. Heat makes a man do crazy things.

But he's over her now. Yes, sir.

"Well?" Mia asks anxiously as Derek returns from the airline's lost-luggage counter, which was too far to walk in feet that are not only swollen, but now bloodily blistered. "What did you find out?"

"I found out all the luggage from your flight was picked up off the carousel. There was nothing left on the belt after the last passengers got their bags."

"But I didn't get my bags."

"I know."

"Derek, where are my bags?" she asks, clutching his sleeves, thinking of all those beautiful outfits she bought yesterday — her version of a trousseau.

"Don't worry, we'll figure it out. They want you to fill out this form so they can try to trace it."

"But . . . I need my sneakers." She's whining. But she can't help it.

"We'll get some for you right after the ceremony. I promise."

"But . . . I can't get married in these shoes. I can't go anywhere in these shoes. My feet are bloody stumps."

To his credit, he doesn't say whatever it is that he might be thinking. Mia certainly hasn't a clue, and can't find one in his facial expression. Derek is the Stepford Groom, as far as she's concerned.

"Then we'll get you some sneakers before we do anything else."

"Like walk another step?"

He sighs and looks around the airport.

Mia watches him, wondering whether he's searching for (a) *a wheelchair,* (b) *a sneaker emporium,* or (c) *the nearest exit.*

How about (d) *who the hell knows?*

"What size are you?" he asks.

All right, so the answer was obviously B.

At least this will give her a few minutes to regroup, clear her head . . . and maybe make a run for it, bloody stumps and all.

"Hey, before I forget, guess who I ran into last night in the buffet line?" Jonathan asks Dom as they wait at the long registration desk for the desk clerk to finish checking him in.

"Who?"

"Remember the day you interviewed for the job, and you recognized the swimsuit model's picture on my wall, and I told you I met her when she auditioned for that beach aerobics show we're doing?"

"You mean Vera?"

"Right."

"Are you sure it was her and not a mirage?" Dom asks.

"Mirage?"

"I just can't picture her in a buffet line. I never saw her ingest anything other than tepid bottled water."

"She had three green beans on her plate. That was it."

"Then it must have been her."

"It was definitely her. I'd recognize those huge . . ." Jonathan glances at a pair of elderly, eavesdropping women checking in with the next clerk over. "Um, *eyes* . . . of hers anywhere."

"Right. She does have huge *eyes*," Dom agrees.

Now *this* is a sign, Dom tells himself. Vera the swimsuit model being in Vegas at the same time as him is his kind of sign.

Here he was thinking that finding a bride on the plane was a sign that he should be getting married.

Obviously he was dead wrong about that since she is about to marry somebody else.

So *this* is the kind of sign he should be looking for from here on in. A sign that the Single Guy torch is meant to go on burning gloriously high and hot.

"Vera is here in Vegas," he repeats, just to be sure. He can't help but think that it's one hell of an incredible coincidence.

"Vera is here in the *hotel*."

"In the hotel?" All the better. Kismet, that's what it is.

"What is she doing here?" he asks Jonathan, trying to remember why he dumped Vera in the first place. It was over a year ago. She probably got too clingy. They all get too clingy, sooner or later.

"Well, actually, she made it onto the show."

"You mean she's one of the aerobicizing models?"

"Yup. And she's staying here at Mandalay Bay. For the conference. She's with us." Jonathan fishes into his pocket and produces a scrap of paper with something scribbled on it. "Here's her room number. You said you dated her, right? Why don't you look her up?"

"Oh, thanks, but, uh . . ."

He's hedging. Why is he hedging?

He has no idea. He only knows that he isn't sure he's in the mood for Vera. "You dated her too, right?" he asks Jonathan. "You should be the one to look her up."

"Dude, I just got engaged."

"Oh." Here we go again, Dom thinks, before he remembers to offer a halfhearted "Congratulations."

"Thanks. It wasn't really my idea."

Is it ever? Dom wonders. Aloud, he asks, "So what made you do it?"

"Colleen gave me an ultimatum. She said if she wasn't engaged by her thirtieth birthday, we were done."

Ah, the old *thirtieth birthday* ultimatum.

Dom can't help comparing it to the *eighty-fifth birthday* ultimatum Mia is facing. Is she the only woman in the world who's getting married because of an ultimatum she didn't initiate herself?

Too bad she's going ahead with it. She would have been the perfect woman for Dom. No clinginess there; no dreamily romantic happily-ever-after pressure, either.

"So Vera . . . she's all yours." Jonathan thrusts the paper into Dom's hand. "I insist."

"But —"

"I'm your boss, Dom. Take the number."

"Is that an order?" Dom asks, amused.

"You bet it is. Otherwise I might get tempted to look her up, and Colleen will find out about it somehow because she always does, and my engagement will be off and my future will be ruined."

When he puts it that way . . . what is there to do but take the number?

"All right, Mr. Chicklet. You're all set," the desk clerk says, sliding his room key and his credit card across the registration desk. "Good luck."

"Hey, thanks," Dom replies with a grin, almost convinced that all he needs to get lucky is Vera's room number in one hand and a pair of dice in the other.

"So," Derek announces ceremoniously. "This is it."

Mia nods, feeling queasy. "Yup. This is it."

This is definitely the Clark County Courthouse, a turquoise concrete and glass rectangle that Derek erroneously claimed was just a short drive from the airport.

An endless drive is more like it.

Or maybe it just felt endless because of the traffic, and because they had nothing substantial to talk about, and because Derek's golly-gee small talk was getting on her nerves, and because the rental car's air-conditioning wasn't working right.

It was so unbearable in the car that she would have been relieved to arrive just about anywhere.

Anywhere other than here. She can't think of anywhere she'd less rather be.

Oh, yes she can. The Chapel of Luv isn't very appealing, either.

That, Mia thinks ominously, is probably another omen that this marriage is doomed.

But what can she do? The poor guy scraped together every last cent he had, flew to Vegas with all his worldly possessions, rented a tux, and thinks he's about to accompany her not only down the aisle, but back to New York. For good.

Plus, he took care of all the paperwork to trace her lost luggage, and he miraculously located a pair of white sneakers in her size. They're just visible beneath the hem of her gown and Carlotta at the bridal boutique would probably have a heart attack if she knew, but walking down the aisle in Keds is the least of Mia's worries.

"Ready to go in and get that license?"

Derek asks, after coming around to open the car door for her.

"All set," she says with false cheer, accepting the hand he offers to hoist her off the seat.

The layers of silk and lace feel like a shroud out here in the relentless Mojave sun, and she quickly lets go of his hand to wipe a trickle of sweat from her brow.

How do the locals stand it? She can't help but wonder why on earth anyone would choose to live out here in this god-forsaken place, where, as far as she can tell, nothing really grows but cactus.

Then again, Nevada natives might wonder how anybody who inherited the legendary Calogera green thumb could possibly live in the concrete jungle she calls home.

Sometimes, she fantasizes about a house in the suburbs, with a real lawn and garden and leafy shade trees. Glancing at Derek, she tries to picture him as master of that imaginary house, as father of her future children.

She succeeds only in conjuring a row of miniature blond farmers in dungarees, and they all look just like Derek.

What about me? I'd be their mother.

But try as she might, she can't begin to

imagine a child who is a combination of them both.

Her thoughts drift to Dominic — and then to an imaginary pint-sized boy and girl who share both parents' black hair and big dark eyes.

But Dominic isn't going to be the father of my children, fictional or otherwise. He's out of the picture.

This blond, blue-eyed actor is her future, and she'd better get used to that.

Dominic awakened to a scream — a shrill, bone-chilling scream that belonged to one of his sisters; he couldn't tell which.

He sat straight up in his bed and looked around the room. Illuminated by the patch of moonlight spilling through the open window, his fourteen-year-old brother lay faceup on his pillow in the opposite bed, mouth open, chest rising and falling rhythmically.

For a moment, seeing Ralphie still sound asleep, Dominic thought he might have dreamed the scream.

Then it came again.

"Help! Rosalie! Dommy! Help me!"

Nina.

Something was wrong with Nina.

Dominic's first thought was that somebody had broken into the house and was hurting his sister. His heart pounding wildly, he swung his legs over the edge of the bed and reached for the baseball bat propped near the headboard.

"Ralphie!" he said in an urgent whisper, and jabbed his brother in the ribs.

Ralphie, who was known for sleeping through anything, didn't even stir.

I should call the police, *Dom told himself frantically as he crept toward the hallway.* I can't go head-to-head with a prowler who might have a gun. *"Somebody help me! It's Pop!" Nina shrieked again.*

Pop.

Something was wrong with Pop.

Somehow, Dominic's legs carried him down the short hall to the master bedroom just as Rosalie rushed past him. By the time Dominic forced himself to peek around the doorway, he found Rosalie crouched on the floor beside his father's sprawled form, sobbing hysterically, and Nina dialing the telephone in a panic.

"Ro, do CPR," she said frantically as she dialed. "You have to do CPR. He's not breathing."

"I don't know how, Nina. You do it!"

"I don't know how, either. He's not breathing. Oh, God. Oh, God, please . . ."

Dominic's mind raced. He should have

167

known CPR. He had taken a course in it last year, part of a new school require-ment. But he spent most of the time goofing off — and flirting with the pretty female instructor. When it came time to be tested and certified, he had no idea what he was doing — and she let him slide right through.

Neither of his sisters saw Dom standing there.

And neither of them saw him turn around and run.

Not for help . . .

Just . . .

Away.

His flight wasn't a conscious choice; it was a shameful, instinctive reaction to the horror of the scene before him.

Don't take Pop, *he prayed to God as he ran blindly through the familiar neighbor-hood streets, oddly still on that hot summer night.*

Please don't let Him take Pop, *he begged his mother in heaven.* We need him here.

He ran despite the oppressive humidity, ran as though he were frantically trying to escape from something . . . or perhaps, as though he were frantically trying to get to *something.*

He didn't know where he was headed until he found himself climbing the chain-link fence surrounding the baseball field behind his high school.

No, his former high school.

Just weeks ago, he had been handed a diploma on a makeshift stage built near home plate. Pop was there in the front row, beaming.

Dominic hurled himself over the fence and landed on his feet. He regained his balance and started running the bases. He didn't stop when he reached home; he ran on to first again, and then to second; he ran the bases over and over until he couldn't take another step.

Then he collapsed in the outfield. Panting, he rolled onto his back and looked up at the stars.

Are you up there, Mommy? *he asked silently, searching the night sky for the brightest star of all, the one Pop once told him was his mother.* Are you with me? Because I've never felt more alone — or afraid — in my life.

Tonight, he couldn't find one star that outshone the others. Tonight, they were all the same.

"Are you up there, Mommy?" he whispered. "Where are you? Please, Mommy.

Please. Pop needs your help. He isn't breathing. Please . . ."

And then he broke off, unable to go on. Dominic cried until he was spent, knowing he should go home, but terrified of what he would find there.

In the distance, he heard sirens.

It was a sound that never fazed him, living here in the city. Sirens blared at all hours; police cars and fire trucks and ambulances racing through the street never gave him pause.

But tonight, their wail filled him with an icy foreboding.

Were they headed to his house?

Were they too late?

Please, Mommy. Please, God. Please don't do this to me. Not again. I can't handle this kind of loss twice in my life. I'm just a kid.

No.

He wasn't a kid. Not anymore. He thought of the diploma his father had proudly framed and hung on the wall back home beside his older siblings' diplomas. He thought of his eighteenth birthday, looming at summer's end.

It's time to grow up, *he told himself.* Time to be a man.

Whether you're ready for it or not.

He should go home and face whatever was waiting. Face it like a man.

He should . . .

But he didn't.

Not for a long, long time. And even when he did, he still wasn't ready to face it like a man.

Filled with shame, he doubted he ever would be.

"Don't forget your purse," Derek tells Mia as she turns away from the car.

Oh, right. Her purse: a small white silk clutch with only enough room for a lipstick, a comb, and the driver's license she'll need for identification purposes. She can't fit her reading glasses in, but that's okay. She can pretty much guess what a marriage license will say.

She tucks the purse nervously under her arm.

"And your bouquet," Derek reminds her.

"But we're not getting married yet," she protests, her voice rising about two octaves higher than usual. She looks around frantically, half expecting to see the Chapel of Luv looming in the shadows of the courthouse. "We're just getting the license, right?"

They'd *better* be just getting the license. She thought she had at least a few more hours to either mentally prepare to go through with the wedding, or gracefully call it off.

"Relax, we're just getting the license," he says soothingly. "But don't you think those orchids will wilt out here in this heat while we're inside?"

"Oh. Probably." Reluctantly, she reaches into the car for the bouquet.

It really was sweet of him to think of orchids for her, even if they are bad-luck yellow.

Everything about him is so . . . sweet.

Almost sickeningly sweet. Like when you eat so many cellophane-wrapped treats you just want to barf.

"Do you know how many florists I had to visit this morning until I found just the right shade of phalaenopsis?" he comments, leaning over to sniff them. "Not so pale that the blossoms are almost white, but not so yellow that they're brassy."

"They're beautiful," Mia assures him.

"Not as beautiful as you are."

She can't help but think he can't really be this sickeningly perfect — and, in his perfection, exceedingly *imperfect* for her.

She'll take a good old-fashioned flawed

human any day over this . . . this . . . this perfect gentleman.

Like Dom Chickalini.

Not to keep bringing him up, but he definitely has his faults, she reminds herself. *I like a man with good, solid, glaring faults.*

No pretenses about Dom Chickalini, that's for sure. He's not trying to convince anybody he's anyone other than himself.

As opposed to Derek here, who has his heart set on earning a living onstage convincing everybody he's anyone other than himself.

"Ready?" he asks, smiling.

"Yes," she says reluctantly.

Then, "No."

"Pardon?"

"Wait, I need a mint or something." Her throat is drier than the desert air.

She leans back into the car and rummages around in her carry-on bag for the roll of Mentos she knew she had, but it's nowhere to be found.

Belatedly, she vaguely remembers that something dropped out of her bag back in the airport. Back when she was in Dom's arms, being kissed senseless.

"How about gum?" Derek asks, offering her a stick he somehow happens to have at the ready. Good old Mr. Perfect. "It's Big

173

Red. Will that do the trick?"

No. No, it absolutely will not do the trick, because Big Red isn't Mentos, dammit, and because Derek isn't Dom.

But she thanks him for the gum and folds it into her mouth, the mouth that Dom was kissing less than an hour ago.

"Got everything you need now?" he asks.

"I think so."

No. No, she doesn't have everything she needs. Not by a long shot. But . . .

Plan A, Mia. You're sticking with Plan A.

Yes. What she needs is a willing groom. Now.

And that would be Derek.

Look at him. He's so earnest.

Or is he?

Maybe that wholesome demeanor is a mask. Some character he's decided to adapt for the latest unfolding drama in his life.

Ladies and gentlemen, playing the lead role of Perfect Groom today will be Derek Jenkins.

If that's even his real name. Maybe it's a stage name. Who knows? Maybe it's all fake, the name, the persona, even the blond hair and blue eyes.

She glances at him, looking for telltale dark roots or a sign that he's wearing contacts, and can't tell a thing.

"How's the gum?" he asks.

How's the *gum?*

Ask a ridiculous question . . .

"It's very chewy," is her answer.

He chuckles. Sort of. Looking into his blue eyes, she can't tell whether he's honestly amused, or perhaps masking an insult.

That's the problem with Derek. The guy is an actor.

So what? All the better. He'll be able to convince Grandpa Junie that he's madly in love with you.

That will certainly make her life simpler.

And anyway, maybe he really is as earnest as he seems. A very earnest, very sweet guy. A sweet, earnest, perfectly perfect guy in whom she's certain she will never have anything other than platonic interest.

So she should have no problem with going ahead and marrying him, right?

Right.

Wrong.

"Ready?" Derek asks.

Mia squints into the relentless glare, thoroughly uncomfortable. She wishes she had thought to grab her sunglasses out of her bag. She wishes her feet weren't so sore and bloody and swollen . . .

And, on top of that, cold.

Yes, the only thing under this blazing desert sun that isn't hotter than the hinges of Hades is Mia's ice-cold feet.

It's all because Derek isn't Dom.

Frustrated, she wonders if she's doomed to spend the rest of her life with his name on her mind and his kiss on her lips.

Dom, Dom, Dom.

If you think his name over and over in your head, it sounds like some kind of yoga chant.

Dom . . . Dom . . . Dom . . .

Will this be my mantra from this day forward?

She tries his full name instead.

Dominic Chickalini.

Domin—

ic!

Dominic!

His full *name* . . .

The psychic's prediction . . .

"Hang on, Derek," she says, putting her hand on his arm as he starts to walk toward the courthouse.

"What? Is your dress stuck on something?"

No. But I am.

"Derek . . ." Mia takes as deep a breath as her corset will allow and looks him squarely in the eye. "We have to talk."

Chapter Seven

Vera the Swimsuit Model is just as stunning as Dom remembers, with flowing honey-colored hair, honey-colored eyes, honey-colored skin, and the biggest pair of silicone-enhanced boobs he's ever seen.

Yes, she's the proverbial California golden girl, albeit one with a New Jersey driver's license and a thick Bayonne accent that pops up every so often to ruin the sun-kissed aura.

Still, Dom can't help but notice heads turning as he leads her through the crowded casino at Mandalay Bay after dinner up the strip — which consisted of the Bellagio's legendary full buffet for Dom, and a forkful of lettuce for his date.

No, it isn't much fun to dine with Vera.

But that isn't why he stopped seeing her last year.

Nor was it because she got too clingy.

No, it was because Vera the Large-Breasted Swimsuit Model is as dumb as a post.

The first five minutes in the restaurant with her were brain numbing.

The prospect of an entire evening is . . . well, even more brain numbing.

The only way Dom can possibly salvage the night is by winning big at craps, which is what he intends to do here in the casino. With any luck, Vera will eventually wander off in search of . . . well, whatever it is swimsuit models wander off in search of in these situations. Certainly not food or a good book, in Vera's case.

"Are you good at this?" Vera asks him as they find room at a craps table.

"I'm pretty good," he lies, studying the possible bets.

"How do you play?"

"It's complicated." He gingerly stacks two red five-dollar chips on the Don't Pass box. "Why don't you watch me for a while and —"

"Can I play, too?" She gestures at the chips in his hand.

"Sure," he says reluctantly, offering her a red chip. "Just put it —"

"Ooh, I like the green ones better." She plucks one from his fingers and presses it to her enormous bosom, which is spilling out of her low-cut neckline. "This thingie matches my top, see?"

Yes, and the green thingies are twenty-five bucks apiece.

He clenches his jaw and watches her survey the table.

"I think I'll go for Any Seven," she tells him. "Seven is my lucky number."

"No, don't do that." He stops her in the nick of time, before she plunks down the chip with brazen, clueless confidence.

"Why not?"

"Trust me, it's a sucker bet."

"But seven's my lucky number."

"Trust me," he says again, not willing to kiss twenty-five bucks good-bye all in one shot. Not just yet, anyway. And certainly not when it's not even his bet. "Just put it on the Pass Line. That's a safe one."

She shrugs and obliges with a casual, "If you say so, hon."

Hon? Dom's inner Confirmed Bachelor cringes at the endearment. He wants to remind Vera that they aren't in a relationship, and inform her that they will never *be* in a relationship.

But the game is on, the boxman passing a hand over the chips and announcing, "All bets down."

The stickman, standing beside Vera, asks her, "Want to shoot?"

"Shoot?" she repeats, and Dom, reading her frighteningly simple-to-read mind, realizes it's as blank as her gaze.

She opens her mouth, either to ask the stickman what he's talking about, or to tell him she doesn't even have a weapon.

Then he offers her the dice, and a lightbulb goes on in her hazel eyes.

"Oh." She giggles, looking at Dominic. "He meant —"

"The dice. Yeah. Go ahead, Vera. Choose two and throw them."

She obediently chooses two, a decision that takes her much longer than it should, but nobody's complaining. Probably because as she leans forward to study the dice, her cleavage is on full, gravity-defying display.

She looks at Dom. "How do I shoot them?"

"Just throw them so they bounce off the far side of the table."

She does, and the dice aren't the only things bouncing off the table. As she bends over to watch their progress, her ample bosom verges on toppling out of her neckline.

Realizing he's the only guy at the table who isn't jaw-droppingly intrigued, Dom glances down to see what she rolled before anybody else, including the four male table operators. When he sees the two and five, his own jaw drops.

"Seven!" the dealer at the far end announces at last, and a cry goes up among the bettors.

Vera sends an accusatory look in Dom's direction. "See? You should have let me put my thingie on seven. I told you that was my —"

"You win," he says incredulously. "When the shooter's Come Out roll is a seven, it's an immediate win."

"I win?" she squeals, and jumps up and down. Her ample breasts are also jumping up and down. The boxman, the dealers, the stickman, and the other male players pause intently to take note.

"Did you win, too, Dom?" she pauses to ask belatedly.

"No."

"Why not?"

"Because Don't Pass loses when a new shooter rolls a seven, that's why not."

She looks momentarily contrite. Then the dealer puts a second green chip on top of Vera's first and slides them toward her.

She scoops them up and resumes the cheerleader act, making it plain to see why she was cast in the beach aerobics TV program. As if there were any doubt.

"That was fun," Vera tells Dom, pocketing the two green chips the dealer gave her, and linking her arm through his.

181

Fun? He's had more fun losing a wad of dollar bills down a subway grate.

She's still breathless from her exhilarating *I won I won I won* routine as she asks, "What should we do next?"

Next? All of one minute — one roll — at the craps table and she's talking about moving on?

"Oh! I know! Let's go dancing."

Dom shakes his head. "Nah, I want to play craps awhile. But you go ahead."

"By myself? But I can't dance by myself."

I think you just did, he thinks, untangling himself from her grasp and putting two red chips on the Field.

"All bets —"

"Oh, what the heck." Vera quickly plops her green chips on Any Seven and looks at Dom. "My lucky number," she explains.

"Yeah, I know."

"Oh, maybe I shouldn't put both of my thingies down at once." She reaches out and snatches one chip back, then freezes as a collective gasp goes up among the players.

"Once the chips are down, you don't touch them," Dom says, wincing.

"Oops!" She presses a hand to her mouth and giggles charmingly.

It might be Dom's imagination, but he

could swear the burly stickman giggles right back at her as he offers her the dice.

"Oh, I just had a turn," she says graciously.

"The rule is that you control the dice until you lose," Dom tells her.

"Oh! That's so nice. What a sweet little rule. Thank you." She takes them from the stickman, rolls again.

A seven, and she's won. Again.

The crowd is treated to more joyous squeals. More spectacular jumping.

"Did you win, too, this time, Dom?"

"Nope."

In no time, the crowd around the craps table is two-deep and all male, Vera is on a bona fide roll, and Dom is down to one red chip and a monster headache.

"Hey, Vera, I'm going to go play some slots. I'll be back."

"See you," she replies gaily.

He could have told her he was boarding a shuttle to Venus and she'd have said the same thing.

He walks through the casino, halfheartedly feeds some quarter slot machines until he's depleted his coin supply, then looks around, wondering what he can do next.

He eyes the roulette wheel, the baccarat

and blackjack tables, trying to muster his usual kid-in-a-candy-store enthusiasm. But all he feels is an oddly unfamiliar indecisiveness.

Does he dare?

He's never felt so unlucky in his life — nor has he ever felt this uncomfortable in his own skin. Yes, what's up with that?

Dom's never been any good at gambling . . . but it never really mattered until now. He could blow thousands of dollars in Atlantic City with his buddies, then go out for a nightcap without a qualm, telling himself it was only money.

Yeah, well, it's still only money. And he's making a lot more of it now than he ever has before. And he's here in Vegas, so he might as well gamble.

What have you got to lose? he asks himself. Or rather, the old, carefree Dom asks the new, oddly restrained Dom.

You have everything to lose, the new Dom replies.

Oh, come on. Money is everything?

No.

No, money most certainly is *not* everything.

Dom has already lost something far more important than money today. Something that, given the chance, could very well have the potential to become his "everything."

He glances at his watch. It's almost midnight.

By now, the enchanting Ms. Mia Calogera has become Mrs. Somebody Else and is undoubtedly enjoying her wedding night in a fabulous bridal suite.

All right, *there's* an unwelcome image he definitely needs to block out immediately. Dom's searching gaze falls squarely on the nearest poker table.

I'm in, he tells himself firmly, and makes a beeline for it.

Standing in the jasmine-and-orange-blossom-scented lobby of the enormous Mandalay Bay megaresort, Mia has finally reached the end of the road. Mentally, physically, and emotionally.

She sinks wearily into the nearest sofa and concludes that if she had any doubts as the bizarre day progressed, they've vanished.

It's official.

She's truly lost her mind.

After more or less leaving Derek at the altar — all right, *en route to* the altar by way of the Clark County Courthouse — did she calmly and sensibly return to the

185

airport and catch the first flight out of Vegas?

No, of course she didn't.

That's what a sane person would have done. A sane person who had cab fare and a plane ticket at the ready.

Only a self-diagnosed madwoman would hightail it over to the Mandalay Bay Hotel at the far end of the strip and spend the remainder of the day and the entire night frantically combing the vast premises for the man she was *supposed to* marry.

Upon what did she base that logic?

Why, upon a kooky, Starbucks-drinking psychic who predicted that Mia's future husband's name would start with a *D* and end in a *c* or a *k*.

It makes perfect sense . . . provided one is a raving lunatic.

Mia rubs her burning shoulder blades and wishes she could curl up on the sofa and sleep until next week.

What's stopping you? she asks herself wryly. *You've already made quite the spectacle of yourself.*

She cringes just thinking of how she must have looked, literally running through Mandalay Bay's public space in her wedding gown and white Keds like a deranged wedding chapel escapee.

Bride on the Loose. What an image.

She searched every inch of this place, from the casino and sports book to the enormous pool, shops, and restaurants. In fact, ironically, the only place she didn't bother to check was the wedding chapel.

Maybe she should have. Maybe Dominic Chickalini met a beautiful woman and, inspired by Mia, decided to get married.

Right, that's about as likely as . . .

Well, as Mia convincing him to marry her.

Which was her intention when she showed up here hours ago to find him.

Okay, now that she's come back to her senses, she realizes that even if she finds Dom, she's not going to get him to marry her. Not tonight; probably not ever.

But she has to find him, because she desperately needs him. He's the only person she can turn to; the only one who can even begin to bail her out of this mess.

"Excuse me," a voice asks, and she looks up to see a cuddly couple dressed in a bridal gown and tux.

"Yes?" Mia asks, knowing what's coming because it's been happening to her pretty much from the moment she arrived.

"Do you know which way we go to find the wedding chapel?"

She points them in the right direction with what she hopes is a not-too-hollow-sounding congratulations.

If you don't find Dom, she thinks wryly, *you can always lead paid, guided tours of this place.*

No, she has to find him. He's here somewhere. Here in this hotel, or somewhere on the strip, or at least, somewhere in town.

Sooner or later, she assures herself, *he'll turn up.*

Just probably not today.

Make that tomorrow morning, which, to her surprise, is what today has long since become.

According to Mia's watch, it's a quarter after two — a.m., she's fairly certain, although you never know.

That's the thing about these self-contained superhotels in Vegas. Without windows or readily accessible exits, it's almost impossible to keep track of time passing.

She's so utterly exhausted she can't possibly walk another step.

So here she is, and here she'll stay, right back where she began the futile quest, in the lobby.

Maybe she should just go ask the desk clerk to try calling Dom's room again. Repeated efforts have yielded generic voice mail, and she didn't leave a message.

What would she say?

Hi, Dom, it's Mia from the plane, and I didn't get married to Derek because I would much rather be married to you; I am, in fact, destined to be married to you?

Uh-huh. He'll think she's a raving lunatic, same as she does.

Same as Derek did, when she broke it to him that she couldn't go through with the wedding.

She should have just told him she had cold feet, and left it at that.

But no. She had to ramble on nervously, telling him she had met another man on the plane, a man with whom she had fallen in love at first sight.

Love at first sight?

Yes, just like Mom and Dad, and look how well that turned out for them.

She doesn't *love* Dominic, so why on earth did she have to phrase it that way? For Pete's sake, she doesn't even *know* Dominic.

Well, at least she found out that Derek's gentlemanly act was just that. He was hardly a graceful jiltee. In fact, he was a nasty, angry jiltee who demanded that she pay him for his expenses, which of course she gladly did. In fact, she gladly handed over the certified check she had brought, just to shut him up.

That shut him up, other than to utter a curt "Fine. Good-bye."

As she watched him drive away, Mia felt nothing but relief.

Until she remembered that her carry-on bag — with her wallet, which contained her cash, credit cards, ticket home, and lost baggage claim — was still on the seat.

All she had was a bouquet of unlucky yellow orchids, and a useless white silk purse that contained only a comb, a lipstick, and her driver's license.

If it weren't for a kindly elderly couple who spotted her tearfully loitering outside the courthouse, she would probably still be there. But they offered her a ride, no questions asked, to the only place she could think of to go.

Mandalay Bay, of course.

Dom is the only person she even knows in Vegas. She's counting on him to at least give her enough money for a room and cab fare to the airport.

Or maybe even marry me.

See, this is why she's certifiably insane. She can't seem to get past the idea that Dominic Chickalini is meant to be her husband.

Would she feel that way if his name were

Fred Chickalini or Walt Chickalini or *anything-that-doesn't-start-with-a-D-and-end-in-a-c* Chickalini?

No.

Well, maybe.

Stifling a huge yawn, Mia forces herself up, off her swollen, aching feet. Maybe it's time to try Dominic's room again. And, if he's still not there, to finally leave a message.

After all, she asks herself, *what do I have to lose?*

Three hours and three maxed-out credit cards later, Dom walks into his room to find the red message light blinking on the phone.

Who could it . . . ?

Vera, he remembers suddenly, and his heart sinks.

He forgot all about her, what with all the excitement of winning thousands of dollars in a crazy run of good luck — and then losing it all, and then some.

Now look at him. He isn't just in debt up to his eyeballs, he's a jerk who abandoned his date to the craps table wolves.

Not that she seemed to mind at the time. But she eventually must have realized he wasn't coming back. She probably got worried. Then, most likely, angry.

He sits on the edge of the bed and takes off his shoes, asking himself if he's really in the mood to listen to a message from her right now. She puts on a good act, with the cooing and eye-batting, but he's willing to bet the don't-mess-with-me Jersey girl in her comes out full force if you cross her.

It would serve him right, having to listen to a voice-mail tirade after his behavior this evening.

Then again, there would be plenty of time for retribution.

And he has a seven o'clock breakfast meeting.

That reminds him . . . the message might not necessarily be from Vera. He is, after all, here on business. What if somebody called him with something urgent and work-related?

Leaning back against the pillows, still fully clothed, Dom tells himself he'll get up, wash up, and change in just a few minutes.

Then, before officially turning in, he'll check his voice mail.

Definitely.

"Excuse me," Mia calls down the corridor after a disappearing chambermaid. "Miss?"

On the verge of disappearing around a

192

corner, the woman pauses and turns around. "Yes?"

"I'm sorry," Mia says apologetically, closing in on her like the smooth-talking con artist she's become, "I went down to the lobby to find a lingerie shop and get a little wedding night gift for my new husband, and I seem to have locked myself out of our room."

"Which room was it?"

"That's the problem," Mia tells her, overcoming her delirious exhaustion and mustering the strength to paste a suitably sheepish expression on her face. "I don't remember."

This is never going to work, she tells herself. She should just go back down to the lobby and wait on the sofa where she told Dominic, in her voice mail, he could find her.

The problem is, she found herself dozing off, and the next thing she knew, a security guard was standing over her. Why she assured him she's a guest of the hotel without even being asked, she'll never know.

All she could think was that he might kick her out onto the strip, and then what?

There was nothing to do but pretend she was heading up to her room.

And then, of course, come up with this brilliant plan to break into Dominic's room.

The trouble is, she has executed the brilliant plan half a dozen times now, and it has yet to succeed.

"This place is so huge," she tells her latest potential pigeon, "and I was so excited and distracted . . . you know how it is, being a newlywed on your wedding night . . ."

If the maid knows how it is, she isn't letting on.

"Anyway," Mia goes on, undaunted, "I guess I got lost. Can you help me?"

The woman looks her up and down dubiously, just as every other chambermaid has.

But unlike the others, this one doesn't send her back down to the lobby. Maybe she, too, locked herself out of her room on her wedding night. Or maybe this is her last night working here and she just doesn't give a damn about the rules.

"What's your name?" she asks sympathetically.

"Chickalini," Mia tells her, elated. "Mrs. Dominic Chickalini."

Chapter Eight

"I just couldn't go through with it, Dom. Not after meeting you. Do you believe in love at first sight?"

"Not until I met you," he croons, and pulls Mia into his arms, down into the billowing cloud of king-sized bed.

Her white wedding gown seems to melt away and all at once, she's naked. He gently caresses her warm, silken, herbal-scented skin, first with his hands, then with his lips, feeling her quiver beneath his touch.

"I've wanted you from the moment I saw you on the plane," she whispers, stroking his hair.

"I've wanted you, too. I couldn't think of anything else. But I thought you were gone forever."

"No. I couldn't stay away. I knew I had to find you."

"Oh, Mia . . ."

"Marry me, Dominic. Please. Marry me."

"It wouldn't be platonic," he warns,

lying on top of her, poised to sink into her.

"I know. I wouldn't want it to be."

"And it wouldn't be temporary."

"I don't want that, either. I just want you, Dom. Forever. Until death do us part. Please, Dom . . . say you will."

"I will." And with a jubilant kiss, he —

At the sound of a loud explosion, Dom is brutally jarred out of the most realistic erotic dream he's had since high school.

Dazed, he examines his startlingly plush surroundings.

He definitely isn't back in his childhood home on Thirty-third Street in Queens, that's for sure.

But it takes another moment for him to figure out where he *is:* in Vegas, at Mandalay Bay, in bed — or rather . . . *on* bed? Yes, he's lying on top of the busy tropical print duvet, fully clothed.

What the . . . ?

There's another explosion — only it isn't an explosion.

Somebody is knocking at the door. Urgently.

As he rolls across the king-sized canyon, it all comes back to him.

Mia . . .

No, that wasn't real. That was a dream. A frustratingly unconsummated dream, unfortunately for him.

But the rest of it — the business trip, Vera, the casino — that's all authentic. For all he knows, he's about to open the door to an irate swimsuit model. Or worse.

As harsh reality sinks in, he remembers to wonder if he could possibly have overslept and is now late for his breakfast meeting.

Another burst of loud rapping at the door keeps him moving.

An irate boss would be even less welcome right now than an irate swimsuit model.

Looking around for a clock as he staggers across the room, he finds a table and sees that it's not morning yet. At least, not a reasonable hour.

Who the heck is pounding on his door at 4:42 in the morning?

It must be Vera. Who else could it be?

Did I even tell her my room number? he wonders, arriving at the door and leaning toward the peephole, fully prepared to see Vera in her skimpy, low-cut, twenty-five-dollar-chip-colored top.

Positioning his eye at the peephole, he blinks the last bit of bleariness out of it, then focuses.

You're still asleep, he realizes. *This is definitely not happening in real, waking life.*

Because there on the other side of the door is — quite literally — the woman of his dreams.

"I'm really sorry — did I wake you up?" is all Mia can think of to say after stepping over the threshold into Dom's room. He's fully clothed, but rumpled, and a growth of five-o'clock stubble shadows his jawline. She has always gone for clean-shaven men, but in this moment, she can think of nothing sexier than a masculine hint of beard.

Stop it, Mia. This isn't about sexy. This is about sleeping.

And not, as sexy as Dom may be, with him. She might be attracted to him; she might, in fact, have had ulterior motives when she set out to locate him earlier. But at this point, numb with exhaustion, all she's looking for is a place to catch a few hours' rest, and he's the only one who can help her.

"Wake me up?" he echoes, closing the door after her. "At this hour? Of course you didn't wake me up."

She examines his face as he seems to be wondering whether or not to lock the door. His stubbly-yet-just-as-beautiful-as-she-remembered-it face. "Are you being sarcastic?"

"What makes you think that?"

"You're being sarcastic," she decides, wishing she could kick off her sneakers and take a nosedive into the inviting king-sized bed. At least it doesn't look slept in, although the duvet is wrinkled.

But he's apparently decided to leave the door unlocked, as if to provide ready access out of here without wasting a moment's time.

A horrifying thought crosses Mia's mind. *What if . . . ?*

She quickly looks around for evidence of a female visitor.

"You're alone, aren't you?" she asks, hoping there isn't a woman here with him.

The room seems to be empty, but the bathroom door is slightly ajar. Did a scantily clad female make a run for it when Mia showed up?

"Yes, I'm alone."

Is he telling the truth?

Why wouldn't he? Why would he hide a date from Mia, of all people? For all he knows, she's newly married.

But if you were newly married, she reminds herself, *what would you be doing here with him?*

"What are you doing here?" Dom echoes her thoughts as he crosses toward the window, turning on lamps as he goes.

The question might be straightforward, but his demeanor is not. She didn't miss the swift, sidelong glance that just slid over her in a disconcertingly intimate route. It should have made her instantly uncomfortable; instead, it sparked the embers left smoldering back at the airport in the wake of his kiss.

Her heart pounding, she manages to sound almost flippant as she tells him, "I had nowhere else to go. Trust me, if I did, this is the last place I'd be."

"What happened to the honeymoon suite?" He's come to a halt beside the wide window's drawn curtains, having turned on every light in the room, perhaps in an effort to diminish any semblance of romantic lighting.

"I don't know," she says, wishing he'd come closer so she could see the expression in his inscrutable dark eyes. "I never got there."

"Derek jilted you?"

"I jilted Derek."

"Really." He folds one arm across his middle, bends the other upward and rests his chin on his hand, studying her.

She takes a few steps into the room, un-invited. *"Really."*

"Why did you jilt him, if you don't mind my asking? And I take it you don't mind, considering that you're here."

"I don't mind."

No, but she can't tell him the truth. Not the whole truth, anyway. She can only tell him the part that has nothing to do with her attraction to him. Because now that she's alone with him in a hotel room, staring at him across a big, inviting, empty bed, she's not just dealing with sparks and embers.

She's playing with fire. And in her state of exhaustion, there's no way she'll keep from getting burned.

She tells Dom, "Derek was . . . well, he was just icky."

"Icky?"

"I can't think of how else to describe him." She walks closer, half expecting him to back away, into the drawn curtains, but he holds his ground.

He's still watching her intently, and she's pretty certain she sees a flicker of amusement in his eyes as he asks, "Icky, how?"

"Icky like . . . I can't describe it."

He shrugs.

For a long moment, neither of them says anything.

She watches the amusement fade from

201

his expression, giving way to an intent gaze that stirs something to life in the vicinity of her empty stomach. But this newly awakened hunger has absolutely nothing to do with food.

"I just need more from you, Dominic," *Jennifer said, shaking her head, watching him squirt more ketchup onto his french fries. "This casual dating isn't enough."*

"I don't know what to tell you, Jen," he said, thinking that the back booth of the student union might just as well be surrounded by iron bars. He was feeling increasingly imprisoned here, where they had been hashing out their relationship for hours now.

Rather, she'd been hashing it out.

He'd sat there pretending to listen and munching his way through several orders of fries, and wishing they could just go to the movies as planned.

There was a new Harrison Ford thriller playing just off-campus — the rare, ideal win-win "date" film, in Dom's opinion. He couldn't stand those sappy girly movies, and most girls didn't like action adventure. But every woman he had ever met liked Harrison Ford.

"Tell me that you'll try harder," Jennifer

was saying. "That you'll give more."

"I've given all I have to give."

"No, you haven't," she protested.

"Well, what exactly is it that you want?" he asked, hoping she would say something like "a date to the winter ball" or "a heart-shaped necklace for Valentine's Day" — something he could manage without feeling as though he was compromising anything other than his immediate future.

"I want a commitment," she said, and just like that, her fate was sealed. "That's what I deserve."

"I told you, Jen . . . I think we're too young for commitment."

"Well, I think you need to grow up," Jennifer replied. "You're graduating this semester. You're going out into the real world. You can't go around like a schoolboy forever, dating every pretty girl who comes along for the rest of your life, Dom."

Oh, yes I can, *he thought an hour later, as he bought two tickets for the Harrison Ford film.*

"I'm so glad I ran into you at the union, Dom," Jennifer's sorority sister Shannon said happily. "I've been dying to see this movie."

"Yeah, me, too," he said, putting an arm around her as they walked into the darkened theater.

"Actually," she said, lowering her voice conspiratorially, "I haven't really been dying to see the movie . . . I've just been dying to go out with you. Are you sure you and Jennifer aren't dating anymore?"

"I'm positive," he said, with only a passing flicker of sadness.

Jennifer was a great girl, but she was far too possessive. She was, in fact, just like all the others. You shared a few laughs, a couple of romantic evenings, and Bam! Things got way too complicated, way too fast.

Maybe I'd be more willing to hang around, *Dominic told himself,* if I could just meet the right girl.

Yes. Somebody fun-loving, and smart, and pretty, and caring . . .

Then again, every girl he had ever dated fit that description.

That was the problem. None of them stood out from the crowd. None of them were different enough to make him want to give up all the others. Why should he?

Commitment? Who needs commitment? *Dominic thought contentedly as he leaned back in his seat with Shannon snuggled against his side. Commitment was for old people. Like his sister Nina, who was thirty-seven, hugely pregnant, and had just announced her engagement to the baby's father, their next-door neighbor Joey Materi.*

But come to think of it, Nina had always said she was never getting married or having children.

She wanted to get out of Queens and travel around the world. She wanted to be free.

Kind of like Dominic did.

Now look at her. Tied down with a baby and a husband-to-be. It wouldn't be long before she realized she'd made a huge mistake.

It had to be a mistake, because people didn't change. Not that drastically.

I guess that means it'll never last, *Dominic thought sadly.* Poor Joey. He's going to get his heart broken.

He thought of Pop, crying into his pizza dough on that long-ago summer's day. The unsettling image had stayed with him, try as he might to forget it.

Oh, well. At least that can never happen to me, *Dom reassured himself.* Because if you don't fall in love in the first place, you can't ever get hurt.

"You still haven't told me why you're here, Mia."

He remembers my name!

Well, he should, she sternly reminds her frivolous inner self. After all, she certainly remembers his.

That it happens to be the catalyst for this impromptu nocturnal visit is information she intends to keep to herself, at least for the time being.

"I did tell you why I'm here," she tells him.

"Refresh my memory."

"I had nowhere else to go. And I mean that in the most literal way. I've got nothing but this wedding dress and this purse, which," she goes on, holding it up, open wide for his inspection, "doesn't contain a single penny."

"He robbed you?" Dom is beside her before she can refute it. There's no mistaking the sudden aura of protective chivalry about him. She can't help but find that even sexier than the way he just looked at her, and the five-o'clock shadow.

"Robbed me? No, not . . . not exactly."

"Let me guess. He 'pretty much platonically' robbed you?"

She scowls. "No. He didn't rob me at all."

Quickly, she explains how Derek took off with her carry-on bag. He probably didn't even realize it was in the rental car — although she can't help but think he must have eventually figured that out. Giving him the benefit of the doubt, even if he did try to track her down and return her belongings, he wouldn't have the slightest idea where to find her.

"So now I'm broke," she concludes.

"Yeah, well, join the club."

Her eyes widen. "You're broke, too?"

"I lost some money in the casino."

"How much?"

He tells her.

She shakes her head. "You shouldn't carry that kind of money around in Vegas."

"I wasn't carrying it around. I charged it."

"That's even worse! How are you going to pay it off?"

"With my paycheck, when I get back home," Dom tells her, so casually that she figures he must have it covered. "You still haven't told me where I come in."

"You happen to be the only person I know in town. So . . ."

"So you were hoping I'd rescue the damsel in distress?"

"No," she replies wryly, gesturing at the cursed white beaded wedding gown, "but

I'm definitely hoping you'll rescue the damsel in this dress. I've been trapped in it for twenty-four hours now."

He laughs.

So does she. She can't help it. Maybe it's the ridiculousness of the situation, maybe it's utter exhaustion, maybe it's sheer relief at having found him at last. Whatever the cause, she's feeling positively giddy.

"What is it that you need, exactly?" Dom asks kindly, and she wants to throw her arms around him in gratitude.

All right, not just in gratitude. But passion is out of the question for the time being.

"I need a place to sleep, for one thing," she reluctantly admits, and at his startled look, adds quickly, "Not here with you, of course."

Not that the thought hasn't entered her mind . . . and his, if his reaction is any indication.

"Of course," he agrees casually, but his sightseeing eyes betray him once again. "So you want me to . . ."

"Well, before I knew you were broke, I wanted you to loan me the money for a room. I'm just exhausted," she rushes on, flustered, feeling the heat in his gaze reflected in her undoubtedly flushed face, "and I would love a place to take a hot shower and rest for a while."

"Great, I'll get you a room."

"Are you sure . . . I mean, would that be okay?"

"It would be fine."

"Thank you."

"It's no problem," he says, already heading for the bedside phone. "I'll call the front desk and get you set up."

"You don't know how much I appreciate this. I'll pay you back the second I get home," she promises. "Which leads me to the next huge favor. I was wondering if —"

"I'll get you a plane ticket, too," he assures her, no questions asked.

"That would be —"

She breaks off as he shushes her with a raised hand. He says into the phone, "Yes, I need another room, please, right away."

Mia allows herself to lower gingerly onto the edge of the bed, relieved, depleted, unable to stay on her feet for another second.

Has she ever been this exhausted in her life?

Not to mention uncomfortable. The corset is digging into her ribs, her feet are blistered and throbbing . . .

But now, thanks to Dominic, she's only a few minutes away from a room and a bed of her own. She can strip off the wedding gown and undergarments, soak her feet in a hot tub, get some much-needed rest . . .

"No, no," he's saying, "this room is perfect. It's not that. I mean, I need an *additional* room . . . yes . . . no, for right now."

Listening, Mia fights the urge to lie back on the bed, but swiftly loses the battle. She allows herself to sink back into the duvet, wondering if any bed, anywhere, has ever been this luxuriously inviting.

Because she's momentarily cast her willpower — and better judgment — to the wind, she then allows herself to imagine just how this particular bed could become even more inviting.

That, of course, would involve Dominic undressing and slipping beneath the sheets with her.

Good God, that's a vivid image. Vivid enough to make her blush all over again — *if* she had the energy for blushing.

As it is, it's all she can do to close her eyes in a halfhearted effort to banish the sensual and wholly inappropriate image she just conjured.

Ah . . .

Tired.

She's so, so very tired . . .

"Are you sure?" Dominic is saying into the phone.

It's as if his voice is coming to her from across a great distance.

Mia yawns. She should really sit up.

But that will make her corset dig into her ribs again. At least when she's lying down, it isn't as constrictive.

Still, she really should sit up. Really.

And she will. In a few seconds.

"Nothing else?" Dominic's voice asks, somewhere in the distance. "Can you please just check again?"

Mmmm.

This bed is so comfortable she could just about fall asleep right here, right . . .

"Hey, what happened to you and Vera last night?" Jonathan asks, making a beeline toward Dom as he strides into the meeting room after lunch with two female media buyers who are in from New York for their client's trade show.

"Um, I have no idea what happened to her," Dom tells his boss. *And no way to begin describing what happened to me.* "Why?"

"I heard from the people who are doing her show that she left town with some high-rolling Arab sheik she met in the high-stakes poker room. I thought maybe the producer had the story confused, and they were talking about you."

"Yeah, right." Dom shakes his head, not the least bit surprised — or disappointed — by this latest development. "People are always confusing me for a high-rolling Arab sheik. I hate when that happens."

Jonathan chuckles. "Well, I'm glad it isn't you. MAN needs you."

"I thought MAN also needed Vera."

"Hell, *mankind* needs Vera."

"Well, I hate to break it to you, but it looks like we've lost her."

"Listen, there are plenty of other swimsuit models in the sea. I'm just wondering why. Last time I saw you and Vera on your way to dinner, I figured you were destined for at least a hot night together, and the next thing you know, she's skipped town without you. What the heck happened?"

"She wasn't my type, I guess."

"Not your type? She's every guy's type, Chickalini." Jonathan pats Dom on the shoulder and says sympathetically, "Don't worry, I'm sure you'll find somebody else by tonight."

Worried? Who's worried?

Thinking of Mia, asleep in his bed, he shrugs. "You never know."

As he and Jonathan take their seats for the meeting, Dom wonders if he did the right thing, letting her stay. Isn't he just asking for trouble?

Well, it isn't as though he had much choice in the matter. When he hung up from his phone call with the front desk and saw that she had fallen asleep, he tried to wake her up. He really did.

Well, he tried without actually reaching out and shaking her awake. He was afraid to touch her, knowing that ignoring the forbidden thoughts running through his mind would require a strict hands-off policy.

But he did call her name loudly and repeatedly.

All right, twice. And maybe not as loudly as he should have.

But seriously, he had every intention of asking her which hotel she'd prefer since Mandalay Bay was sold out, and he did plan to get her a room elsewhere.

He just couldn't seem to wake her up.

Not only that, but the night was just about over, anyway. How much sense would it have made to send her packing at that point and pay a whole night's room rate out of his own pocket?

It wasn't just about money. No, sir. But the fact that Dom had lost a bundle last night is definitely an issue. It's going to take him months — maybe *years* — to pay off those gambling charges on his credit cards.

What was he thinking?

He wasn't thinking anything. His brain had obviously fallen into the clutches of old, reckless Dom.

It was also old, reckless Dom who, driven by those same steamy, forbidden thoughts, considered crawling into bed beside Mia as she slept. She looked so beautiful — and vulnerable — with her eyes closed and her hair tousled on the pillow. It was that vulnerability that caught him off-guard — and convinced him to stay away from her.

So he spent the remainder of the night alternately dozing in a chair by the bed and watching her sleep from that safe vantage point. He couldn't quite shake the bizarre dream about her; to have her materialize in his room was almost too overwhelming a turn of events. He wasn't quite sure what, if anything, he was supposed to do about it.

He took a shower and got dressed long before the clock was set to go off, and turned off the alarm setting before he left the room. She never even stirred.

For all he knows she's still there, sound asleep.

At least, he hopes she is.

She might have awakened and left . . . not that it's very likely. Not without money, or a change of clothes.

She's more or less a prisoner in his room until he gets back, and it took all his self-restraint not to dash up there between meals and meetings to check on her.

That, of course, would be a seriously irresponsible thing to do.

He needs to prove himself in his new position, and it wouldn't do to go disappearing in the middle of the conference day.

Mia will just have to wait.

Which will give him time enough to figure out just what he's going to say to her when he does see her.

"How was lunch?" Jonathan asks, shattering his thoughts.

"Lunch?"

"With those two buyers."

"Oh! Lunch! With those two buyers! It was great. I think they liked our package." And one of them, the more attractive one, definitely liked Dom's package, judging by the looks she kept giving him across the table.

Dom's attempt to flirt right back at her resulted in unaccustomed awkwardness on his part.

The problem was, he just wasn't interested. Everything about her was wrong, from her rail-thin, petite stature, tailored suit, and pale, fair-skinned comeliness to her all-business wheeling and dealing.

Try as he might to keep his mind on media sales, his thoughts couldn't stop wandering from the boardroom to the bedroom and a tall, curvy, Mediterranean beauty in a bridal gown who had probably never seen an office cubicle or spreadsheet in her life.

Chapter Nine

After emerging from the longest, hottest, most eagerly anticipated shower of her life, Mia slips into the plush white terry cloth robe hanging on a hook on the back of the bathroom door. As the sleeves fall past her fingertips and the hem hits her ankles, she's enveloped in the all-too-familiar masculine scent of Dom's cologne.

The waft of fragrance is enough to send a shiver of intrigue through her, try as she might to dismiss it as a chill. Being here, in Dom's room, among Dom's things, is the next best thing to being with him.

She still can scarcely believe that he didn't send her out to a room of her own, as planned, and can't help wondering whether he spent the rest of the night in bed beside her. Not that she was actually *in* the bed until after he left, but still . . .

The idea of sharing a bed with Dom, even on top of the duvet, fully clothed — and fully unconscious — is decidedly titillating.

Standing in front of the mirror, she wipes away a patch of condensation and checks her reflection to see whether she's any the worse for wear after yesterday's ordeal.

To her surprise, she doesn't look the least bit haggard. Aside from some smudged eyeliner at the base of her lashes that wouldn't wash off in the shower, she looks like her usual self.

Given the grueling physical and emotional marathon that had begun at the airport back in New York, what *isn't* surprising is that she feels as though she's taken a beating. She can't help but wonder if she'd be any more sore and battered had she jumped out of the plane somewhere over the Grand Canyon. *Sans* parachute, but wearing a tourniquet in the vicinity of her waist and rib cage.

What a relief it was to take off the corset and dress at last . . . and anticlimactic to say the least, considering that it took her almost a half hour to single-handedly unfasten the row of elusive, tiny buttons up her back. She would probably have gone ahead and ripped the bodice apart, if she'd had anything else to wear.

The thought of donning that getup again now is about as appealing as marching up the strip in the midday desert heat wearing a down parka.

Maybe it wouldn't be so bad without the corset . . . but of course, it won't fit her any other way. That's what she gets for not allowing enough time for fittings. Say, fourteen months instead of two days.

She takes her time towel-drying her hair, looking over the array of toiletries on the counter as she does so. It isn't snooping, really. Not if she doesn't touch anything. She tells herself that she's simply looking for something she might use as eye makeup remover.

Hmm. Toothpaste and deodorant brands say a lot about a person. Old Spice and Crest indicate, at least to Mia, that Dom is no pampered metrosexual despite his appearance. No, he's clearly more of a man's man, down to earth and old-fashioned. Apparently, he's also effortlessly good-looking and robustly healthy, judging by the lack of styling products or prescription medications visible in his open leather Dopp bag.

Does she dare use his hairbrush?

She gazes into the foggy mirror at her damp, tangled black tresses.

Does she dare *not* use his hairbrush?

Mind made up, and feeling vaguely like a ransacking prowler, she reaches into his Dopp bag and feels around for it. When her fingertips encounter a telltale foil-wrapped package, she can't help but pull it out.

Just looking at it, she feels her pulse pick up a little. Granted, she's seen condoms before. But finding them here, in the hotel room of a man to whom she's wildly attracted . . . well, it seems to have triggered a series of naughty images in her brain.

Yes, she knows, intellectually, that a virile man like Dominic Chickalini wouldn't be opposed to a little extracurricular activity on a business trip. But this blatant evidence of his sexual preparedness is a virtual beacon as far as Mia is concerned, spurring intimate visions of an aroused Dom actually using them.

With her.

Stop that! It isn't going to happen.

If only Mia could remember *why* it isn't going to happen.

My goodness, it's hot in here, she thinks, waving at the steam still wafting in the air. Dropping the foil packet back into the Dopp bag, she searches her suddenly spotty memory for what it was she was looking for in there in the first place.

Oh, right. His hairbrush.

She finds it and uses it, along with the blow-dryer hanging on the wall.

Then she carefully cleans Dom's brush of telltale evidence. As she pulls the dark strands from the bristles, she can't help but notice, once again, that his hair is precisely the shade of her own.

Not that it means anything.

Nothing other than that length is all that distinguishes his hair from hers. Oh, and that they would probably make a striking couple.

You're really out there, Mia, do you know that?

She sticks her tongue out at herself in the mirror and notices, once again, the smudged eye makeup. It doesn't look bad, really. The faint charcoal outline rimming her lashes makes her eyes look bigger, and perhaps more seductive, than usual.

Returning the brush to Dom's Dopp bag, she considers using his toothbrush, or even calling down to the desk for one. She quickly decides neither option is a good idea and winds up squeezing a dollop of Crest on her index fingertip instead. After rubbing her teeth with it, she rinses with the hotel's mouthwash.

There. Kissably fresh.

Not, she reminds herself sternly, that she's likely to kiss anybody any time soon.

Turning her attention to her wardrobe

options, she acknowledges that she basically has none.

At least, none that appeal to her fashion aesthetic or her claustrophobic urge to leave the room. She can either wear this robe, or the wedding gown she placed on a hanger in the closet, or nothing at all.

Maybe, if they were staying up the strip at Caesar's Palace, she could fashion a bedsheet into a toga and blend in with the Roman atmosphere of that hotel.

Here at Mandalay Bay in the pseudo seaside tropics, she'd have to dress like a fish. Oh, or a mermaid. Not likely.

Yawning, she realizes she'll either have to stay put in the room until Dom shows up again or don the dreaded wedding gown again.

If she chooses the latter option, she'll certainly get more use out of it than she intended, which is a nice perk, given the astronomical amount she paid for it. Not many people get more than one day's wear out of the most costly garment they'll ever purchase.

Then again, not many people put on a wedding gown in the morning without eventually making it down the aisle before the day is through. It's almost a shame that Mia's dress didn't get to serve its original purpose . . . though it isn't, by any means, a shame that she isn't married to Derek.

Still wearing the robe, she exits the bathroom and returns to the relative arctic chill of the next room. Brrr. She pulls the robe's shawl collar up a bit and shivers.

The bed is still rumpled. She had awakened sometime midmorning to find herself fully clothed on the bed, and no sign of Dom. After a brief moment of embarrassed panic at the realization that she had fallen asleep before he could get her a room of her own, she crawled beneath the covers for another few hours' sleep.

She awakened only when the maid tried to come in, and sent her on her way after accepting an armload of clean towels. She should probably make the bed now, she decides, looking at it.

Now, she halfheartedly fights the powerful urge to strip off the robe and slip between the toasty, butter-soft sheets once again.

Toast. Butter. Good Lord, she's famished.

But she's just as exhausted as she is hungry.

Yes, she managed to get some much-needed rest in the wedding gown, but it would have been much more comfortable to sleep without it.

Does she dare return to that cozy warmth and catch forty more winks au naturel?

She wonders where Dom went this morning and what time he'll be back. It's early afternoon now.

She decides she probably has at least a few more hours with the room to herself. After all, this is a business trip. He's probably . . . well, doing business. During business hours.

It can't hurt to at least see what those soft cotton sheets would feel like if you weren't tourniqueted into a wedding gown, right?

Wrong.

Wrong?

What if Dom walks in?

Okay, *that* would be a problem.

Which is why she can't actually take a nap. She'll merely climb into bed for a minute or two, just to warm up. She won't even let her head hit the pillow this time.

Brooding through his meeting, Dom ponders the cosmic significance of his predicament.

All right, maybe not predicament, per se.

Then again, what else do you call it when

there's a beautiful, wedding-gown-clad woman in your confirmed bachelor bed and marriage on your confirmed bachelor mind?

He figures deeper meaning has to be there somewhere.

After all, he was raised to believe that everything happens for a reason. That coincidences never are; rather, they're part of something bigger, some divine plan.

How else could he begin to explain a beguiling bride crossing his path twice in one day? Especially on a day when he had already actually begun to contemplate settling down at some point.

Yes, but you can't marry her. This isn't a fantasy sequence where absolutely anything can happen. This is real life, your life, and you know the ground rules.

Well, he can't just say good-bye to Mia again, either. At least not yet. She's under his skin in a way no other woman has ever been; he has to find out what makes her different. If, indeed, she really is.

Maybe she's just like all the others and it's Dominic who's suddenly different.

Maybe, as much as he hates to admit it, Maggie was right about him growing up and settling down.

But that doesn't mean it has to be with Mia.

Or even that it has to happen any time soon.

I just want you, Dom. Forever. Until death do us part. Please, Dom . . . say you will.

I . . .

Won't!

No way. The thought of forever with *anyone* — including the seductive dream bride in his hotel room — still strikes him with fear.

Maybe he's no longer tempted to bed every swimsuit model or boardroom barracuda who crosses his path, but he isn't ready for death, either.

Not death, you moron. "Until death do you part." As in, marriage.

For old Dom, there would have been little to distinguish the two.

Even new Dom isn't anxious to embrace the idea. Sure, he might be turning the corner, becoming more adult about how he conducts his life. But that doesn't mean he's ready to take the plunge.

Baby steps are definitely in order. He'll start today by acknowledging that eventually, he might actually get married. Then, maybe in a few . . . er, *years* . . . he can work himself up to actively seeking someone to date on a regular basis.

"Coffee?" Jonathan asks, passing a white Styrofoam cup to him.

He realizes the meeting has hit a temporary lull.

"No, thanks." A tremendous yawn escapes him, as if to contradict the caffeine-free reply.

"Are you sure? You look like you can use it."

"You're right." He yawns again, filling the cup from a plastic carafe.

Watching him, Jonathan asks, "So if you weren't up all night with Vera, who were you with?"

"If you must know . . ."

"I must. I'm an engaged man. My only hope now is to live through the sexual adventures of my fellow man."

Dom laughs. Humorlessly. Then, choosing to leave Mia out of this lest his covetous coworker get the wrong idea, he informs Jonathan, "I didn't lose any sleep through sexual adventures. I was in the casino most of the night with a bunch of card sharks from L.A."

"What'd you do, gamble away your life savings?"

"And then some," Dom says, wincing at the thought of all those credit cards he so foolishly maxed out.

At the time, it didn't seem like a bad idea. After all, he had been up. Way, way up. Then he started losing. Not just his winnings, but his increasingly frantic investments in the jackpot he was convinced lurked right around the corner.

It happens to the best of us, bub, one of the L.A. card sharks said, consoling him with a pat on the shoulder as he left the table.

Yeah, well, it isn't going to happen to Dominic ever again. There was no joy in it. Any of it.

Not even winning, when you get right down to it. Which is odd.

Maybe in the wake of meeting — and then losing — Mia, he was trying unsuccessfully to replace her with something bigger, better. Like . . .

Vera.

And . . .

Money.

When he started winning in the casino, nothing was enough. No stack of chips was tall enough to lift him to the emotional summit he perhaps subconsciously sought. Why, he doesn't know. In the past, he might have been fulfilled by a gambling payoff . . .

Or a shallow, stupid swimsuit model on his arm.

Not anymore. He's changed.

So. Starting today, he's going to take full responsibility for himself. No more careless slipups, financial or otherwise.

It's time Dominic Chickalini got control of his life.

"You lost big, huh?" Jonathan is asking.

"Huge."

"Want to try to win it back? I was thinking of hitting the casino after this meeting."

"I thought we were supposed to have drinks with those marketing guys."

"That got pushed back to after dinner. We've got some time off this afternoon, and there's a craps table out there calling my name. What do you say?"

"I say there's a craps table out there calling my name, too. And it's saying —" He intones in a faraway voice, " 'Stay away . . . stay away . . .' "

"Yeah, but you might have a change of luck. You never know."

"No, I know. Trust me." He shakes his head, and says from behind his hand as he covers a huge yawn, "I think I'll take a rain check."

"Okay. Maybe you should just go back to your room and crawl into bed for a while."

"You have no idea," Dom says thoughtfully, "how tempted I am to do just that."

Mia daringly, decisively, slips out of the robe and tosses it onto a chair.

Instantly chilled in the air-conditioning, she hurries over to the bed, scrambles in, and pulls the covers up to her chin.

Just to warm up a little.

Just to see what it feels like, to be in this incredibly luxurious bed without being confined to a corsetlike garment for the duration.

Ah, this is better. Infinitely better. An apt reward for the most challenging — and yes, downright physically uncomfortable — day of her life.

Well, Fuji would certainly be proud of her stamina, not to mention her minimal food intake.

Come to think of it, she hasn't eaten since the airline meal yesterday. Sometime last night, her stomach's incessant growling gave way to survival mode, and her appetite eventually seemed to have shut down.

Now, however, it's back with a vengeance.

Wouldn't it be nice to pick up the phone and order a nice hot room-service meal?

Wouldn't it be even nicer to forget all her troubles and snooze away the rest of the afternoon just like this?

Go ahead, Mia tells herself. *Go for it.*

You deserve it — the room service and the nap.

But before she can make another decadent decision, she hears somebody fumbling at the lock on the door.

Praying that it's just housekeeping again, she burrows into the duvet and calls, "Who is it?"

"It's me," Dominic says, opening the door and stepping into the room. "Who did you think it could possibly be?"

Closing the door behind him, he looks around for Mia and spots her right where he left her. Only this time, she's actually *in* the bed.

Should he really be this happy to see the woman who might single-handedly have usurped his precious plan for a lifetime of bachelorhood?

Who cares? The point is, he's thrilled to see her.

The whole way up to the room, he worried that he might find it empty. He has no idea where he thought Mia might go, but the thought of her leaving without at least giving him a chance to . . .

What?

What is it that you want a chance to do?
Say good-bye?
Kiss the bride . . . again?
And then what? Run away? Again?

She says something in a muffled voice, and he sees that she has the covers pulled up to her nose.

"What did you say?"

"I said," she lowers the covers an inch at most, "I thought you were the maid."

"Yeah, well, I get mistaken for her all the time. Her, and rich Arab sheiks."

"Huh?"

"Never mind."

He puts his room key on the bureau and crosses the room, opening the curtains to let the sun in.

To the north, the strip lies at his feet in all its glory, outlined against a magnificent blue desert sky. Glancing down at the faux Manhattan skyline of the New York, New York resort in the foreground, he's instantly reminded of home — and that Mia shares it.

Maybe, he thinks, they can actually see each other when they get back and things settle down. Maybe he can ask her out on a date or something . . . well, normal.

Yet somehow, the idea of dinner and a movie after all they've been through together seems almost too . . . innocuous.

Okay, so what are you going to do instead? Marry her?

"Where have you been all day?" she asks behind him, thrusting him out of that disturbing tangent, thank God.

"I've been in meetings." He turns to look at her, wondering why she isn't getting out of bed. He can't help but notice that her dark hair is falling in loose waves that beg a man's fingers to comb through them, and that her dark eyes seem larger, softer, than before.

"Are they over?" she asks.

Caught up in his errant desire to take her into his arms and kiss her senseless, it's his turn to ask, "Huh?"

"The meetings. Are they over?"

"Until dinner. How do you feel?"

"Hungry," is the immediate reply, and he realizes she probably hasn't eaten all day.

"Why don't you get up," he suggests, "and I'll take you somewhere to get something to eat before we get you a room or a flight out of here."

Anything to prolong her inevitable departure.

She hesitates. "That sounds good, but . . ."

But she wants to stay here with him, so that he can take her into his arms and kiss her senseless?

He finds himself holding his breath, willing her to say it.

When she doesn't say anything at all, he prods, "But . . . *what?*"

"I, um, don't think I can get up. At least, not with you standing here."

"Why not?" he asks, a split second before he spots the terry cloth bathrobe tossed carelessly on the chair a few feet from the bed, the wedding gown hanging in the open closet across the room, and a lacy white Victorian-looking undergarment with garter fastenings draped over a doorknob.

A slow grin spreads over his face. "Oh. I get it."

"I just . . . the dress was so uncomfortable and, um, after I took a shower —"

She took a *shower?* The images conjured by that nugget of information all but steal his breath away.

"— I couldn't bring myself to put it back on."

"Gotcha." He nods, trying to banish the thought of Mia, nude and lathered with suds, beneath a jet of steaming water. He succeeds only in replacing it with one of Mia, nude, in his bed, her soft skin and silken hair fragrant with soap and shampoo.

Swallowing hard, he asks, "Do you want me to . . . leave?"

"No!" she says quickly. Too quickly, for somebody who purportedly isn't the least bit interested in him. "Don't leave."

So she wants him to stay.

But only platonically, he assures himself. She isn't inviting him to do what he's all too tempted to do. He's got to be imagining the sexual tension hovering in the room like a cloud of casino smoke.

"I mean," she goes on tentatively, "it's your room. You don't have to leave. Maybe you could just . . . turn your back?"

"Sure." He pivots obediently, exhales in an effort to calm himself . . . and realizes he's facing the window.

What if the glass is reflective? He doesn't dare find out. Hearing the bedsprings squeak behind him, he abruptly says, "Wait!"

"What?"

"What, uh, are you going to wear?" he improvises, trying to check the glass.

"Oh." The bedsprings squeak again. "I guess I didn't even think about clothes."

Wishing they weren't an immediate necessity, he admits, still facing the wall, "I didn't, either."

"Okay," she tells him after a moment.

"You can turn around. I'm covered up."

Yes, and what a shame that is, he thinks, turning back to face the bed and finding the blankets securely tucked beneath her chin once again.

"Ooh, I like this one," Mia exclaimed to Grandpa Junie, spotting a row of exquisite pale pink blooms atop the nearest plant's towering stem. "The flowers look like butterflies!"

"Very good, Bella," he said in his Italian accent, looking pleased. "Its botanical name is phalaenopsis, but most people call it a moth orchid."

"That's the one I want," she said, leaning over to gently hold the top waxy blossom to her nose. Just as she realized that it didn't have a scent, the slender stem snapped off in her fingers. Horrified, she said, "Oh, no! Grandpa! Look what I —"

"It's all right."

"But . . . we'll have to buy it now," Mia protested, knowing that they didn't have the money for unexpected expenses.

They came to the nursery on Saturday afternoons just to browse; rarely to buy. Not fully grown plants, anyway. Grandpa Junie propagated most of his plants from seed packets and from cuttings. Then the fragile seedlings vied for sunlight on the windowsill of the small apartment's lone southern exposure.

"We'll buy it," he said now, lifting the moth orchid carefully and examining the pot for a price. "It's a good orchid for a beginner to grow. They bloom for months."

"But this one isn't blooming at all anymore," Mia pointed out. "I ruined it."

"No, you didn't. It will blossom again."

"But you said once before that orchids take seven years to grow a flower."

"No, Bella, not all orchids. If you accidentally injure a phalaenopsis by breaking off a flower spike, a new bloom will soon appear right where it was wounded."

Mia smiled sadly, thinking that life was sometimes like that, too. Her heart was broken when her parents turned their backs on her, but then, slowly, it was healed by her newfound love for Grandpa Junie and Nana Mona.

Still . . .

"I can't let you buy this for me," she said, shaking her head. "I'll earn the money to pay you back somehow."

"No." Her grandfather shook his head stubbornly. "I'm buying it for you. It will be your sweet sixteen gift."

"My birthday was over a month ago, and

you already gave me a gift," Mia protested.

"Yes, but not a store-bought one."

"Yours was better," she said with a smile, thinking of the small bedside table he'd built out of scrap wood and painted her favorite shade of pink.

"Well, you can put your new moth orchid on your new table, and watch, and you'll see what will happen. I'll bet," he said, leaning conspiratorially close, "the flower that replaces the old one might be even more beautiful."

"What if there is no new flower?" Mia asked. "What if I just killed it, and nothing ever grows on this ugly old stem again?"

"It will, Bella," Grandpa Junie promised. "You just have to have patience, and have faith, and nurture the roots with water and with light. You'll see. There will be a new flower someday."

She put the plant on her new table, and she watered and watched it for days, weeks, months. Every morning, she told her grandfather, "There's still no bloom. I told you I killed it."

"No, Bella. Just be patient. Just have faith."

She tried. Really, she did.

But eventually, she gave up. One day, she decided it was time that she stopped *wasting her time on a dead, dried-up old stalk. So she stopped watering, and she stopped watching, and she stopped hoping.*

And one day, not long afterward, Mia woke up, opened her eyes . . . and found herself looking at a waxy pale pink bloom that was, indeed, more beautiful than the original.

"I can't put that wedding gown back on," Mia informs Dom resolutely, the words partly muffled by the bed quilt she has pulled up past her chin.

"Are you sure?"

"I'm positive. No way."

"Well, um, it's not like you have a choice."

"I know, but . . . maybe you could go shopping and find me some clothes? Just one outfit, not anything expensive . . . just enough to get me home."

Now there's an interesting prospect. He pictures Mia in Vera's low-cut blouse, then in a wholly inappropriate series of lingerie items, starting with the one draped over the doorknob. Was she actually wearing that thing? With thigh-high stockings?

"There's a mall right downstairs, here at the hotel. I could go shopping for you," he agrees, his voice cracking embarrassingly, "but . . . I mean, by the time I do that, and get back up here, it's going to be time for me to go to my next meeting. I won't have time to take you out to eat, or to another hotel, or to the airport, if that's what you . . ."

"Oh." She nods. "Then I guess I'm indefinitely stuck here, naked, in your bed. Is that what you're saying?"

"No!" Embarrassed, he shakes his head vehemently. "That's not what I meant. I meant, of course I'll get you some clothes, and you can leave right away."

She smiles faintly, the expression on her face impossible to read. "I didn't mean you had to do that, either."

All right, is it his imagination, or is there a seductive gleam in her eyes and a sensual note in her tone?

"I don't want to inconvenience you," she tells him. "And I'm feeling absolutely ravenous."

"For what?" he asks, trying to decipher hidden meaning in her words.

"I don't know. I only know I have never felt this . . . I don't know, empty. Never in my entire life. I really, really need something now."

Are they still talking about food? he wonders.

"I hate to ask," she goes on, "but . . . I really can't do this without you."

Were they *ever* talking about food?

"What . . ." He pauses, clears his throat, and asks hoarsely, "What do you need me to do, exactly?"

"Maybe you could just lend me a shirt or something to put on for now, and order room service?"

Oh. Definitely food.

Deflated, he says, "Sure. But what about —"

"When you're done with your meetings, you can get me some clothes and get me out of here. If you don't mind being put out. I'm so sorry."

"No, it's okay. I can do that," he agrees, reluctantly relinquishing his more provocative ideas and reminding himself it's definitely better if they keep things strictly platonic.

"I can definitely do that. In fact," he adds, realizing he had barely touched his breakfast or lunch, "I'll get room service for myself, too."

"Here's the menu." She snakes a long arm, still bearing the remnants of a summer tan, from under the blanket.

She retrieves a menu from the bedside table and waves it at him.

"Don't you want to look at it first?" he asks.

"No, I already know what I'm having."

"What?"

"A cheeseburger."

"How do you know they have one?"

"I just do." She nods at the menu. "Go ahead, decide what you want."

It takes him only a moment to settle on the cheeseburger. He calls in the order for both of them, including a couple of bottles of water at her request.

Hanging up the phone, he tells her, "Sorry. I know you're hungry, but they said it'll be at least forty-five minutes."

"That's fine. I can make it that long."

Right. Forty-five minutes with nothing to do but sit here and wait?

He puts the menu back on the bedside table and looks at her. He's surprised to find her watching him.

"Thank you," she says softly, and unexpectedly.

"For room service? It's on my company. They're footing the hotel bill, so don't worry about it."

"No," she says, shaking her head, "not just the room service. Thank you for everything. You didn't have to help me last night, but you did."

"Well, what can I say? I'm a great guy," he says with a laugh.

"No, don't, Dom." She reaches out an arm — a naked arm, he can't help noticing once again — and touches his sleeve. "Don't downplay what you did. It was really big of you to take me in when I had nowhere else to go."

"Look, Mia, I have to tell you . . . I'm no hero," he says, flustered by her heartfelt expression and by his desire to lean over and kiss the smattering of brown freckles on her bare shoulder. "If I were . . ."

He trails off, unable to say it.

"What?"

"If I were a hero," he says, "I wouldn't have walked away from you in the first place, the way I did back at the airport. That was the last thing I wanted to do, and I wish I hadn't."

There. It's out there. His true feelings and vulnerability have been exposed to a woman he's crazy about.

This is a momentous milestone in Chickalini history, and she seems to realize that.

She's staring at him, wide-eyed. "You mean . . . after you kissed me . . ."

He nods.

She smiles ruefully. "I wasn't going to

bring that up, but now that you did . . . why did you do that?"

"Kiss you? Or walk away?"

"Both."

He shrugs. "I kissed you because you asked me to."

She smiles tightly, looking away and shaking her head, as if she doesn't believe that's the only reason.

"And I walked away," he goes on, "because you didn't ask me *not* to."

"What if I had?"

"It doesn't matter. You wouldn't have, because you were on your way to your wedding. Remember?"

"Oh. Right. I remember." Her tone is clipped.

"Look, what was I supposed to do? Ask you not to get married?"

"You could have. You knew it wasn't a real marriage."

"Is that why you called it off? Because you want a real marriage?"

"No," she says sharply. "I don't want a real marriage now any more than I did then. I told you, I don't believe in any of that. I just need a husband, in name only, so that I don't lose millions of dollars."

"Still?"

"What do you mean?"

"I mean, you *still* need a husband?"

"Do you *see* one at my side?" she asks wryly, gesturing around.

Dom quirks his mouth, realizing the only person at her side is . . .

No.

No, he most certainly is not going to step into this trap.

He'd better make that clear right now. "Look, Mia, if you're asking me to —"

"I'm not!" she cuts in, so vehemently that he can't help but take offense. "Trust me, I'm not asking *you* to marry me."

"Why not?"

She lifts her chin with what he imagines is a hint of her grandfather's Sicilian stubborn streak. "Because all I need from you is a place to stay, and help getting back home."

"What about a cheeseburger?" he asks, to break the tension.

The corners of her lips twitch. "I'll take that, too. But nothing else."

Oh.

He should be relieved.

He should be thrilled.

He should be anything *but* disappointed. So why is he?

He wants to ask her what's wrong with him; why she isn't interested in marrying him. But he can't quite bring himself to get the words out because, after all, he doesn't want to marry *her.*

And anyway, she's touching his sleeve again. The unexpected gentle warmth of her fingertips, even across the cloth barrier of his shirt, trips a switch inside him, activating a fierce yearning for . . .

For the impossible.

"Listen, I'll figure something out when I get back to New York," she's saying, oblivious — or is she? — to the heated desire humming to life within him. "Maybe I'll just wait to make any decisions about my future until I meet Grandpa Junie's guy."

"No!" he protests, wishing the distracting ache of longing would subside. Instead, it grows stronger with every second, like a fuel-burning missile getting ready to launch.

"What?" she asks in surprise. "Maybe he won't be so bad."

"You mean . . . you might go ahead and *marry* him?"

She shrugs, not answering, and begins to move her hand away.

He catches it in his own. "Don't do that, Mia."

She looks at him, apparently as surprised by his words, and by his fervent grasp, as . . . well, as *he* is.

Warning bells are clanging in his brain.

Abort mission. Repeat: Abort mission.

"Don't marry some desperate gold digger, Mia," he finds himself blurting. "That's what this guy is going to be. And it would be a huge mistake."

She probes his eyes, startled, intrigued. "Why? And anyway . . . what do you care?"

"I care because it would be wrong. You're too . . . too . . ."

"What?" she asks, almost breathlessly.

He doesn't answer, just leans over and takes her into his arms.

"What are you doing, Dom?"

He just shakes his head and kisses her, no longer willing or even able to fight whatever it is that's happening between them.

If their first kiss back in the airport was sweetly romantic, opening the door to a realm of sensual possibilities, their next is boldly erotic, rocketing them over the threshold to the land of no return.

Dom's lips devour Mia's as he presses her back against the pillows; she goes willingly, pulling him down on top of her.

Now the plush bedding is a hindrance to be wriggled away and tossed overboard, exposing her bare skin to the air, and to his eyes.

There is nothing shy about his gaze as it

flicks over her, then returns to meet her own with reverent awe.

"You're amazing," he whispers, and lowers his mouth to the hollow above her collarbone. He nuzzles her there, and she relishes the wonderfully rugged texture of his manly unshaven face against her skin.

With captivating expertise, he slides lower to lap at one breast and then the other, sending shimmers of heat to her very core.

Fingers buried in his hair, she holds him to her as he expertly tweaks her arousal using his tongue, his mouth, his hands in the most unexpected ways. Somewhere in the back of her mind, she acknowledges that this man is a masterful lover, yet she doesn't care to ponder the comprehensive experience that undoubtedly led to his expertise.

Right here, right now, nobody else exists. Nobody but the two of them. The world has fallen away with the discarded duvet and his hastily shed clothing, and there is nothing left but exquisite sensation.

Mia closes her eyes and perhaps for the first time in her life, simply allows herself to *feel*. Not to think, not to question, not to analyze, not to hope . . .

Just to *feel*.

His lips are everywhere: nuzzling softly

against her ear, then grazing her inner thigh with the promise of pleasures to come.

She tugs him up to kiss him deeply, exulting in the way his tongue performs an erotic waltz with her own as he holds her in his strong, muscular arms, rocking with her.

When she can no longer bear the sublime agony of him, naked, against her, she raggedly whispers, "Please . . ."

Dom lifts his head and looks into her eyes as if to make sure this is what she wants.

"Please," she says again.

With a nod, he tells her, "I'll be right back."

She watches him dash for the bathroom; thinks of the foil packet she spotted in his Dopp bag.

She knew then, she realizes, with a small twinge of guilt. Perhaps even before then. She knew this was bound to happen if she stayed. She wanted this to happen. Her being here, waiting in his bed when he returned, was no accident.

Somewhere in the back of her mind, she knew she could not possibly bring herself to leave this room, this man, without surrendering to some wanton need he'd awakened deep inside her.

Now he walks back to the bed and as she

drinks in the potent, masculine sight of him, a curious calm envelops her. An odd familiarity almost, as though they've been together a thousand times before; as though they've always been together. *Belonged* together.

Look at him; he's a stranger, she attempts to remind herself, but the very idea is ludicrous. He isn't a stranger. Somehow, he isn't.

He sinks back into her arms, kissing her tenderly, and his voice is appealingly husky as he asks, "Are you okay?"

She nods, unable to find her own, hoping that her gaze will tell him everything he needs to know.

He smiles . . . smiles!

Struck by that seemingly incongruous expression, Mia nevertheless finds herself returning it — and fittingly so, for this, she realizes in a burst of clarity as a thousand butterflies flutter to life and are released within her, is what joy feels like.

Giddy with elation, thoughts careening every which way, she gives her head a little shake and murmurs, "This is so . . . so . . ."

How can she begin to tell him what she's feeling? That in all her life, in her wildest imagination, nothing has ever stirred her in this way?

"Shh . . ." He brushes a finger against her lips, then kisses the spot. "I know."

"Do you . . . ?"

Do you feel it, too? she wants to ask, but she doesn't dare.

"Yes," he says softly, "I feel it," and she can't help but wonder how he could possibly have read her mind.

Dom moves into her with excruciating care, kissing her passionately at precisely the moment they're joined. She senses a spontaneity in the act and tells herself that it's okay to believe, if only for the moment, that he, too, is experiencing a profound depth of emotion he's never before encountered.

His movements are flawlessly choreographed with her own, an exhilarating cadence that carries them closer, closer still, breathtakingly close, to the pinnacle.

"Mia," he gasps, "I can't —" He grunts, his eyes closed, his jaw clenched with the effort of restraint.

She can't reply, for a storm of sparks has exploded within her.

She can only clutch his shoulders and hold on, quivering, as the power of his own climax sends him into molten spasms above her.

All she can think, as they hold each other close, still panting in the wake of passion, is that there's no going back now.

Chapter Ten

Forty-eight hours later, Mia is lounging on Dom's bed, painting her toenails a glossy poppy red, when she hears him at the door.

"You aren't supposed to be back yet — and you're not supposed to be spending any money," she scolds, looking up to see him enter the room with a bouquet of tropical flowers in one hand and a shopping bag in the other.

"I know, but the meeting ended early and I saw these" — he waves the bouquet — "and this" — he waves the bag — "and I thought of you."

"Stop spoiling me," she orders, suppressing her delight.

"No." He locks the door, then crosses to the bed, sniffing the air. "What's that stink?"

She returns the brush to the bottle and waves a bare, crimson-tipped foot in the air under his nose. He captures it and kisses her toes, then her ankle, then her shin.

"Wait, stop," she says, laughing and

wriggling out of his grasp. "You're going to get wet nail polish on your suit."

"Who cares?"

"It won't come off."

"Who cares?" he asks again. "That was my last meeting." He loosens his tie. "All I have is one more casual dinner with buyers later, and I'm home free."

Mia's heart sinks.

Sure, she already knows that they fly back to New York tomorrow.

She has, in fact, thought of nothing else since she woke up this morning, naked in his arms for the second day in a row.

She just doesn't want to be reminded that leaving here will mean being anything but "home free" for her.

He bought her a plane ticket on the same flight he's on, and even downgraded himself from first class, despite her protests, so they can sit together.

But they haven't discussed what's going to happen when they actually land. Avoiding the topic has been surprisingly easy.

There's so much else to talk about. Being with Dom is like being with a best friend she's known all her life — one with bedroom privileges. Because when they aren't talking, they're making love.

253

"These," Dom says, handing her the exotically scented, bright-colored bouquet accented by fern fronds, "are for you."

She buries her nose in the fragrant blooms. They aren't orchids — he doesn't even know of her passion for orchids — but who cares?

"Thank you," she tells him. "They smell good."

"Better than that nail polish, anyway." He takes off his jacket, his tie, and begins to unbutton his white dress shirt.

"Sorry," she says with a grin, "but I needed a manicure and a pedicure. And anyway, you're the one who bought me the polish."

Along with every drugstore sundry she could possibly require, as well as enough clothing to last the remainder of her time in Vegas.

Her luggage has yet to be traced by the airline, though she has dutifully called a few times a day to check on it, feeling guilty about everything Dom's bought for her. If it weren't for him, she'd probably still be in that wedding gown and corset, or trapped in the hotel room twenty-four–seven.

Instead, while he's at breakfast and lunch meetings, she's been sunning herself by the pool in a skimpier-than-she's-used-to red bikini and matching sun hat, or working out in the fitness center in body-hugging black spandex. While he's at seminars or dinner, she's at the hotel buffet or strolling the strip in a strappy, low-cut black sundress and sandals — flats, as he pointed out proudly, lest it escape her notice that he wanted to spare her healing feet further agony.

In a sense, it's disconcerting to be dressed by a man — by a *lover,* at that. But thanks to the most unusual of circumstances, she's been forced to surrender herself to his visions and whims. She can't help but be amused, and all right, a little flattered, by her new scantily clad, life-sized Barbie Doll image.

Never before has she been on such a wild ride: sexually fulfilled one minute, and utterly insatiable the next. His voracious appetite matches her own, and it seems that the intoxicating intimacy can go on forever, if only they let it . . .

But we can't, she tells herself now, as she has over and over again these last few days. *Or . . .*

Can we?

Oblivious to her wayward thoughts, Dom momentarily stops taking off his business clothes to present her with the shopping bag, from a boutique downstairs at Mandalay Place, the hotel's mall. "Here, this is for you, too."

Peeking inside, she sees a delicate pale pink nightgown. "It's beautiful," she exclaims, reaching in and running her hands over the lace-trimmed silk. "I can't wait to put it on."

"Yeah, well, I can't wait to take it off. This, too," he murmurs, tugging playfully at the robe she's wearing now.

"Wait, Dom —" She holds the bouquet away so that he won't crush it as he sits beside her and takes her into his arms.

He grabs the flowers from her hand and tosses them aside, seizing her mouth in a fervent kiss. She slips her hands into the halfway unbuttoned opening of his dress shirt, needing to feel his warm skin against her own.

Pressing her palm to his chest, she can feel his heart pounding wildly; as she shifts her weight, her other hand grazes his lap and further evidence of his arousal.

I did this to him, she realizes, as awed by her own newly awakened seductive powers as she is by his physical reaction.

He fumbles hurriedly with the buttons of his shirt and she laughingly pushes him back onto his elbows, straddling him in one swift move.

"What about your wet toenail polish?" he asks wickedly.

"Oh, well, I'll start over later."

He willingly allows her to undress him as though he relishes every move she makes. He flashes a lascivious grin up at her as she strips the starched cotton down his muscular arms. She tugs at his fly and eases the zipper down painstakingly, and he lifts his hips to slip out of the trousers and boxers beneath.

"You, too," he says, and with a swish, her robe pools at her bent thighs.

Shirtless, he's magnificent: taut abs, broad shoulders, firm biceps that beg her fingertips' caress.

"Come here," he says with a groan, and pulls her face down to kiss her passionately.

With that, they're off again, tumbling across the freshly made bed, roaming hands stroking heated flesh.

Pulling him upright, she at last straddles his lap once more, facing him, shoulder to shoulder, breast to chest. Her arms encircle his shoulders and her eyes are wide open, locked with his. She savors his rapt expression, visual evidence of her effect on him as he enters her.

Their sweat-slicked bodies slip erotically in time, exquisite friction building potent heat. He moans her name as his body begins to buck beneath hers, pulsating heat within.

Her breath catches in her throat and she closes her eyes, ripples of inner warmth unexpectedly cascading into intense waves of pleasure. Awash on a sea of sensation, she clings to his stalwart frame as she might to a steadfast buoy in a ferocious storm.

At last the raging tide pitches them to a tranquil shore, panting and exhausted, before gradually ebbing.

Mia kisses Dom's brow, strokes his flushed face and dampened forehead. "That was amazing."

"It was." With a groan, he leans back, pulling her with him. He rolls onto his side, their bodies perfectly aligned, and traces her cheek with his finger.

He seems to study her expression for a long moment, then asks, "What are you thinking?"

"That I wish you didn't have to go anywhere for the rest of the day," she admits readily. "I wish we could just stay here, just like this."

"So do I. And I don't want to go home,"

he says unexpectedly, a shadow gliding across his face.

"Tomorrow?"

"Ever."

She laughs, just a little. So does he.

But then he says, very seriously, "I've been thinking about it, Mia."

"Thinking about what? Going home? And what's going to happen when we get there?"

He nods. "I don't want us to stop seeing each other."

"I don't either, but —"

"But you're going to marry this guy your grandfather picked out for you?"

She sighs. "I don't know."

"You don't know? Yesterday, it was, 'I need a husband, any husband.' "

"No, that wasn't yesterday. That was the day before. We haven't talked about this since . . ."

Since Us, she finishes silently, afraid to put a verbal label on what they've become.

"So you've changed your mind about getting married?" he asks.

"That's not an easy question, and you know it." She rolls away from him, sitting up and raking a hand through her tousled hair.

He follows, leaning into her back, slipping his arms around her waist and pressing a kiss on her shoulder. "I don't want to lose you to somebody else."

"I feel the same way."

"But you don't want to lose the money, either."

Money.

The mere mention of it in this setting seems almost ludicrous.

What's money, really? How can it even compare to this . . . well, whatever it is that's going on between them?

"Who cares?" she asks flippantly, turning to look at him.

"Who . . . cares?"

"About the money."

"You do," he answers, frowning. He pauses, watching her intently, and asks, "Don't you?"

"Eh," she says with a wave of her newly polished fingernails. "I think I could probably learn to live without it."

Mia's words hit Dom like a ton of bricks. Gold bricks. Gold bricks she claims not to want or need.

"Oh, yeah?" he asks doubtfully, even as a wisp of hope takes hold within him. "Where?"

"Where, what?"

"Where would you live without money?

Can you afford an apartment?"

"If I get a job, I can." She scowls. "Why are you looking at me like that?"

"Do you have any job experience whatsoever?"

"I worked at the Gap when I was in high school, before Grandpa Junie won the lottery. Oh, and I waitressed."

"Really?" Somehow, he can't quite picture that. "Where?" he asks, figuring she must have been a cocktail girl at some fancy club.

"At Mike's Diner." All right, he definitely can't picture *that*.

"But only for a day," she adds.

"What happened? They fired you?"

"No, I quit," she says indignantly. "What makes you think I got fired?"

"I don't know . . . why did you quit?"

She shrugs. "Look, I was young. I was lazy. And it was hard work. But I'm different now."

"Yeah," he says, "me, too."

"Come on, I'm being totally serious, Dom."

"So am I. I was just like you. I can't tell you how many jobs I started and lost when I was younger. If it weren't for my old man's pizza parlor, I never would have learned how to work hard."

Not, he admits, but only to himself, that he works all that hard now. Yes, he's continued to rise in his field, but it was largely his charisma and good fortune that got him here.

He decides not to tell her that.

Instead, he says, utterly straight-faced, "You know, you can't always take the easy way out, Mia."

If his friends back home could hear him now . . .

"You're right," she tells him. "I already came to that conclusion. That's why I decided not to marry Derek."

"What about your grandfather's . . . guy?" He holds his breath.

"Him, either."

"You're serious?"

"Dead serious. I'm not going to let Grandpa Junie control me. I'll learn to take care of myself. I mean, it's about time, isn't it?"

He's speechless.

"And anyway," she says in a small voice, as though the implications of her bold declaration are beginning to wash over her, "what choice do I have? It's either the money . . . or you."

The money.

Or him.

And she chose him.

He rolls away from her abruptly, swinging his legs over the opposite edge of the bed.

"What's wrong?" she asks.

He shakes his head, his thoughts reeling.

She's willing to give up everything — everything — for *him*. Her lifestyle, her home, her family, millions of dollars. *Everything.*

She's taking an enormous risk, putting herself on the line in a way he never expected. In a way he's never done himself. Not for anyone.

Well, would you? an inner voice demands.

Would he do the same for her?

It doesn't compare, he tells himself.

Wimp.

But it's true.

It's different for him. He already has a job, a home, a life, money — or at least, the means to make more of it and pay off his debt. There's nothing he has that he could give up for her with as profound a sacrifice as she's making.

If there were . . .

Wait a minute.

Maybe there is.

What's the one thing that means more to him than anything else? The one thing he has that he could never fathom giving up?

Not, at least, until now.

Not until her.

"Dom?" she asks tentatively, behind him.

He turns to see that she's pulled a sheet up to her armpits, wrapping it around to conceal her nudity.

He realizes in dismay that she's utterly misread his silence, his turned back.

She thinks, somehow, that he's shut down emotionally; is oblivious to the floodgate that just opened within.

Looking into her dark eyes, he glimpses a vulnerable little girl who watched her parents turn their backs on her when she needed them most.

She thinks I'm going to do the same thing to her.

"Mia, no," he says fervently, too caught up in the barrage of feelings to collect his thoughts; to speak coherently.

He has yet to grasp the momentous decision he's about to make — has in fact, he realizes, already made.

Wow.

Just . . .

Wow.

"Dom?" she asks again, as though she's giving him one last chance not to be the selfish cad everybody — including Dominic himself — has always believed him to be.

But all he can say, for the moment, is, "Don't."

Are you sure? he asks himself. *Absolutely, positively sure?*

It wouldn't be a forever kind of marriage. It would be more of an . . . agreement. Born of necessity, not of love.

But still . . .

Marriage is marriage.

"Don't," she echoes, bitter disappointment vivid in her eyes. "Don't what?"

"Don't give up the money," he manages, above the freight train roar in his brain.

He'd be giving up his bachelorhood. Maybe not forever, but for as long as she needs him.

Is he prepared to do that? Is he really sure?

He looks at Mia.

Yes. Yes, he's sure.

"Don't give up the money? What are you saying?"

Get it together, Dom. Tell her. Tell her, before you lose her.

"I can't let you do it."

"You want me to marry him after all?" she asks dully.

"No," he says, shaking his head in wonder that she just isn't getting it. "I want you to marry *me*."

Chapter Eleven

"Are you sure you want to do this?" Mia asks nervously outside the hotel's Chapel by the Bay the following morning. She's wearing her wedding gown again — along with the unforgiving corset, which is currently digging into her ribs and hip bones.

"I'm positive I want to do this," Dominic says, but he doesn't sound — or look — the least bit reassuring.

What a difference from his impromptu proposal last night. Then, he was full of plans for the two of them; eager to help her keep her inheritance intact even if it meant convincing the world that they were madly in love and ready to live happily ever after.

"You don't have to go through with this, you know," she tells him, pinning a rose — a red rose — to the lapel of his newly pressed dark suit. He chose it himself from the florist's vast selection, before she could mention her passion for orchids.

She was glad she hadn't, after he said, "My mother's first name was Rose, so this seems fitting."

Yes, in light of that admission, a rose boutonniere does seem fitting, as does the bridal bouquet of red roses he chose for her.

It's the marriage charade itself that doesn't seem to fit.

"If you want to call it off now," Mia is compelled to say, "I promise I won't be —"

"No." He silences her with a kiss, then adds, "I want to marry you, Mia."

She nods, thinking that now would be a good time to remind him once again of their deal.

Last night, when the heat of the moment had passed and they were working out the logistics of the plan, they had agreed that despite their budding relationship, it was definitely a marriage of convenience — meaning, it wasn't meant to withstand a lifetime.

In fact, it probably *won't* last forever. Each of them is entirely free to walk away at any time, with the other's complete blessing and understanding.

Or so Mia keeps assuring herself — and him.

It's the only way she can possibly reconcile Dominic's sudden, shocking proposal with the man who kissed her in the airport, then literally ran scared.

But he wasn't running scared last night. Even earlier today, he didn't seem flustered in the flurry of getting dressed and hurrying across town to the Clark County Courthouse marriage bureau.

It was she who grew more and more nervous as they waited in line for their license. By the time they climbed back into the hotel-furnished limo for the ride back here, she felt not only bleary-eyed from the lack of sleep the night before, and painfully constricted by the corset, but sick to her stomach.

Maybe if the whole thing didn't feel so . . . rushed. Maybe if she'd at least been able to grab a couple of hours of sleep. But there was no time. There were too many details to work out, and the wedding had to be this morning. Their flight is scheduled to leave in two hours, and they can't stay any longer. It will be evening by the time they land in New York as it is, and Dom is due back at work tomorrow morning.

"We should go in," she tells him, feeling calmer now that they're actually here.

"Okay." His voice trembles a little.

"Are you sure you —"

"Stop asking me, Mia. I'm positive."

But she can't help noticing that his hand

is shaking violently now as he reaches up to straighten the stem of the rose on his lapel. It swivels askew again, caught in place by the pin.

"Here, let me fix it," she offers, but he shakes his head.

"It's okay."

"But —"

"It's fine," he tells her. "Really."

As if to offset his brusque tone, he smiles at her.

She smiles back, riddled with misgivings, and certain he is, too.

This was much easier last night, when he had his arms around her and they were talking endlessly about how they'd set up housekeeping in her apartment when they got back home, and introduce each other to their families and friends, and how everyone would react to the bombshell news.

Yes, last night, the prospect of getting married in Vegas seemed romantic and exhilarating; amusing, even. Anything but frightening.

In the cold light of day, standing beside the white three-tiered fountain outside the wedding chapel and wearing the gown that failed to make it down the aisle the first time, getting married is nothing *but* frightening.

All right, so maybe this isn't exactly the

cold light of day. With the temperature hovering near a hundred degrees, the only cold thing in Vegas right now is probably Dom's feet.

And her own.

She's bound to get hurt, sooner or later. Why did she agree to this?

Not for the money.

Not this time, anyway — that much is certain.

She would have given up her grandfather's millions in a heartbeat if it meant keeping Dom in her life.

Ironic the way the tables turned so swiftly: that the only way to guarantee Dom will remain in her life is to keep her grandfather's millions, as well.

So everything will work out. You won't have to move; you won't have to find a job. You'll keep your salary and your inheritance and life as you know it.

Dom thinks he's giving her exactly what she wants and needs.

And he's right; he *is*.

He just doesn't realize that her priorities have changed. That all she wants now — all she *needs* — is him.

Yes, she was willing to give up everything else, but there he was, Mr. Right, offering to let her keep it all — *and* to marry her.

How could she possibly turn down an offer like that?

All right, maybe it would have been the safest choice.

If her thoughts weren't clouded by infatuation, and if she weren't being motivated by a probably meaningless prediction by a probably phony psychic, she might have told Dominic that she couldn't possibly marry him. She most likely would have realized that she really did need to grow up, stand up to her grandfather, and take financial responsibility for herself.

Instead, here she is, following in her mother's footsteps, head over heels in . . .

Infatuation, Mia . . . it's just infatuation.

Right.

Here she is head over heels in infatuation, about to walk down the aisle on a whim.

It's the very thing she swore that she would never, ever do.

But this is different, she tells herself. *I'm not in love, like my mother was. And I'm not thinking it's going to last forever, either.*

When you come right down to it, this marriage is actually a levelheaded business agreement on her part. On both their parts, given the gambling debt Dom racked up in the Mandalay Bay casino.

She finally convinced him that paying it off as soon as they get back to New York will be a mere drop in the bucket in the grand financial scheme of things. She can afford it a million times over, and anyway, it's the least she can do in return for his marrying her.

"Ready?" Dom asks, exhaling a shaky breath and looking down at her with those dark eyes that captivated her from the start.

"Ready," she says decisively, and takes the arm he offers.

On a whim, he bends his head and kisses her; a dizzying, soul-stirring kiss that jolts her to the very core.

"I'm glad we're doing this," he says softly. "Just so you know."

She smiles, shaken, unable to speak.

A levelheaded business agreement on her part.

Sure.

You just go on telling yourself that, Mia.

In the chapel, rectangular white columns rise past elegant murals, and sunlight splashes through large French windows framed by filmy curtains.

It was Dom's idea to hold the wedding right here at the hotel, not realizing couples make reservations for the chapels months in advance. The luck he lacked in the casino was with him when he booked the ceremony: the smallest chapel was available this morning.

For a price.

A price he insisted on charging to his lone remaining credit card. He isn't an opportunistic unemployed actor. A bride shouldn't pay for her own wedding.

Never mind that Mia thinks she's going to pay off all his credit cards when they get home anyway.

He isn't about to become a kept man. According to the prenup he just signed, he'll keep his bank account and his own income. If the marriage ends, so will any potential claim to her finances. Which is fine with him. He doesn't need her money. He just needs . . .

Her.

There. He'll admit it. In some capacity, yes, he needs her. But not to the point where he would be here marrying her if she hadn't come to Vegas to get married in the first place. No, if she were just a regular woman he had met on the plane — a regular woman and not a *bride* — he certainly wouldn't be standing here in this wedding chapel.

273

By now, they would long since have had a few laughs, some intimate moments, and gone their separate ways, sailing into the sunset.

Instead, he feels as though he's sailed directly into a tempest, lost in uncharted territory on a raging sea.

A twinge of panic takes hold as he gazes at the plank —

Er, white satin aisle runner.

Father Michael O'Bannon stands serenely at the opposite end, between two towering urns spilling over with fresh white flowers.

Mia had suggested that they locate a Catholic priest, and he wholeheartedly agreed to that, though he secretly doubted it would be possible to find one on such short notice.

Once again, good fortune was with them.

Or maybe it's just that absolutely anything is attainable in Las Vegas.

Dom feels an unexpected pang of regret, looking at the unfamiliar priest in his white robe. He can't help but think of good old Father Tom, the Chickalinis' longtime parish priest back home in Astoria.

If he had ever allowed himself to imagine getting married one day, he probably would have assumed Father Tom would officiate. And of course, he would have pictured the wedding taking place at Most Precious Mother. He was once an altar boy there. He attended Catholic school in the old brick building adjacent to the church. It's where his parents, sisters, and older brother were married; where his mother was eulogized; where everyone in the family, including Dom himself, was baptized.

Well, he never did imagine his own wedding.

So you can't possibly be disappointed, right?

Right.

The priest beckons.

Mia puts her right foot forward, clad in low-heeled white satin pumps. He bought the new shoes for her on his way back to the room after his business dinner last night, and threw the old ones — the ones that tortured her feet — into the garbage can.

How carefree he felt then, laughing with her.

How trapped he feels now, so fraught with tension that his collar and necktie seem to be strangling him, and his breath seems to be permanently caught in his lungs.

"Wait!" Dom blurts, his voice coming out in more of a shout than the intended reverent whisper.

"What is it?"

Yes, what is it? he wonders frantically. *What the hell are you doing?*

He can tell by her voice that Mia is thinking he can't go through with this, that he's about to leave her at the altar.

"My boutonniere," he says, reaching for something, anything, that makes the least bit of sense. "It's . . . it's . . . crooked."

"I know, I tried to —"

"I know. I didn't think it mattered, but . . ."

But it does. He has no idea why, but it really, truly does. If he's going to go through with this — if he's going to walk down this aisle and take wedding vows — he isn't going to do it with a crooked boutonniere.

"Can you . . . ?" he asks Mia, and she smiles. Nervously.

"C'mere. I'll fix it."

He stands utterly rigid as she unpins the red rose on his lapel, telling himself that once it's on straight, everything will be fine again.

No, it won't. You're stalling. You don't care about a stupid flower. You're looking for any reason to put this off even just another few seconds.

"There," she says all too soon, giving his

276

chest a little pat. "You're all set. It's straight now, see?"

Dom takes a deep breath and glances down at the rose, which is indeed straight, and then at Mia.

His *bride.*

"Thank you," he whispers.

"You're welcome," she whispers back, her cheeks flushed with either excitement or worry. Probably both. "Are you okay?"

Dominic nods.

Look at her. She's radiant in her white wedding gown and veil, sunlight falling across her hair. She looks just as she did the first time he saw her, on the plane.

Maybe it really was a sign, he tells himself, and swallows over a sudden lump in his throat. A sign that it's time to stop gallivanting around; time to settle down with just one woman. *This* woman.

Mia's eyes are huge as she gazes up at him, as if she can't quite believe this is really happening.

Neither can he. The last seventy-two hours have been by far the most impassioned, the most shocking, the most — *surreal* — days of his life, culminating in this, the most startling turn of events yet.

I'm actually getting married, he tells himself in disbelief as they start walking down the aisle. *Married. Me.*

How does he feel?

Not as though he wants to bolt from the chapel, which is definitely a good sign.

Maybe the pressure is off because this isn't a *real* wedding.

All right, it *is* real by Vegas standards, and it's quite real by legal standards. Just . . . not by the old-fashioned head-over-heels-in-love standards.

Mia even assured him that she won't hold him to his vows indefinitely, unless he wants to keep them.

We'll take it one day at a time, is what she said. *Whatever happens, happens.*

Marriage. One day at a time. It's the opposite of everything he's ever thought a marriage should be.

Maybe that's why he's here. Maybe the only way anybody could ever coax Dominic Chickalini down the aisle was to give him a potential Out, a *Get Out of Jail Free* card, right from the start.

Yes, as soon as the going gets tough, he's free to get going.

Come on, don't think of that now, he scolds himself, even as he takes note of a red EXIT sign over the door to the left of the altar.

Another sign?

Maybe.

But it seems wrong, somehow, to literally walk down the aisle reassuring yourself with the knowledge that annulment is a viable future option.

Focus on the moment, he commands, and forces his thoughts back to the present.

How do you feel? he asks himself again.

The answer is, *Surprisingly good.*

Yet, as they pass the rows of empty white curved-back seats, he imagines them filled with his family and friends.

Only the front row is occupied, by a chapel-supplied witness.

Dom can't help but miss his brothers and brothers-in-law. If he were getting married back home, they would be groomsmen, wearing tuxedos.

The thought is so potent he can almost see them, Pete and Ralphie, Joey and Timmy, smiling encouragingly from their formal lineup at the altar. Yes, and he can almost hear his nieces and nephews fussing and his sisters and sister-in-law shushing and the church organist, Millicent Millagros, playing the Wedding March.

Here comes the bride . . . dum dum de-dum.

He's aware that the Wedding March actually *is* playing in the background. But it's recorded. He can't help but think of old

Millicent. Fondly, perhaps for the first time in his life. She's getting up there in years, and she frequently hits the wrong chords.

It seems wrong, somehow, to hear the Wedding March flawlessly executed.

Wrong, too, that Pop and Nina and Ro and Ralphie and Pete aren't here to see their son-slash-brother relinquish his prized bachelorhood.

I didn't make it, he realizes with a start, almost stopping in his tracks.

He falters for just a moment, and Mia looks up at him, as if she's bracing herself for him to flee.

He smiles to show her that he's absolutely fine. They resume walking toward the altar, but his thoughts are reeling.

His thirtieth birthday is still days away. The old Chickalini curse — or blessing, depending on how one looks at it — has struck again.

Dom honestly thought he was going to be the one to break it.

But here he is, in the waning twilight of his twenties, about to leave his single days behind for good.

No, not for good, his inner Confirmed Bachelor amends staunchly, albeit a bit hysterically.

For now.

The music has stopped.

"Please face each other and join hands," Father Michael instructs them after a brief opening prayer.

Mia's fingers are cold and trembling as Dom takes them in his own. He squeezes them to reassure her, but looking into her eyes, he realizes that she knows. She knows what he's thinking. She knows that although he's here, about to be joined with her in holy matrimony, he isn't ready for forever.

The corners of her lips quirk and she raises her head in a slight nod.

She's telling me it's okay, he thinks. *She doesn't expect anything more from me than I'm capable of giving.*

He tells himself that for her, this is strictly about preserving her fortune.

Sure, she said she was willing to give up the money for him . . . but when push came to shove, would she really have done so?

Well, you'll never know now, will you?

No, rather than find out, he had to rise to the occasion and throw his bachelorhood into the ring. Why?

Out of guilt?

Out of chivalry?

Out of sheer stupidity?

281

This is wrong. If we can't both be here one hundred percent, then we shouldn't be here at all.

But they *are* here, and if she isn't going to call it off now, he isn't, either. He promised her that he'd hold up his end of the deal, and if nothing else, he'll prove that he's a man of his word.

On the road to responsible adulthood — the road he decided just yesterday he needs to start following in earnest — that's a solid start.

Then the priest asks, "Have you come here freely and without reservation to give yourselves to each other in marriage?"

Freely?

Why does he have to put it that way?

He isn't about to lie to a priest.

Now what?

Now he has to answer the question, that's what. Answer it honestly. That's what grown-ups do.

All right, so . . . *has* he come here freely?

Yes. This was your choice, Dom reminds himself. *Your choice, and your idea.*

But what about . . .

Without reservation?

He finds the answer to that difficult question in Mia's eyes. She's looking at

282

him with such . . . gratitude? Trust? Whatever it is that he sees there, it warms him
to the core.

For now, at least, his doubts have subsided.

I can do this, he tells himself. *I want to
do this. For her.*

The priest is waiting for a reply.

Dom smiles at Mia and his voice barely
wavers as he says, in unison with his bride,
"We have."

"By the power vested in me by the state
of Nevada, I pronounce you man and
wife."

Mia exhales the breath she didn't even
realize she had been holding from the moment she saw the gold band glinting in
Dom's hand as he slid it over her finger.

Wife.

She's a wife.

She's Dominic Chickalini's wife. Mrs.
Dominic Chickalini.

As her newly minted husband leans in to
kiss her, she finds herself wondering
whether it was a good idea to take his
name.

Funny, it hadn't even occurred to her
until they were in the courthouse, filling
out paperwork that was slightly blurry

without her glasses. In all the postnuptial details they discussed last night, a name change never even came up.

She decided on the spot that she'd better do it. Her old-fashioned grandparents wouldn't understand if she didn't.

So now, at this moment, she has officially become Mia Chickalini.

It has a nice ring to it, she decides.

But what if this isn't permanent? a nagging voice asks.

Maybe she should keep her own name and hyphenate.

Mia Calogera-Chickalini.

That's quite a mouthful.

Maybe —

Then Dom's lips are on hers, and mundane details are momentarily swept from her mind.

When he lifts his head, and she sees him smiling down at her, she can almost allow herself to believe that this is permanent. That they'll be together in sickness and in health, for richer and for poorer, all the days of their lives, just as they vowed minutes ago.

For richer or for poorer.

Dom had raised an eyebrow at her as he repeated that part after the priest. She knew that he was thinking of all that money waiting for her — for *them* — back in New York.

But he isn't in this for the money.

Of course he isn't.

He's in this because . . .

Well, it isn't because he's in love with her, either. If he were, he would have said so.

And it's fine with her. She isn't in love with him, either.

They're merely mutually infatuated.

And he married her because . . . because . . .

All right, if not for love or money, why *did* he marry her?

It's a little late to be wondering about that now, don't you think? she asks herself, as Dominic hands an envelope to the priest and makes a jovial comment that Mia doesn't quite catch.

No, she's too busy wondering if the man who just bailed her out of yet another predicament might be an even bigger, bolder opportunist than Derek was.

Maybe the only difference between them is that Derek was icky, and Dom is wildly attractive.

Maybe he saw her — and her checkbook — as the answer to his gambling debts. Heiress to the rescue . . .

Is that what he was seeing when he looked at her last night, offering to marry her?

Distressed, she bows her head to hide the tears that have suddenly sprung to her eyes. Her gaze falls on the bridal bouquet in her trembling hands.

Roses.

Not orchids.

She just married a man who doesn't even know her well enough to be aware of her passion for orchids. It's not that the flowers matter — she loves roses, too; she loves all flowers. But suddenly, she can't help but think that the bridal bouquet symbolizes just how out of sync this relationship really is.

Well, it's too late to do anything about that now.

She blinks away the tears and looks up just as Dominic turns back to her with a grin, looking relaxed for the first time since they entered the chapel.

"Well, Mrs. Chickalini," he says, "shall we?"

Mrs. Chickalini.

Dear God.

She asks, not as lightly as she intended, "Shall we what?"

Shall we commence the masquerade as happy newlyweds?

Dom looks pointedly at his watch. "Shall we grab our luggage and get to the airport before we miss our plane?"

"Yes," she replies, "we definitely shall. Let's hurry. I want to make sure I have enough time to change out of this dress before we leave."

"Are you sure?"

"I'm positive," she tells him, wondering if she can accidentally leave the gown on the hook behind the bathroom door.

Then she reminds herself that she actually made it to the altar in it. The dress might be uncomfortable, but it's destined to be a family heirloom . . . provided she and Dom last long enough to consider themselves a real family.

For richer, for poorer . . .

Well, he's certainly richer now that he's married to her.

What if he makes me fall in love with him, and then walks away?

She's never felt so vulnerable in all her life.

What have I done?

"Congratulations," the chapel's hired witness calls after them as they retreat down the aisle. "And good luck!"

Good luck.

Looking at her handsome, dashing new

husband, Mia can't help thinking that she's going to need good luck, and then some, if she's to survive this ordeal with her heart intact.

Chapter Twelve

It's raining when the jet touches down at JFK Airport.

Raining, and night, and the traffic is horrendous.

Limp with the sheer physical exhaustion that's finally caught up with her, Mia fights back yet another huge yawn and stares bleakly through the windshield from the backseat of the yellow cab. Nothing to see but a string of motionless red taillights before them, reflected in the shiny black pavement.

She's fully conscious of Dominic's presence beside her in the dark. He's put away his cell phone at last and is presumably looking out the side window. He spent the first fifteen minutes in the cab checking his voice mail at the office and leaving messages on other people's voice mail.

He also called his father to say he was safely back in New York but wouldn't be home for at least a few days. Mia gathered from the one-sided conversation that this development wasn't atypical for Dom.

Either his father, whom he adorably calls Pop, didn't remember to ask where he would be staying, or he's so accustomed to his son's not sleeping in his own bed that he no longer bothers.

Which is fine, in theory. Dominic is a grown man; he shouldn't be expected to account for his nightly whereabouts.

But Mia can't help feeling uneasy at the evidence confirming her earlier suspicion that her new husband might be a bit of a . . . cad.

Yeah, well, those days are over, she reminds herself.

And Dom's gentle concern for his pop's well-being is positively heartwarming. He asked several times how his father is feeling, whether he's been eating right and remembering to take his medicine for his heart condition. He also asked about the rest of the Chickalini clan — all of them, individually, using the names Mia recognizes from one of their conversations about his close-knit family.

Still . . .

In all the time he just spent on his cell phone with his father and everyone else, not once did he mention to anyone that he just happens to have gotten married this morning.

It isn't that Mia expected him to trumpet the glad tidings to every colleague he's ever met. But one would think the news is relevant enough to at least be mentioned to his father . . . wouldn't one?

One might, she concedes, if one knew the man in question at all.

I'm married to an absolute stranger, she tells herself incredulously. *I don't know a thing about him, other than his name and the fact that he works in advertising sales, grew up in Astoria, likes red meat, and just gambled away a small fortune on his credit cards.*

Maybe if the plane trip home had been anywhere near the bonding experience they'd shared on the outgoing flight . . .

But it wasn't. Not at all. After a delayed takeoff due to mechanical problems, and an unappetizing coach-class meal, Dom immediately reclined his seat and fell asleep. When Mia leaned her own seat back, the man behind her protested.

Forced to sit uncomfortably upright, she was left to either brood about her new marital status or watch the new Adam Sandler movie, and Mia wasn't in the mood for slapstick. So she brooded about her new marital status for five-plus hours, wedged into the middle seat between her unconscious new husband and a loudly snoring, obese stranger whose girth spilled into her territory.

It was a miserable trip.

She thought she might lighten up once they reached New York, but now that they're here, things only seem worse.

JFK Airport was as chaotic as it always is. Their luggage — Dom's garment bag, and the new duffel he bought at Mandalay Place to hold her new possessions — took forever to come out on the carousel. She wanted to stop at the airline's lost baggage counter and check the status of her claim, but the line there was endless, and Dom convinced her to forget it.

She didn't tell him, as they wove their way through the terminal and the line at the taxi stand, that the lost baggage could stay lost, as far as she's concerned. Everything in it is more or less expendable now that she's back in New York.

She just wanted to prolong the time at the airport because she isn't quite ready to go home and face her grandparents with her big news.

But that's precisely where they're headed. Rather, they were, until traffic ground to a halt a mile from the airport.

Mia initially welcomed the delay, but

now the silence between her and Dom seems strained. She can't think of a single thing to say, under the circumstances, that wouldn't seem trite.

She dares to sneak a sidelong glance at him, and finds him doing the same thing.

He smiles — she can see that much in the dim light — but she can't tell whether it's genuine.

"Excited?" he asks, and she has no idea how to reply.

Excited doesn't begin to cover her current frame of mind.

Traumatized would be more like it, but she decides to keep things positive and shoots the question right back at him. "Are you?"

"Sure."

Sure? His answer is a little too laid-back for her taste.

"When are you going to tell people about us?" she asks.

"People? Do you mean, people in general, or . . ."

"Your family would be a good start."

"We'll tell them together. In person. On the weekend. How does that sound?"

"It sounds fine," she says, relieved that at least he's not planning to hide his marital status indefinitely.

"What do you think your grandparents are going to say when we walk in together and you tell them?" he asks.

"Maybe we shouldn't walk in together," she says quickly. "Maybe you should wait downstairs in my apartment while I go up and talk to them."

"Sure, whatever you want."

She wishes she could see his expression. It would certainly be helpful to know whether he's as affable as he sounds, or is merely agreeing because she didn't really give him a choice.

"So do you think they'll like me?"

Surprised by his earnest tone, Mia can't help but answer with a confidence she doesn't feel. "Of course they'll like you. You're a nice Italian boy from Queens, aren't you?"

"Who's easier to win over? Your grandmother or your grandfather?"

"My grandmother, definitely. She'll make you some lasagna and watch you eat it. If you tell her you love it, she'll be on your side for life."

"What if I don't love it?"

"You lie. When it comes to her cooking, she's very sensitive. And very vain. She thinks she's the best cook in the world, and all you have to do is agree with her and she's yours."

"Is she the best cook in the world?"

"Absolutely."

"Then no problem. What about Grandpa Junie?"

"He's a little tougher." Understatement of the year. "Talk to him about stuff you have in common, and you'll be okay."

"Like . . . ?"

"Like . . . loving Nana Mona's lasagna. Because I guarantee you will. And on Sunday, she'll win you over with her gravy and meatballs."

"You mean spaghetti sauce." His tone is good-natured, but she senses that she's hit a sore spot.

"We call it gravy."

"Yeah, well, we call it sauce. And actually, my aunt Carm makes it for us on Sundays, and we all have dinner together at noon, so . . ."

"Yes?"

"You said your grandmother makes her sauce on Sundays, too."

"Gravy. At noon."

"Gravy," he echoes impatiently. "At noon? What are we going to do?"

"About . . . ?"

"Obviously, we can't be in two places at once every Sunday."

"Not at once, but . . . maybe your family

can change their time."

"Impossible." He shakes his head. "Maybe yours can."

"Impossible."

They stare at each other.

"Now what?"

"What else? We'll alternate. One Sunday with my grandparents, the next with your family."

"I don't know." He frowns.

"You mean you've never missed a Sunday spaghetti dinner at home in your life?"

"Maybe a few," he concedes. "All I mean is that it's going to be confusing, switching off like that."

Discarding that minor detail, Mia goes on, "What about music? Frank Sinatra and Connie Francis — do you like Frank Sinatra and Connie Francis?"

"I like U2."

"Who doesn't? But what about Frank and Connie?"

"I hope you know that's a major cliché."

"What?"

"That all Italian-Americans are fans of Frank and Connie."

"I also know that it's pretty much true. Do you like them?" she persists.

"Do you want me to serenade your

grandfather with 'My Way' and 'The Summer Wind,' or what?"

Exasperated, Mia says, "All I want you to do is either tell my grandfather you like them, or pretend you do."

"Okay, okay, I like them."

"Really?"

"What do you think? I'm a nice Italian boy from Queens, remember?"

"Good. So you can talk about my grandmother's lasagna, Frank and Connie, and I don't know . . . the Mets."

"The Mets?" he asks in a tone that sinks her spirits.

"You're not a Mets fan?"

"Yankees."

"But . . . you're from Queens."

"I hate the Mets. My whole family hates the Mets. We're Yankees fans."

"Can you at least pretend to be a Mets fan?"

"Pretend? Are you kidding?"

Apparently, that translates into *No*.

"Terrific." She shakes her head. "Whatever you do, then, don't bring up baseball. My grandfather is a die-hard Mets fan."

"Terrific," he says flatly.

They fall silent.

Mia contemplates the deeper meaning beyond Dominic's alliance to the Mets' crosstown rivals. The first thing Grandpa Junie did after winning the lottery was buy season tickets at Shea Stadium, which is conveniently located just a few stops down the number seven line. Prime box seats.

What if, in an effort to bond with his new grandson-in-law, Grandpa Junie invites Dominic to a game? She pictures him sitting there in Yankee pinstripes, jeering the players, then being pelted with garbage by rowdy Mets fans. In her dismal fantasy, Grandpa Junie is the leader of the angry mob.

"Dom," she says tentatively, "maybe —"

She breaks off with a wince as the cabdriver blasts his horn at the unmoving vehicle in front of them and utters an ominous foreign word that must be a curse. It sure as heck isn't a friendly little greeting.

"Maybe what?" Dom asks.

She was going to say, *Maybe you should just go home to your house, at least for tonight.*

But that seems like the easy way out . . . doesn't it?

What are you so afraid of?

Are you afraid Grandpa Junie won't approve of your marrying a Yankees fan?

Or are you more afraid that in the grim light of New York City day, you might wake up and realize you made a huge mistake?

Or . . . that he will?

"Mia?" He reaches over and feels around for her hand. Finding it, he squeezes it in his warm grasp.

It's now or never, she tells herself, nerves frayed. Either you admit to him that you're having second thoughts, or you finish what you started.

"Mia?" he prods again. "Maybe . . . what?"

So he has faults. He isn't perfect.

That's part of the Chickalini charm. You willingly chose him over Sticky Icky, remember?

"Never mind," she says, leaning her head on his shoulder and squeezing his hand in return.

Stepping out of the cab after paying the driver, Dom immediately relaxes a little.

This is home — maybe not his familiar block, but it's still his neighborhood, and friendly territory.

After the arid heat out west, he welcomes the damp September chill in the air; even welcomes the drizzle.

I could never live in Las Vegas, he concludes as he steps over the running current in the gutter, inhaling the refreshing New York City air.

Too many warm, sunny days in a row just wouldn't feel . . . natural. Or interesting.

No, he definitely prefers a few rumbling storm clouds rolling in every now and then, just to shake things up a little.

"Is this it?" he asks Mia, nodding up at the building before them as he shoulders his garment bag and the duffle.

"This is it."

The building is nondescript enough: the quintessential small four-story brick building on a side street lined with other buildings exactly like it, a smattering of small trees, and cars parked along the curbs bumper to bumper.

"It's nice," he says, because he has to say something and because it *is* nice. Not as homey as his father's two-story, vinyl-sided house with a concrete stoop that's perfect for lounging and watching the world go by.

But this place is nice in a different way. The low shrubs and tiny patches of grass that front the foundation are neatly trimmed, and there's a border of impatiens, still in full healthy bloom. Fixtures on both sides of the double doors emit a misty glow, and lamplight spills from the windows on the floors above the street.

Mia leads the way up the steps.

"You don't have your keys," he points out. "Do you have to get somebody to buzz you in?"

"Nah." He watches her glance furtively over one shoulder and then the other to make sure nobody is lurking nearby. Then she reaches for the outdoor thermometer hanging on the wall near the door. The case pops off, and she retrieves a key.

"Ingenious," Dom comments, thinking that would be a good idea for his father's house. He's always losing his own keys, and has climbed in a back window or camped out at Nina's next door on more than one occasion.

"It's because of my grandfather. Sometimes he forgets his keys. And he lost them once. He says he's getting old and senile."

They step into the vestibule, where Mia pauses to check one of the metal mailboxes. He watches her riffle through a tremendous stack of envelopes, magazines, and catalogs.

"That's quite a bit of mail for a few days away," he comments.

"Oh, I always get a lot of mail."

From the looks of it, she's quite the avid

consumer. He can tell just by glancing over her shoulder that she's an advertising executive's dream demographic, with numerous store credit cards, a penchant for mail-order shopping, and subscriptions to every women's periodical he can think of.

Reminding himself that if it weren't for him, she would be facing imminent impoverishment, he can't help but feel vaguely . . . all right, for lack of a better word, *used*.

Granted, the marriage was *his* idea.

And he *did* manage to convince himself back in Vegas that she isn't a shallow, coldhearted, money-hungry manipulator, as he initially believed when he heard about her original wedding plans on the flight out.

Still . . .

Faced with the blatant reminder that she has a vast amount of money, and that getting married to him ensures she gets to keep said money, he's losing confidence by the second.

Maybe she had him fooled all along.

Maybe she very cleverly tricked him into becoming an unsuspecting, infatuated pawn in her avaricious little game.

Maybe —

"Let's go up," she says, and he realizes

he could lose himself in that faint, beguiling smile of hers and not give a damn
who or what she really is.

*"Mia? Your order's up," bellowed Bobby,
the short-order cook, then reached out
and dinged the little counter bell to
summon her even though she was less
than a yard away.*

*In the process of untying her grungy
apron, she paused and glanced up at the
plates containing chicken croquettes,
sloppy joes, and the lumberjack special.*

*She should probably deliver just this
one last order before she walked out of
Mike's Diner forever . . . even if she wasn't
planning on sticking around to drop the
check or collect her tip from that particular
table, or any of her others.*

Are you sure you want to quit? *she
asked herself, fighting a little twinge of
guilt as she arranged the plates on a tray
the way she had been taught just hours
ago.*

I'm positive. This is the worst job ever.
It's dirty and noisy and my feet are killing
me and I smell like I just crawled out of a
deep fryer.

*But if she quit, how was she going to
pay her community college tuition for the*

spring semester? Grandpa certainly wouldn't be able to help her. Not on his Social Security income. And she wouldn't ask him, anyway. He and Nana Mona had enough financial worries.

All right, so maybe she could put school on hold for a while. She had no idea what she wanted to be, anyway. Everything she thought sounded even remotely interesting required a four-year degree. She couldn't afford tuition for that much college.

True, Lenore kept talking about the financial aid grant she was getting from her school up in Utica, and how Mia should put in her application. But she kept stalling.

Maybe it was just that she didn't want to go away to college yet.

Or perhaps ever.

The thought of moving away from Grandpa Junie and Nana Mona made her too sad. They took care of her in a way nobody ever had. Why would she want to go off on her own into the world when she had everything she needed right here in Queens?

But Grandpa Junie and Nana Mona weren't going to live forever. What would happen to her when they were gone?

She couldn't bear the thought of it. So she quite simply didn't allow herself to think about it. Ever.

"There you go," she said, depositing the plates in front of the three men sitting in a booth in her section.

"Hey, miss . . . you forgot my bacon," called the Lumberjack Special.

"Oh, sorry." She returned to the kitchen and put in the order, forced to wait another few minutes and ponder her next move.

Not the specifics of quitting. No, that was well thought out, right down to every word she would say to the manager.

She'd been planning her farewell speech pretty much ever since she waited on her first table this morning, a quartet of little old ladies who ran her ragged and left all of forty-five cents on a thirty-dollar tab.

I'm just not cut out to be a waitress, *Mia told herself.*

Just as she wasn't cut out to be a salesgirl at the Gap back in high school. But at least she had lasted more than a day at that job.

Only because of the employee discount, *she reminded herself. Not that she ever looked halfway decent in any of those clothes.*

Well, working in a diner wasn't going to help her with her weight problem, that was for sure.

She grabbed the plate of greasy bacon and returned to the booth.

"There you go, sir," she said, and set it down in front of Mr. Lumberjack Special.

"Miss, can I get some more coffee?" one of his companions asked.

"And more butter for the bread?"

"And some ketchup for the eggs?"

"And a couple of extra napkins?"

Clenching her jaw, Mia retreated once again, wishing she could fling off her apron and walk out of here right now.

"Mia!" a voice called. "Is there a Mia Calogera here?"

"I'm Mia," she replied, hoping they weren't assigning her to yet another table. How was she supposed to quit if they wouldn't let her catch her breath to do it?

"You have a telephone call," the waitress said, gesturing at a phone on the wall behind the counter. "Better make it quick."

Grandpa Junie, *she thought, crossing over to the phone, her heart pounding.* Something must have happened to him. Or maybe Nana Mona. She'd been complaining lately about chest pains.

"Hello?" Mia said breathlessly,

snatching up the receiver.

"Mia?" It was her grandfather's voice, and it was oddly high-pitched. Almost frantic-sounding. That meant something had happened to Nana Mona.

How will I get through this? *she wondered, as panic welled up inside.* How will I live without my nana?

Steeling herself for the worst, she asked, "Grandpa, what is it?"

For a moment, he was talking such gibberish that she couldn't translate a word he was saying.

Then she heard the one word that made sense.

The one word that changed her life, all of their lives, from that moment on.

"Lottery," she repeated incredulously. "Grandpa, did you just say . . . ?"

"I won, Mia!" he shouted triumphantly. "We're rich. You quit that job and come on home. You'll never have to work again a day in your life."

Dominic takes everything in as he follows Mia through the marble corridor, lit by chandeliers and furnished with cushy benches. This might be a private residence, but it reminds him of the lobby of an upscale Manhattan doorman building, albeit on a much smaller scale.

Even the elevator is luxuriously appointed with carpet and mirrors. Glancing into one, Dom is taken aback by the dark circles under his eyes and a liberal growth of five-o'clock shadow. He's still wearing his wedding suit, and his boutonniere is sadly wilted.

You look like hell, he tells himself, realizing that he hasn't had a sound night's sleep since he left home, thanks to Mia. If she wasn't pounding on his door in the wee hours and taking over his bed, she was in it, naked, providing an erotic — and yes, entirely welcome — distraction from sleep.

Then last night, with all the prewedding plans, he hadn't closed his eyes any longer than it took to blink. And the measly few hours' rest he managed to get on the plane was more teaser catnap than deep rejuvenating sleep, that's for darned sure.

All right. So you're wiped out. Snap out of it. This is your wedding night, remember?

Yes, but it doesn't feel like a wedding night — and not just because there's no honeymoon suite. Mia seems to have grown more distant with every moment that's passed since they exchanged their *I do*'s. He's been telling himself she's just nervous about presenting him to Grandpa Junie, but he isn't so sure.

"You look fine," she says quietly behind him, and he realizes she's caught him still staring into the mirror.

"Fine?" He snorts. "I look like I haven't slept in days."

"Well, you haven't. Neither have I. Look at me."

He looks at her. Big mistake . . . or is it?

Remembering precisely why he fell under her spell in the first place, he fights the urge to take her into his arms as he says, "You look beautiful, same as always."

Her expression softens. "Yeah, well, you look pretty good yourself," is all she says.

He shakes his head at the lie, thinking it's a good thing he'll have some time to freshen up in her apartment before the big meeting with her grandparents. He'll take a shower, shave, change into something more . . .

More what?

As the elevator arrives on the second floor, he wonders what he should wear to make the best impression on the old guy. Definitely not his favorite Derek Jeter jersey, that's for sure.

Is it really possible that he's not only *married,* but married into a family of *Mets fans?* No, not only that, but he's been asked by his supposedly sane new wife to pose as one of them?

It's one thing to pretend a sweet old Italian grandmother's lasagna is the best in the world. It's quite another to feign allegiance to one's archenemy.

How could she even suggest such a thing?

How well does he know her?

Not at all. She's a total stranger, and a Mets fan, and your wife.

Good Lord.

Breathe, he reminds himself, feeling a flicker of panic rising within. *Just breathe. It's not as bad as it seems.*

No, he realizes, as the doors slide open. It's worse. Far worse.

For there, standing in the hallway, gaping through thick bifocals into the elevator, is an elderly man with a shock of thick white hair, a cane, and a watering can.

A man, Dominic realizes, who can only be the notorious Grandpa Junie.

"Bella Mia," the old man says, and pulls her into his embrace.

"Grandpa! What are you doing here?" she blurts into his sturdy-for-a-soon-to-be-eighty-five-year-old-man shoulder beneath his cashmere sweater.

"I was watering your plants. Somebody had to. They were —" He releases her, puts his gnarled hands around his own throat, and makes a horrible retching sound, as though he's dying of thirst.

"They were not. I watered them the morning I left."

"What?"

"I *said,*" she raises her voice and checks to see whether he's wearing his hearing aid, "I watered them the morning I left." He's wearing the hearing aid, but he probably doesn't have it turned on. He frequently forgets, and resents being reminded.

"Things dry out fast," he says, after taking a moment to obviously decipher what she said. "Your basil was a drop away from shriveling up."

"The basil, fine. But what about the orchids? The cattleya brassolaelia and the odontoglossums are ephiphytes, Grandpa. They need to dry out between waterings."

"I know they do. They were dry, they were dry."

"Well, I have plenty of watering cans. You didn't have to lug yours up here."

"I like mine better," he says stubbornly.

Then he shifts his accusatory glance to Dominic. "Who's this?"

Mia falters.

She glances at her, um, *husband,* wondering if now is the time to break the news.

To her shock, Dominic saves the day, stepping out of the elevator to firmly shake her grandfather's hand and say in a booming voice even Grandpa Junie should be able to hear, "I'm Dominic Chickalini, sir. It's nice to meet you."

"Chickalini?" Grandpa echoes, as Dominic slips his foot between the doors to keep them from closing.

Mia shoots him a grateful glance.

The last thing she needs is for her grandfather to be stuck here on the second floor with them for any longer than is absolutely necessary. She definitely shouldn't tell him about the marriage here, standing in the hall, on the spur of the moment. Better to wait until he's comfortably settled in his favorite chair upstairs, and she's figured out how best to break the news.

It isn't that she expects him to be disappointed, because, after all, she's done this for him. Married is what he wants her to be.

And married is what she planned to be, anyway. She was planning to come home today with Derek as her husband.

Yes, but I didn't have feelings for Derek. I didn't care whether Grandpa Junie liked him or not. He was just my token groom.

Dominic is . . .

Well, technically, she supposes he's just her token groom as well.

Her token groom with whom she's fallen in . . . into *infatuation.*

"Chickalini . . ." Grandpa appears to be trying to place the name. Then his black eyes light with recognition and he asks, in his Italian-accented English, "Any relation to Cheech Chickalini from Astoria Boulevard?"

"He's my uncle."

Mia exhales in relief. Chalk one up for Dominic.

Grandpa grins, revealing the row of fancy white dentures he bought to replace his uneven, coffee-stained prelottery teeth. "Cheech Chickalini. How is the old son of a gun? I haven't seen him in the barbershop in years."

"Well, sir, I'm afraid that's because Uncle Cheech hasn't had hair in years."

Grandpa Junie — still blessed with a headful, of which he's very proud — laughs heartily.

Mia relaxes a bit more.

"How about that," he says. "Old Cheech

Chickalini lost all his hair. I bet his lady friend isn't too happy about that, huh?"

"Anita? Oh, she's fine with it."

"Anita? Last I knew, his lady friend was named Delores."

"Delores?" Dom shakes his head. "They broke up years ago."

"That's not surprising. Cheech always was a Casanova. He never stayed with anyone for very long. Not even his wives."

"Um, no sir." Dominic shifts his weight uncomfortably and now seems to be avoiding Mia's gaze.

She can't help but wonder just how much he has in common with his Casanova uncle.

"Eh, no great loss," Grandpa Junie says with a wave of his gnarled fingers. "I never liked that Dolores. She dressed like a *putana*. Why are you wearing that flower?"

Dominic, unaccustomed to Grandpa's seamless conversational segues, blinks in confusion — and then dismay.

Mia clears her throat pointedly and says, loudly enough that he can't possibly not hear — or pretend he didn't hear — "Um, Grandpa? The elevator?"

"Come back upstairs with me, Bella," her grandfather says, taking her arm, sending a stern look in Dominic's direction. "You'll wait for her in there."

"Definitely," Dom says, clearly relieved. "Do I, uh, need a key?"

"It's unlocked," Grandpa Junie informs him, his sharp old eyes falling again to Dom's lapel. "That flower —"

"Grandpa," Mia cuts in, "I told you that you have to stop leaving the door to my apartment unlocked."

"Who's going to walk in there besides family?" Grandpa asks, pulling her into the elevator. "I own the building. There's nobody here but us. And him," he adds, shooting another glance in Dom's direction.

Mia heads off the potential question *Who is he, anyway?* with a terse, "Well, you never know. The neighborhood isn't as safe as it —"

"It's safe," Grandpa proclaims, and she wearily clamps her jaw shut, knowing there's no sense in arguing, just grateful the boutonniere seems to have been forgotten for the time being.

As the elevator doors slide closed, Dom sends Mia a last look that obviously reads *Good luck.*

Yeah, right. She's starting to wonder if her luck vanished along with her luggage in Las Vegas.

Chapter Thirteen

With Mia safely upstairs, Dominic is left to explore her apartment alone.

As he walks toward the closed door, he reminds himself that regardless of what he finds behind it, this is going to be his home for . . . well, for however long he stays married to Mia.

It might be a few days; it might be a lifetime.

A lifetime.

A lifetime of *forsaking all others*. That, after all, is what he vowed to do this morning in the chapel.

Forsake all others.

It just sounds so . . . unfriendly.

Relax. Don't think about that now, he tells himself, as the inevitable panic stirs to life right on cue, somewhere in his gut.

But it doesn't turn into the churning wave of panic he might expect. No, it's more of a slight ripple.

He frowns, wondering what that means.

Does it mean that at last, after all these years, it's actually happening? The profound, life-altering "IT" his sisters and Maggie predicted all along?

Is the perennial bachelor really open to settling down?

Or is he simply too jet-lagged to get all worked up about his marital status now?

He opens the unlocked door, steps cautiously over the threshold, and deposits his bags on the floor, feeling around for a light switch. He finds one, right where it should be. So far, so good.

Nice foyer.

Really nice.

Marble floor, potted ferns, elaborate sconces, a couple of paintings that look, to his untrained eye, like authentic art. At least, authentic as opposed to the framed posters in his room back home.

He advances to the next room, the heels of his dress shoes tapping hollowly on the floor. Again, he pauses to turn on a light.

This must be the living room. A bit too formal for his taste, and the color scheme is much too feminine. But it's still beautiful. And huge. He could fit the entire first floor of his father's house in here with room to spare.

There are lush green plants everywhere. Many of them have long stems and bright blooms. He finds himself recapping the conversation Mia just had with her grand-father about watering the plants. Who knew she even had a green thumb? It certainly comes as a surprise to Dominic. She doesn't seem like the kind of woman who would want to get her hands dirty.

Guess you don't know her as well as you thought you did, he tells himself as he bends over to sniff the nearest blossom.

He finds that it's unscented and wonders what good a flower is if it doesn't smell nice. Mia seems like the kind of woman who would like flowers that smell like flowers.

Then again, who knows what she really likes?

Pushing aside a twinge of uneasiness, he pursues his tour.

An Oriental carpet in shades of cream and pale pink lies centered on the polished hardwood floor. Pastel rose silk draperies cover what he assumes is a wall lined with windows. The furniture is off-white, luxuriously upholstered, and looks as though nobody has ever sat on it.

He tries, and fails, to picture himself sprawled on that elegant sofa with a beer and a bag of chips, watching the World Series.

Dominic, whose greatest pleasure in life is watching the World Series with beer and chips, feels a pang of regret. Are those days over?

Is he doomed to view the World Series in this . . . this . . . pink nest?

Wait a minute . . . there isn't even a TV in here. What kind of living room doesn't have a TV? Now it's time to start worrying. Forget the little ripple of uneasiness; this is a tidal wave of bona fide panic.

Calm down. It's probably hidden behind a fancy panel or something. He looks around hopefully. The room seems to have fancy everything except fancy panels.

Well, all right, then maybe there's a plasma television on the wall behind those curtains.

Feeling as though he should go back and take off his shoes first, he gingerly crosses the carpet and peeks through the curtains.

Nope, just windows.

Maybe Manhattan's distant skyline would be visible if it weren't a rainy, misty night, and if he turned off the lamps in the room. Right now, there's nothing to see but his own reflection staring back at him.

It isn't pretty.

Letting the curtain fall across the glass again, he turns away. No need to spend another moment confirming that he's had better days, appearance-wise. He makes his way through the rest of the apartment in search of a hot shower. If he locates a television set somewhere along the way, life will be good.

Adjacent to the living room is a formal dining room. He takes in the chair rail and crown moldings, the hutch filled with delicate pink china, and a big oval table that doesn't look as though it's ever been laden with platters of food or surrounded by hungry family members. In the center is another one of those long-stemmed potted flowers that don't have any scent.

Dom wistfully thinks of the weekly Chickalini Sunday spaghetti dinner, which he is now destined to experience on a strictly semimonthly basis.

Why did he have to be such a stickler about it with Mia? It's not as if he hasn't blown it off regularly over the years, along with countless other family gatherings.

Maybe because these last few months, he's made more of an effort to spend time with everyone.

Or maybe because the reluctant newlywed in him childishly resented having to meet her halfway on this. On anything.

His stomach growls fiercely.

Okay, so he needs a shower, a television, and a snack. All the comforts of home. So far, he's oh-for-three.

He walks through a butler's pantry and, optimistically, into an enormous kitchen. It looks like a magazine picture, with polished granite countertops, restaurant-quality appliances, and custom cherry cabinets. He knows they're custom — and cherry — having learned more than he'd ever want to know about kitchen cabinetry last spring when Maggie and Charlie remodeled their new brownstone.

Nice cupboards . . . and lots more of those potted flowers . . . but where's the food? Does anybody ever actually cook in here?

He checks out the hanging rack lined with top-notch copper pots and pans, the under-cabinet recessed lighting, the backlit stemware displayed on glass shelves behind paned glass doors.

Opening the built-in, cherry-paneled refrigerator door, suddenly needing a beer, Dom is dismayed by the lack of potential snack items.

Well, she's been away. What do you expect, leftover pizza, a monster hero sandwich, chocolate cake?

That would be great, actually. His stomach growls again.

He checks the meat and cheese compartment and finds nothing but a small bowl of baking soda. In the crisper, there are two lemons, a lime, and a clear plastic box of organic mesclun salad greens that look exactly like lawn clippings to him.

Even the condiments in the door are lackluster: plenty of imported mustard, but no mayo or ketchup. Fat-free marinades, lemon juice. The milk, which expired yesterday, is skim. There are ominous-looking little green things called capers but no nice, normal olives. Nothing whatsoever to nibble on. Even the pickles — at least they *look* like pickles — are strange. They're labeled *cornichons* and they're about the size of a fingernail clipping.

Then . . . bingo! Back on the top shelf, he tracks down a couple of Molsons among the bottles of water and fancy salad dressings and helps himself to one. All right, so there's hope for her after all.

Still, Dom can't help but compare this sleek, gleaming kitchen to the cluttered, perpetually crumb-littered one in his father's house.

Back home, the kitchen has reportedly been the same since 1973. The cabinets are dark wood, the appliances are olive green, and the countertops are harvest gold Formica. The wallpaper is covered in groovy daisies, and the white ruffled curtains are trimmed in red rickrack. Cereal boxes are perpetually stacked on top of the fridge, which is covered with magnets and all the nieces' and nephews' artwork.

The best thing about the kitchen at home, in Dom's opinion, is that there's always leftover pizza from the restaurant. And Pop usually keeps on hand a stick or two of pepperoni, cheese, some good olives, Italian bread.

His stomach rumbles again, loudly.

All right, time to get out of the kitchen.

Carrying his open beer, he tours the rest of the sprawling showplace. No wonder she doesn't want to give it up. He almost can't blame her for wanting to marry any old stranger just to keep her lifestyle intact.

But she didn't marry any old stranger, he reminds himself. *She married me. And I married . . .*

Money.

Big, big money.

It's a good thing, he concludes, that he didn't quite grasp the extent of her wealth before he agreed to marry her. If he had, he might question whether his own intentions were really all that noble, or if he, too, might secretly harbor an inner shallow, coldhearted, money-hungry manipulator.

I could get used to this place, he tells himself, strolling down a wide, white-carpeted corridor. *I could definitely get used to it, pink froufrou frills and all.*

There are closets galore, a couple of impersonal-looking obvious guest rooms with polished wood furniture, and three bathrooms, all with deep whirlpool tubs and walk-in steam showers.

There's an actual gym, filled with state-of-the-art exercise equipment.

There's an actual greenhouse, with a potting bench and rows of potted seedlings, blooming plants, tropical-looking full-sized trees.

And there's — *yes!* — a den, complete with that enormous wall-mounted plasma television. He instantly forgives Mia for all that pink; even for the lack of sandwich fixings.

This room is more comfortable than the living room. The furniture isn't exactly masculine — on the contrary, it's floral chintz — but at least he can picture himself sitting here, watching a ball game on that glorious TV.

A *Yankees* ball game.

His spirits buoyed, he reaches for the knob on the last door, knowing Mia's bedroom must lie beyond.

Oh, yes. It's her bedroom, all right. Her luscious floral perfume wafts to his nostrils as he crosses the plush white carpet.

Or maybe it's the flowers he's smelling after all, he realizes, bending to sniff the pale pink bloom that's growing out of a pot on the bedside table. It doesn't have a scent. He can't help but notice, before he glances away, that it does have one distinctive characteristic: the distinctly contoured blossoms look just like butterflies.

Her bedroom furniture is light wood. The clean scent of lemon polish lingers in the air with her perfume, or her soap, or her laundry detergent — whatever it is that makes her smell so good.

The bed is king-sized, covered in a downy white cloud of a duvet and a double row of matching pillows. The filmy curtains at the window and the upholstery on the fainting couch are also white.

He opens the door to the adjoining bathroom. More white, from the marble floor to the gleaming fixtures to the fluffy towels hanging beside the sink to the white long-stemmed flower growing from a white pot beside the sink.

Should he take a shower now, or wait? If he takes one now, he'll be ready to go out to dinner as soon as she gets back. Maybe they can bring her grandparents along and make it a nuptial celebration.

Then again, if he waits, he might be able to convince her to join him in a Jacuzzi bubble bath, and they can order dinner in.

So what do you want to do?

It all depends on whether he's more ravenous for food . . . or for her.

I'll wait, he concludes. *Definitely.*

Dom can't help but feel as though he's already left a telltale bold smudge on the master suite as he casts one last longing look at the bed. He'd like nothing more than to find his way there with Mia in his arms, make passionate wedding night love to her, and then fall asleep.

But that can't happen . . . at least, not yet.

He wonders how she's doing upstairs with her grandfather. Maybe Grandpa Junie was thrilled by the glad tidings — although, having met the man, Dom has to admit that it's hard to imagine his being overjoyed by anything that he didn't orchestrate in its entirety.

But overall, he wasn't so bad, Dom thinks as he works his way back to the kitchen, just to make sure he didn't miss a stray stick of pepperoni in the refrigerator. *I'll win him over in no time.*

★ ★ ★

Mia is prepared for her grandfather to ask her about Dominic as they ride up to her grandparents' quarters, but he doesn't.

He doesn't say anything at all. He faces straight forward, holding the watering can and his cane with one hand and rubbing his jowly chin with the other, his bushy white eyebrows furrowed in thought.

She considers asking him how he enjoyed his European vacation, but she's afraid he'll bring up the arranged marriage thing right here and now. She has no doubt that somewhere in Sicily, an eligible bachelor is packing his bags and waiting for the official summons to Astoria, Queens.

When the elevator doors slide open on the third floor, she's instantly greeted by the delicious aroma of Nana Mona's homemade meatballs and tomato gravy.

"What's going on, Grandpa?"

"What?"

"I *said,* what's going on?"

He opens the door, which, of course, is unlocked. "What do you mean, what's going on?"

"What's up with the gravy?"

"What do you mean, what's up with the gravy?" is his maddening counter.

"Nana Mona's making it on a weekday?

327

Now?" she adds, checking the time on the hall grandfather clock as they pass it.

"What's the matter with now?"

"Now is *late,* Grandpa. That's all."

To say that her grandparents are creatures of habit is putting it mildly. Without fail, Nana Mona starts frying meatballs every single Sunday morning before seven o'clock Mass. Without fail, she serves a complete spaghetti dinner every Sunday precisely at noon.

Never during the week. Ever.

On weeknights, she might make farfalle with butter and peas, or rigatoni with olive oil and garlic, or fettuccine Alfredo, or even her famous lasagna.

But she never, ever, makes spaghetti and gravy on a weeknight. And she and Grandpa Junie always sit down to their evening meal by four-thirty sharp.

"I missed my spaghetti this week. I didn't fly back from Sicily until Sunday night," Grandpa Junie explains, leading the way through the room along the plastic runner, past the gilt-framed paintings of the Italian Riviera, the still-wrapped-in-plastic Victorian reproduction furniture and fringed lampshades.

"So Nana Mona made it for you today?" Mia asks incredulously, still trying to wrap her mind around the curious turn of events.

"Not just for me."

Uh-oh. Thinking of Dominic waiting for her upstairs, and knowing what Fuji would say about ingesting simple carbohydrates at this hour, Mia shakes her head. "Oh, no, thanks, Grandpa, I'm not —"

"Come on into the kitchen," Grandpa cuts in, either because he didn't hear her protest, or because there's no room here for argument. "You'll come, and you'll see."

"See what?"

"I brought a little something back for you from Sicily."

A little something?

Oh, no.

Last time he went abroad, he brought her back a thick gold necklace that had been blessed by the pope. It was adorned with a crucifix big enough to hang on a wall. She wore it once and had a crick in her neck for a week.

He also brought her Italian figs. Lots of them. More Italian figs than one human being should ever have to face in one sitting. He picked them himself, from the tree in the backyard of Fungi Calogera, her second cousin once removed.

Mia doesn't even like the darned things. Not the kind that grow on trees, anyway. But Grandpa Junie had caught her nibbling a Fig Newton right before he left, and he said, "You like figs? That's not a fig. I'll show you a real fig."

The next thing she knew, he was presenting her with ten pounds of them, which he had smuggled back to New York in his suitcase, hidden in the pockets of his packed clothes.

Searching her mind for any misleading information she might inadvertently have given him lately, she's afraid to wonder what he brought her this time.

"Dom, where have you been?" Nina asked, pouncing on him the moment he walked in the door.

"I went out for a few beers after work with my friends," he said, throwing his briefcase down on a chair that was already heaped with jackets and somebody's diaper bag. "Why?"

"Because, you moron, it's Pop's sixty-fifth birthday. You were supposed to pick up the cake and be here by six, remember?"

"The cake!" Dominic smacked his head in dismay. Nina had ordered a special low-

sugar, low-fat cake from a bakery near his office.

Thanks to Pop's heart condition, he wasn't supposed to have regular cake — or regular anything — anymore.

"I forgot all about it," he admitted to Nina.

"How could you?"

"I got busy at work," he said. He wanted to point out to his sister, yet again, that being in account management at Blair Barnett Advertising wasn't exactly conducive to relaxation.

But before he could go on, Nina told him, "Pop kept asking where you were. And Joey had to run down to Carvel and pick up an ice-cream cake. You know Pop's not supposed to have that stuff."

"Did he eat it?"

"It's his birthday, Dominic. What do you think?"

He shook his head. "Sorry, Nina. I blew it."

"You sure did. Just like you blew it last week when you were supposed to meet Ralphie at Penn Station."

"I already said I was sorry for that," Dom reminded her — not that he really was sorry. Not much, anyway. Not for that.

In his opinion, if his kid brother was old

enough to be living away at Saint Bonaventure University, he was old enough to get himself home from the train station when he came back to New York for winter break.

It wasn't Dom's problem that Ralphie had so much luggage to carry. He wasn't his kid brother's keeper. That was Nina's self-appointed position.

"Yeah, well, being sorry doesn't undo the damage, Dominic."

"I told you I was stuck at the office that night working on a client presentation, remember?" he said indignantly. "I couldn't go to the train station. I have responsibilities."

"And this family is one of them," Nina informed him. "Only you seem to keep forgetting that. Just like you seem to keep forgetting that it's your duty to help out in the pizza parlor with the rest of us."

Here we go again, Dom thought, his mouth set grimly.

"I have a job," he pointed out. "A demanding job."

"We all have other demanding jobs," Nina said, probably considering chasing around after two little kids a demanding job.

"I just wish you'd pull your weight

around here a little more, Dom," his sister said. "Maybe you can get by on your good looks out in the real world, but don't forget that around here, you're just one of us."

He brushed by her, heading toward the dining room, where he could hear the rest of the family talking and laughing. He didn't have a present for Pop, but he'd make up something. Something great. Something better than what he'd received from anyone else.

Dom would promise him . . . orchestra tickets to see Connie Francis the next time she was in town. Or . . . box seats at the Yankees' Opening Day next spring.

That was one of the great things about Dom's job. He could snap his fingers and perks like that were his, at no cost. It was one of the reasons he'd chosen to go into advertising in the first place.

"Dom, wait," Nina said, behind him, grabbing his sleeve. "I'm sorry to be so harsh. But I worry about you."

"Don't," he said shortly. "Because I swear I'm fine. When I'm not abandoning people at the train station or ruining their birthday parties, that is."

"Come on, baby brother. We just miss you around here," Nina told him, squeezing his arm. "That's all. You always

seem to have a million other more important places to go. I just wish you'd hang
around more."

"I'm sorry," he said, thinking he hadn't
felt this guilty since he snuck out to go to
the prom with Donna DiLorenzo a decade
ago.

Wait a minute. Yes. Yes, he had.

He thought of the night his father almost
died. The night he ran away.

"It's okay," Nina said, forgiving him now,
same as she had then.

She reached out and hugged him. "The
way I figure, someday, you'll grow up and
settle down and then we won't be able to
get rid of you," she said with a laugh. "You
and your wife and kids."

"Don't count on it, Nina. I really can't
see myself married."

"Don't rule it out, either. You're going to
meet someone and realize that there's
nothing more important in your life than
living it with her."

The trouble with Nina, Dom thought,
and not for the first time, was that she
thought she knew everything.

He couldn't help noticing lately that,
trapped in her own narrow little world of
marriage and motherhood, she really
didn't know much of anything at all.

*At least, not about the real world. And
not about him.*

"Mona, look who's back," Grandpa announces, escorting Mia into the kitchen.

Standing at the stove, stirring a pot,
Nana Mona looks up. Her glasses are
slightly fogged from the steam, but her
crinkly old eyes are smiling behind them.

"Mia! There you are!"

"Hi, Nana." Mia crosses the room to kiss
her grandmother's wrinkled cheek, comforted by the familiar sight of her in
scuffies and an orange-spattered apron tied
over one of the knit tracksuits she wears
every day. Her salt-and-pepper hair is
tucked back in a bun, and she's wearing all
her favorite gold jewelry, as usual.

"How was Las Vegas?" she asks Mia.
"Did you bring back big winnings? Luck
runs in this family, you know."

"I know, but —" Mia breaks off,
catching sight of the strapping stranger
seated at the kitchen table.

He has longish, wavy blond hair,
bronzed skin, and the chiseled bone struc-
ture and muscular build of . . . well, of
Fabio, she can't help thinking.

"Vincenzo, *this*" — brimming with
pride, Grandpa Junie takes her hand and

335

leads her over to the table — "is Bella Mia. You see? Didn't I promise you that she's just as pretty as her pictures?"

Promise? Pictures? Why would this nodding, grinning stranger have —

Oh.

So this oversized nonfig is the "little something" Grandpa Junie brought back for her.

"Mia, *this,*" Grandpa goes on, placing her hand squarely in the beefy palm the faux Fabio offers, "is Vincenzo Palermo. And he's *from* Palermo."

"You see? He's *from* Palermo, and his *name* is Palermo," echoes Nana Mona, who frequently feels the need to reiterate her husband's more clever utterances. "How 'bout that, Mia?"

"How 'bout that," she mutters through tight lips, her thoughts whirling.

She never thought her grandfather would actually import his hand-selected fiancé at this stage of the game. She figured he would go, pick out a good prospect the way he picked fruit from Cousin Fungi's backyard orchard, and maybe bring back for her approval a picture, a phone number, a note.

But no. Not Grandpa Junie. For all she knows, he's reserved the chapel at Saint

Theresa's for a wedding tomorrow.

Well, you should have expected this, Mia tells herself, while noting that the apparently mute Palermo from Palermo is staring up at her with smiling yet oddly vacant Mediterranean blue eyes. *You know Grandpa Junie likes to do everything his way.*

"What do you think? You like him?" Grandpa asks slyly, nudging her in the ribs.

"Does he speak?" she asks, and then, realizing that sounds rude, she tacks on, ". . . English? Do you speak English, Mr. Palermo?"

"Si," he says, or maybe, *"See."*

As in, *See how well I can speaka the English,* or *See how I can smile and speak and make eyes at you, all at the same time.*

"Vincenzo grows orchids back in Sicily," Grandpa Junie announces.

"That's nice," Mia replies with a tight smile, when she realizes everyone seems to be waiting for a response to this momentous revelation.

"Vincenzo said he was hungry for gravy and meatballs," Grandpa says next, "so I promised him the best in the world."

"I don't know if mine is the best in the

337

world," Nana Mona tells her husband with false modesty.

"You know it is, Mona," Grandpa Junie insists. "Your gravy is the best in the world."

"Well, if you say so."

"Listen, you guys enjoy your dinner," Mia pipes up, "and I'm going to —"

"We're all going to sit down and eat together in a few minutes," Grandpa Junie cuts in, wearing a Case Closed expression that tells her his hearing aid is coming in loud and clear, but her words aren't registering.

"Can I speak to you for a second, Grandpa?" Mia asks tersely. "Privately?"

He shrugs and looks at Nana Mona, who is back at the stove, breaking bunches of dry spaghetti in half and throwing them into a loudly boiling pot. "How long before the pasta is cooked, Mona?"

"Eight minutes, al dente," she replies, reaching for the timer on the stove and setting it. "You like al dente, Vincenzo?"

"Si," is the reply, or maybe, "See."

As in *See how big I'm smiling? That shows you how much I like al dente.*

"We'll be right back," Grandpa Junie promises.

"In eight minutes," Mia says, and drags him into the next room.

"Where are we going, Bella?"

"First to your office, so I can talk to you alone," Mia tells him. "Then upstairs. I want to show you a little something I brought back from Vegas."

"For me?"

"Kind of," she concedes. "But mostly for me."

"Su-*weet,*" Dominic murmurs, gazing at the impressive larger-than-life image of the newest Yankees pitcher warming up on the mound.

Aiming the remote at the television, he takes it out for a spin, flipping from YES Network to ESPN to MAN. All the essentials are accounted for, but he soon realizes she gets over nine hundred other stations, some that although he knew of, he has never seen.

I could definitely get used to this, he tells himself, settling on a movie channel that's showing *Animal House,* one of his all-time favorites.

He takes off his jacket and tosses it over a chair, not bothering to protect the boutonniere. His tie comes next; then he loosens the collar of his dress shirt, unbuttons the cuffs, and rolls up his sleeves.

Better. Much better.

Even the flowery couch is growing on him. He leans back into the cushions and debates kicking off his shoes and putting his feet up on the glass coffee table.

He'd better not. What if his feet smell? Or what if Mia enforces a strict no-feet-on-the-glass-coffee-table rule? After all, the place doesn't exactly look lived-in.

Again, Dom pictures the house where he grew up, and his sisters' nearby homes. Kids, crumbs, and chaos. It must strictly be a Chickalini thing.

He closes his eyes and tries to picture the scene through the eyes of his new bride.

Mia doesn't strike him as a snob, but you never know.

Irked by the mere idea that she might not be charmed by his family, Dom bends over and defiantly unlaces his dress shoes.

He kicks them off, takes a cautious sniff, and decides his feet smell just fine. Maybe not like herbal soap or those flower blossoms in her bedroom, but these are his feet, and Mia had better just learn to deal with that.

He leans even farther back, crosses his legs, and props his heels on the table. *Aaaah.*

Heaven.

Stretching and yawning, he checks his watch, wondering how long Mia has been upstairs. Five minutes? Ten minutes?

He bends his elbows and clasps his hands at the back of his aching neck, then yawns again.

He wishes she'd hurry. He's starved, and if they're going out to dinner, he'll need to take that shower.

We'll need to take that shower, he amends with a slow grin, feeling, for the first time in ages, as though he hasn't a care in the world.

Chapter Fourteen

"You weren't very friendly to Vincenzo," Grandpa Junie informs Mia as she closes the door to the den.

"I don't even *know* Vincenzo."

"Well, what did you think of him?"

"I thought he was very . . . large."

"What?" He conveniently cups a hand to his hearing aid. "Speak up. I can't hear you. What did you say? Isn't he a charmer?"

No. Dominic Chickalini is a charmer. Vincenzo is merely . . . large.

Mia sighs. "Why does it matter what I think of him, Grandpa?"

"He's a wonderful man. Has a heart of gold, that one."

"I'm sure he does." A heart of gold that complements his platinum hair.

"He'd give you the shirt off his back."

Yes, the better to show off his pecs and abs.

Maybe she isn't being fair. For all she knows, Vincenzo Palermo from Palermo is a wonderful guy just oozing with personality. But she already has one of those, thank you very much.

"Your grandmother loves Vincenzo," Grandpa informs her. "Mona doesn't make gravy and meatballs on a weekday for just anyone, you know."

"I know, I know. But why is he here?" Mia cuts off that question with, "Wait, before you tell me that, let me tell you my news."

"News? What news?"

"Sit down, Grandpa."

"That's okay. I'll stand."

She goes to his desk and pulls out his upholstered leather chair, rolling it over and positioning the edge of the seat against the back of his legs. "Please sit, Grandpa."

"Why? I like to stand."

Mia sighs inwardly, knowing that if she were insisting he remain on his feet, he would be heading for the nearest chair.

Stubborn. That's what he is. Impossibly stubborn.

"I wanted you to be the first to know . . ."

"Know what?" Grandpa Junie asks suspiciously.

"This." She thrusts her left hand at him, waiting for him to notice the gold wedding band on her fourth finger.

"Red nail polish," he says, apparently

not only selectively deaf, but perhaps also legitimately blind. "Nice. So what?"

"No, *this*." She bends the knuckles on her left hand and points at the ring with her right, holding it up to his nose.

He gasps. "You're . . . married?"

"I'm married."

He plops himself into his chair and murmurs something in Italian. She's not sure what, exactly, but it invokes God and the Blessed Mother, and there seems to be some possibility of Grandpa Junie's imminent death from shock.

"I told you that you should sit," she says, kneeling on the floor at his feet. "Are you all right?"

He nods unconvincingly.

"Well, are you . . . happy for me?"

"You're married. I don't believe it."

"It's true. Really."

"But . . . when? Where? And who?" he remembers to ask, belatedly.

"I eloped to Las Vegas with Dominic."

"Who?"

"Dominic. Chickalini."

No reaction.

"The guy upstairs?" Mia prods.

Still no lightbulb.

She wonders if her grandfather is stubbornly pretending not to know what she's talking about, or if his eighty-four years and eleven and a half months are beginning to take their toll, rendering him half-deaf, half-blind, and totally forgetful.

"You know his uncle Cheech?" Mia prods.

"What? Cheese?" he asks blankly.

"No, Grandpa, *Cheech*. Cheech Chickalini. Your friend."

"Him? He's not my friend," Grandpa Junio says with an irritated wave of his hand. "I can't stand that guy."

Terrific. "Why not?"

"Because he's a Casanova, that's why. They all are."

"All the Chickalinis are Casanovas?"

"You bet."

"Exactly how many Chickalinis do you know?"

"Two," he says decisively.

"Two?"

He counts off on his fingers. "Cheech, and that one upstairs."

Rather than point out that he doesn't exactly "know" that one upstairs — perhaps because she might then be forced to admit that she doesn't exactly "know" the one upstairs, either — Mia says, exasperated, "Grandpa, you can't make an assumption about an entire family's characteristics based on one person."

"Two. Two persons."

"Grandpa —"

"You know the old saying."

"Which old saying? The one about the Chickalinis of Astoria being a pack of roving Casanovas?"

"No, the one about the apple not falling far from the tree."

"But that doesn't mean —"

"Certain things run in families. For instance, take the Calogeras," he says, warming to his subject. "The Calogeras are all very good looking and very smart."

She snorts at that.

"What?" he asks indignantly. "Are you going to tell me that's not true? Can you think of anybody in our family who isn't very good looking and very smart? No, you can't. Because that's a family trait."

Apparently, so is immodesty, Mia thinks, shaking her head in exasperation.

"Now, you take the Chickalinis —"

"Grandpa, you can't confuse genetics with broad generalizations. We're talking about my husband, remember?"

Husband.

Will she ever get used to saying it? Thinking it?

"I know," he says heavily, the cantankerous spark having faded from his eyes. "But I didn't have any say in this."

"You still don't."

Realizing he didn't hear her, she quickly decides not to repeat the harsh words. He has a right to be taken aback by the news that she's gone and gotten married without his blessing.

Just as she has a right to defend her husband.

Husband.

Nope. She'll never get used to it.

"Grandpa," she says, softening her attitude if not her voice, "Dom's here to stay, regardless of whether you like him."

Here to stay . . . for how long?

"I thought you wanted me to get married," she goes on, shoving aside the nagging doubts. "I thought you'd be happy for me."

"I didn't even know you were going with this fellow."

"I know. I'm sorry. We've been dating for . . . a while."

It isn't a lie, she tells herself — and God. *"A while" is a relative term. I'm safe as long as he doesn't ask me to define it in months.*

If that does happen, she'll be forced to admit the truth: that when it comes to her premarital dating relationship with Dom, "a while" can be defined in hours.

"Why didn't you tell me you were going with him? Why didn't he come to me to ask for your hand? What kind of a man doesn't ask for a woman's hand? I'll tell you what kind. A real Casanova, that's what kind."

Rather than point out that a real Casanova might be less interested in a woman's hand than some of her other parts, Mia hedges, "Dom *wanted* to ask you for my hand, but . . . you were away in Sicily. Remember?"

"Of course I remember. You think I could forget already? I just got back." He shakes his head. "This Chickalini Casanova couldn't wait until I got back?"

"We were anxious to get married, Grandpa."

"Why?" His old eyes sharpen. "Are you in trouble?"

"Trouble?"

"Don't tell me!" He slaps his head. "A bambino on the way? Is there? Tell me!"

Mia opens her mouth.

"No, wait! Don't tell me!" He clutches his head, shaking it. "Is there a baby? Tell me, Mia! Tell me now!"

"No! No bambino on the way! Absolutely not."

"So then why did you elope to Las Vegas?"

"Because we were . . . madly in love," she says, before thinking better of it.

"Ah. Madly in love." He nods in disgust. "I know all about madly in love. Your mother was madly in love when she got married."

"I know she was, Grandpa, but —"

"Look what happened to her. It ruined her life."

"Look what happened to *you*. You're madly in love with Nana Mona. Did that ruin your life?"

"I wasn't in love with her when I met her. It was an arranged marriage."

"Yes, but you fell for her right away. You say it all the time, Grandpa. And you're still madly in love, fifty years later."

A glimmer of promise returns to his gaze. "You're right. I am still madly in love."

She squeezes his crepe-papery old hands in both of her own. "Be happy for me, Grandpa. I'm settled down, just like you always wanted. That is what you wanted for me, right?"

"Yes," he admits. "That's what I wanted."

"And he's Italian, Grandpa. From right

here in Astoria. What more could you ask for?"

He shrugs, looking down.

When he lifts his head to meet her gaze, she's stunned to see tears in his eyes.

"What is it, Grandpa? What's wrong?"

"I could have asked for more. I could have asked to see you walk down the aisle, Bella. I would have liked to be the one to give you away. That's all."

A lump rises swiftly in her throat. "Oh, Grandpa, I . . . I'm sorry. I didn't know."

She had honestly thought he just wanted to see her married. She didn't realize he might want to *see* her *get* married.

"It's okay," he tells her. "I'll live."

But he doesn't sound so sure.

Then he asks, "What about Vincenzo?"

Oh. Him.

"What about him?" Mia asks, fighting the urge to check her watch. She wonders anxiously what time it is, what Dom is doing upstairs, what he thinks of her apartment.

"You were supposed to marry Vincenzo, Bella."

"I don't even know him!" she protests. "You wanted me to marry a complete stranger?"

Way to go, Mia. Nothing like sounding — and feeling — like a total hypocrite. Except Grandpa Junie doesn't know about that.

"Stranger. What stranger? You'd get to know him right away. He has a heart of gold. He'd give you the shirt off his back."

"I know, I know . . . but so would Dom, Grandpa. Come on. Let's go downstairs and meet him. I promise you're going to love him."

"He should come up here to me if he wants to meet me. Go get him."

"But what about Vincenzo?"

"Oh." Her grandfather nods. "Him, I'll have to go talk to. I just hope he's not too upset when he finds out he's lost you."

"Trust me, he'll survive."

"Nana Mona is going to be so disappointed. She loves Vincenzo."

"Come on, Grandpa. She loves him? That's a pretty strong thing to say about somebody she's known all of a day."

"What's not to love?"

Rather than stir things up again, Mia simply says, "She'll love Dominic, too."

"We'll see."

"We *will* see." A pause, then Mia presses, "*When* will we see?"

"Tomorrow. Mona will make lasagna, and you'll bring your husband to dinner."

Husband.

Yes. It definitely has a nice ring to it.

"Tomorrow, I'll bring my husband to dinner," she agrees, smiling.

"Good. Four-thirty sharp."

"Four-thirty sharp?" Dom echoes in disbelief, staring up at Mia from his sprawled position on her flowery couch. He hasn't moved in a good relaxing while, except to quickly lower his feet from the coffee table when he heard her come in.

"Four-thirty sharp."

"Sometimes I haven't even finished lunch by four-thirty."

"I know, but that's what time my grandparents eat." She folds her arms.

"Mia, I can't come to dinner at that hour on a weeknight. Do you know what time I'd have to leave the office to be here by then?" He shakes his head, and can't help but notice that she's blocking his view of the television screen on the wall behind her.

This is his favorite scene in *Animal House*; the one where John Belushi destroys the Bohemian professor's guitar on the stairs.

"You could leave at four-fifteen and take a cab," she suggests.

"That'll never happen. I've been out of

the office for a few days as it is. I'm lucky if I get out of there by six-thirty or seven on a normal night."

"But this won't be a normal night. It's the night after your wedding night. The night you're meeting your new in-laws."

"I understand that, and I'm looking forward to it. But I can't be in Queens by four-thirty," he says firmly.

She says nothing, but the lips he's been dreaming about kissing in the shower have tightened into a straight line that looks difficult, if not downright impossible, to cross.

"I know!" he exclaims, after a moment's desperate brainstorming. "Why don't you and your grandparents come to the city and I'll take us all out to a celebratory dinner? We can go down to Little Italy, or up to Arthur Avenue," he adds, thinking a cozy Italian trattoria will be just the ticket.

They'll order a nice antipasto, a good Chianti, some veal, some pasta, some cannoli and espresso . . .

His stomach growls in hearty, audible agreement.

"My grandmother is making lasagna," Mia replies in a tone that suggests the prospect of Nana Mona's lasagna precludes any other dining possibility. Ever.

Not that Dom doesn't love lasagna as much as the next Nice Italian Boy from Queens, but . . .

"You can't just order me to leave work in the middle of the afternoon," he tersely informs his wife, who is rapidly living up to his worst nightmarish nagging wife cliché.

"*Order* you?" she repeats indignantly.

"Isn't that what you just did?"

"No, I *invited* you."

"Well, unfortunately I have to decline the invitation due to a prior commitment."

Speaking of commitments, is it too late to back out of this one? he finds himself wondering. He glances down at the gold wedding band he bought less than twenty-four hours ago with what was left of his credit. Right about now, he wouldn't mind marching over to the window and tossing it out.

Funny how things can change so quickly. Just a few minutes ago, he was relaxing pleasantly on the sofa daydreaming about a bubble bath with his bride.

He looks up at her.

Then, when she moves her head slightly he looks past her, at the television, where John Belushi as Bluto is saying, "Sorry," with a sheepish shrug. Dom has never before watched him utter that line without cracking up, but there's nothing funny about it now. There's nothing funny about anything.

Is this what happens when you get married? he wonders glumly. *All the joy goes out of life?*

Then . . .

Come on, you big lug. You know better than that. Look at Nina and Joey. Rosalie and Timmy. Maggie and Charlie.

The world is made up of happily married couples, remember?

"Come here," he says impulsively, and reaches up to tug Mia's hand.

"What?" she asks stubbornly, not moving.

"Come *here*." He pulls her down onto his lap.

She laughs a little. "What?"

"Talk to me. Like a real person. Not like Wifezilla."

He waits for her to be offended, but she laughs again. Just a little. "I'm not a Wifezilla."

"Are you sure?" he asks, brushing a strand of hair back from her face. "Because you just scared the heck out of me. I thought I glimpsed my future and it was henpecked."

"Hey, watch it there, Casanova."

"Casanova?" Terrific. Her grandfather has been telling her tales about his uncle Cheech, probably trying to convince her that he's cut from the same cloth.

"Never mind." She shakes her head. "You just have to work with me on this, Dom. Grandpa Junie feels so bad about not being at our wedding. I just want to make it up to him somehow. I want you to come to dinner tomorrow night, and I want him and Nana Mona to meet you and fall in love with you."

Yes, but you *haven't,* he wants to point out. *You don't even believe in love, remember?*

Sure he remembers. That's one of the reasons he married her. Because it wasn't about love and forever. Because she was a safe bet. Because she was willing to give him an out.

But you're not taking it, he informs himself sternly. *Not yet, at least.*

No. Because this isn't a game. This is marriage. The real deal.

And he's a man. The real deal.

Maybe he was, until just the other day, a mere kid masquerading in grown-up clothes. But not anymore. He told himself he was ready to grow up and take some responsibility.

Yeah. So how about it?

"Listen," he says, very reasonably, stroking Mia's dark hair, "why don't we go up to your grandparents' place right now? That way, I won't have to wait until dinner tomorrow. I can get to know them right —"

"You can't," Mia interrupts quickly. "You definitely can't go up there right now."

"Why not?"

"Because there's something I, uh, forgot to mention when I was telling you what happened."

"What is it?" he asks, sensing that it's something rather . . . hugely important. Otherwise, she probably wouldn't look as though she's ready to bolt from his lap.

Maybe her grandfather decided to cut her out of the will anyway, because she didn't invite him to the wedding. It sounds like he was pretty upset about that.

Well, if that's the case, we'll just live on my salary, Dom decides. *We'll move in with Pop, and we'll —*

"My grandparents have a visitor."

"A visitor?" In the Chickalini household, where visitors are as common as dust bunnies, this would hardly be cause for a lap-bolting news bulletin. "Yeah? Who is it?"

"His name is Vincenzo, and he happens

357

to be a little *souvenir* my grandfather brought back for me from Sicily."

Dom's eyes widen. "You mean . . ."

"Oh, yes." She sighs. "My mail-order groom, fresh from the Old Country, is sitting at my grandparents' kitchen table as we speak."

"Oh."

That *is* news. Dominic himself has never sat at her grandparents' kitchen table and this interloper is making himself at home, probably dunking a biscotto in his coffee and thinking he's part of the family.

Well, you're not, Dom informs his unseen nemesis, a bit irrationally jealous. All right, *a lot* irrationally jealous. *I'm part of the family. And you're out, Vincenzo.*

Except that at least for the time being, Vincenzo seems to be in.

"What's he like?" he can't help but ask, bristling at the mere notion of Mia with another man.

"He's a beefcake."

"A beefcake?"

For a moment, the word "beef" merely triggers his salivary glands.

Then the old romantic rivalry mechanism kicks in, and he pictures a brawny stranger vying with him for Mia's hand.

Wait a minute. Dominic has already *won*

her hand. Mia is with him now. She'll never be with another man . . . not if they can make this marriage thing work.

He gazes with pride at the gold ring on her finger, identical to the one he was just thinking of throwing out the window. There's something to be said for that *forsaking all others* vow after all.

"You know," Mia is saying. "He's just your basic garden-variety Mediterranean godlike specimen."

"He's a *god?*" Dom scowls. "Is that supposed to make me feel better about any of this?"

"Well, actually, I didn't know you didn't feel good about it," Mia says, and he sees that the corners of her mouth are twitching in amusement.

All right, so he's letting his jealousy show. So what? He has a right not to be thrilled about some . . . some Mediterranean *god* who sailed across the ocean to steal his wife.

"Do you want me to call you a beefcake, too?" she asks teasingly, running her fingertips over his triceps. "Hmm? Is that what you want?"

He feels himself stirring to arousal at her slight touch. He shifts her weight on his lap, holding her so that she can't possibly be mistaken about what he wants.

"Do you realize this marriage hasn't been consummated yet, Mrs. Chickalini?" he asks against her mouth, before he kisses her. Hard.

"Come on," she whispers, pulling away, taking his hand. "Come with me. I'll show you around the place. We'll start with my bedroom."

"Is that an order or an invitation?"

"It depends. I wouldn't want you to feel henpecked or anything."

"Feel free to peck away," he says with a grin.

Chapter Fifteen

"I can't believe I'm doing this," are the first words out of Dominic's mouth when he walks into the apartment the next afternoon at 4:28.

"You made it!" Mia quickly sets aside the bottle of water she has been drinking and throws herself into his arms. "I knew you would."

Actually, she didn't know any such thing. She had spent the afternoon pacing around the apartment, jumping every time the phone rang, certain it would be Dom calling to tell her he couldn't get away from the office after all, despite the promise he made last night, during a lull in the multiple marriage consummations.

But Dom only called once, wanting to know what kind of wine he should pick up to bring to her grandfather.

The other calls were from Lenore, her oldest friend, and from Fuji, her trainer. She neglected to share her glad tidings with either of them. Maybe because she was afraid of jinxing the marriage, which,

for the time being at least, is going remark-
ably well.

Lenore, of course, was expecting to hear
all about her wedding to Derek.

"I couldn't go through with it," was all
Mia could tell her.

"I knew it!" Lenore said triumphantly. "I
knew you weren't cut out for it."

"For what? An elopement with somebody I'd never met?"

"No. Marriage. Just marriage in general.
Not to be mean, but you're not the wifely
type, Mia."

"Why not?" she asked, utterly offended.

"Because when you're married, you have
to compromise a lot," said Lenore, the veteran of a five-year marriage — and an ongoing bitter divorce. "Face it, Mia . . .
you're just not very good at compromising."

She wanted to argue with her friend, but
there was no time.

All right, truth be told, there was plenty
of time, but she couldn't seem to think of a
convincing argument.

The truth is, she *isn't* very good at compromising, and she knows it. But that
doesn't mean she can't learn. It doesn't
mean she wouldn't make a damned good
wife, if she set her mind to it.

Still . . . between the conversation with Lenore and Dominic's "Wifezilla" comment the night before, Mia was left thinking she might just harbor some serious control issues.

But she's determined to work through them. For Dominic's sake.

And for your own. Because you don't want to lose him.

"I'm so glad you're here," Mia tells Dom now.

"There's going to be hell to pay tomorrow when I get to work, but who cares?" He tosses his briefcase on a chair, then turns and seems to catch sight of her for the first time. "Mia! You look . . ."

She smiles. "Thank you."

"I mean, you always look great, but I've never seen you so . . ." He trails off, shaking his head, blatant admiration radiating in his gaze.

"Thank you," she says again, twirling around so that he can see the simple black designer dress. "Until now, you've never seen me in my own clothes, other than the wedding dress — not," she adds quickly, "that I didn't love everything you bought for me."

"That reminds me . . . did you hear from the airline about your luggage or from

Derek about your carry-on bag?"

"What do you think?"

"I guess you didn't. That stinks."

"C'est la vie," she says with a shrug, thinking she's lost other far more important things in her life, and survived.

"Oh, these are for you." He hands her one of the two bouquets in his arms.

"Wildflowers!" she exclaims. "And they're all shades of pink!"

"Yeah, I thought you might like that color just a little," he says wryly, gesturing at the adjacent living room with its pastel color scheme.

"Thank you, Dom," she says sincerely, not caring that they aren't orchids — that she still hasn't even told him about her passion for orchids. Nor has he even commented on the many species growing around the apartment . . . or even on the greenhouse where she cultivates them.

Sooner or later, you'll share the orchids with him. It's not that big a deal, she tells herself.

"These are beautiful," she tells him, inhaling the wildflowers' sweet fragrance.

"Not as beautiful as you are," he says softly, and her heart skips a beat.

Funny how she could only squirm when Derek said almost the exact same thing just the other day. Coming from him, the compliment didn't ring true.

Coming from Dominic, the words are poetry.

"These are for your grandmother," he says, gesturing with the other bouquet as she sets hers in a handily empty vase on the console table.

"And this" — he holds up an elaborately wrapped gift package from the liquor store — "is for your grandfather. I got the red."

"The cabernet?"

"The Chianti. Is that okay?"

"It's fine. He'll be thrilled." She pours the remainder of the drinking water from her bottle into the vase, and makes a mental note to add more later. "When did you have time to get any of this?"

"Right after I lied to my boss about going out on a sales call. Do I have time to shave before we go upstairs?"

"No, we'll be late. Let's go."

She pulls him out the door, wine in hand.

"You seem so calm," he says as they step into the elevator.

"I am calm," she lies, concluding it's probably best not to tell him she's so nervous she feels like she's going to throw up or faint or both.

All day, disastrous scenarios have been running through her head.

What if Grandpa Junie calls Dominic a Casanova to his face?

What if Dominic doesn't like Nana Mona's lasagna and it shows?

What if the subject of baseball comes up?

What if she's forced to admit that she actually met Dominic on the plane to Las Vegas?

Mia is silent as the doors slide closed, telling herself that even if any of the above come to pass, they'll survive. If her grandparents don't approve of her new husband, then so be it.

The elevator lurches into motion and Dom asks conversationally, "What did you do all day? Did you work?"

"No, Nana Mona didn't need me," she says, deciding not to tell him about her earlier conversation with her grandmother, who showed up on her doorstep moments after Dom left for the office.

That would be the conversation in which Nana Mona cried over not being at her only grandchild's wedding, and all but accused Mia of eloping with a total stranger just so that her grandfather wouldn't disinherit her.

"Nana! I would never do such a thing!"

she protested, praying that God wouldn't strike her dead on the spot.

He didn't.

But He did throw Vincenzo into her path one last time. She ran into him in the lobby as he was leaving for the airport. He bowed and kissed her hand — the one that wasn't wearing a wedding ring — and sadly told her in broken English that he was sorry things didn't work out between them, but he wished her well.

Or maybe, for all she knows, he simply told her to go to hell. His English *was* pretty broken and her Italian is hardly fluent.

"I should have shaved," Dominic comments, checking his reflection in the elevator mirror as they bump to a halt.

"No, you shouldn't have. I like the rugged look."

"You're not the one I'm trying to impress," he reminds her, and exhales shakily as he holds the door open for her.

"You're really, really nervous," she realizes, surprised.

"Well, what would you expect? I already met your grandfather once, remember? He wasn't exactly a gentle old soul."

"He'll love you," she assures him, hoping her voice doesn't sound as hollow as her hopes are.

★ ★ ★

"Grandpa? Nana Mona?" Mia calls, leading the way over the threshold into her grandparents' apartment.

Grandpa Junie materializes immediately, almost as if he's been waiting behind the door. He's looking quite dapper in a three-piece suit and a bow tie, cane in hand.

"Hello, sir," Dominic says, reaching out to shake the other hand firmly. The old man's fingers are cool and dry. Dom wonders whether his own are as moist and warm as they feel. Grandpa Junie doesn't wipe off his fingers on his dress pants, which he chooses to interpret as a good sign.

"Welcome to the family, Dominic," is the perhaps cursory but nonetheless infinitely reassuring reply.

At least, Dom is reassured until he glances at Mia, who is planting a kiss on her grandfather's cheek. Her mouth is smiling but her eyes are worriedly pessimistic.

"Thank you. This is for you, sir," Dom says, handing over the bottle of wine.

He takes a deep breath to steady his nerves, and notes the tantalizing aroma of lasagna.

Ah. Now *that's* reassuring. In his experience, food tends to make a lot of things better.

"This is for me?" Grandpa Junie looks pleased as he props his cane against the wall and unwraps it.

"I hope you like it. Mia mentioned you're a wine connoisseur."

"A what?"

"A connoisseur, Grandpa," Mia repeats loudly.

"What, connoisseur," Grandpa says, throwing up the hand that isn't clutching the bottle. "I've been drinking wine since I was ten."

Dominic laughs.

"I'm serious."

"He's serious," Mia says. "But Grandpa, you've got that wine cellar now, and you enjoy going to tastings."

Grandpa Junie shrugs.

"Look at this," Mia persists. "I know you're going to like it."

"What is it?" Her grandfather holds the bottle at arm's length, squints; brings it up almost to the tip of his nose, and squints again.

"Felsina Fontalloro," Mia says, reading the label over his shoulder. "Nineteen ninety-seven. That was a very good year."

"I'll say. It was the year I won the lottery." Grandpa Junie grins. "Thank you, Dominic. Let's go have a glass. What do you say?"

"That sounds great," he blurts with perhaps a little too much overt enthusiasm.

But he can't help it. He definitely could use something to take the edge off his nerves right about now. A glass of wine or two — or three or four — should at least put a dent in his anxiety.

"One glass," Mia the Mind-Reading Wifezilla whispers to him in a warning tone as her grandfather leads the way to the back of the apartment.

Taking a cue from Grandpa Junie, Dom pretends not to hear her.

Everything about the place is ornate, from the gilt mirrors and gold velvet sofas to the tasseled amber silk brocade draperies and countless lamps whose bases are carved to look like cherubs.

Most of the furniture is wrapped in transparent, straight-from-the-factory plastic, just like at Dom's aunt Carm's house. There's even a series of plastic runners protecting the plush wall-to-wall carpeting in each room they cross, reminding Dom of a network of railroad tracks.

He remembers what Mia said about her grandparents' being poor before the lottery win, and finds that he's touched, rather than amused, by all the protective plastic.

They still aren't used to having nice

things. He imagines it would be the same way in his house if Pop were to become an overnight millionaire. Come to think of it, though, Dom can't think of anything his father would even change if that happened. The only thing he's ever wanted is something all the money in the world can't buy.

She was the love of my life, Dominic.

Poor Pop, Dominic thinks, suddenly missing his father fiercely. But he can't go home yet. Not until the weekend. His sisters are planning a birthday dinner for him on Saturday night, and he's bringing Mia along.

Don't think of that now, he tells himself, feeling the tension rise another notch at the mere notion of presenting his bride to his family. *One potentially traumatic event at a time.*

In the kitchen, Dominic is greeted by a stout woman in an apron, standing by the enormous restaurant-sized stove. Her salt-and-pepper hair is pulled back to reveal a face that was probably once very attractive. It still is, really. Just rounded and wrinkled.

And worried, he realizes, noticing the way she's looking at him.

Grandpa Junie relieves an equally fretful-looking Mia of the introductory duties.

"Mona, this is Dominic Chickalini. Dominic, my wife."

"It's a pleasure to meet you, Mrs. Calogera," he says politely, shaking her hand.

"Oh, you can call me . . ." She falters, as if she isn't quite sure *what* he should call her.

"Call her Mona," Grandpa Junie booms, rescuing the rest of them from an exceedingly awkward moment. "And call me Carmine."

"Grandpa, nobody calls you Carmine," Mia protests.

Dominic, who can't imagine calling the old man Grandpa or Junior or, God forbid, Junie, speaks up quickly. "Carmine is fine, sir."

"How about that glass of wine?"

"Thank you, sir," Dom says gratefully.

"We'll go drink it in my den while the women get dinner on the table," Mia's grandfather adds, and Dom's heart sinks.

He looks helplessly at Mia, who shrugs, just as helplessly.

Dom has no choice but to accept a glass of Chianti and follow her grandfather to the den, where he closes the door with a click that seems much more deafening — and threatening — than it probably really is.

"Have a seat," Grandpa Junie — er, Carmine — offers. "Not there."

"Oh . . . sorry." Dom rises awkwardly from the nearest leather chair.

"There."

"Thanks." He moves a few feet over to the leather couch. It makes an embarrassing sound when he lowers himself into it. Alarmed, he looks up to make sure the old man doesn't think he passed wind.

Grandpa Junie doesn't appear to have heard. He's either too hard of hearing, or too busy settling himself in the chair he just reclaimed from Dom.

"Ah, that's better." He groans loudly as he sinks back in the seat. "The old bones aren't as willing to budge as they used to be. You know, there aren't many things all this money of mine can't buy. Youth is one of them."

What about your granddaughter? Dom wants to ask. *Is she another? Or do you honestly think you can buy her, too?*

Maybe if he'd had a full glass of wine — or the whole damned bottle — rather than a couple of sips, he'd ask that question.

Oh, who is he kidding? He would not.

He wouldn't, because there's already a clear-cut answer, at least in his own mind.

Obviously, Grandpa Junie's money can

— and did — buy Mia's compliance. And, for all the old man knows, it bought Dominic's as well.

"You didn't have a lot of money growing up, did you, Dominic?" Grandpa Junie asks rather shrewdly — and, Dom can't help but notice, with unnerving clairvoyance.

"No," he admits.

"Are you wondering how I knew that?"

"How?" Dom asks reluctantly.

"I did a little digging around today. Big Pizza Pie, huh? I know that place. And I knew your mother."

Dom feels as though he's been punched in the gut. "My . . . mother?"

"Years ago," he says with a nod. "Little Rosemarie Valerio. Had a voice like an angel. She used to sing in the church choir at Saint Theresa's."

"Saint Theresa's?" Dom shakes his head. "You mean, Most Precious Mother."

"No, Saint Theresa's. That's the only church I've ever gone to."

"Are you sure?" asks Dom, since Most Precious Mother is the only church he — or, as far as he knows, his late mother — has ever gone to.

"I'm so sure I named my only daughter after it. Only she hated the name. Wasn't big on church, either, that one," he adds grimly. "But your mother . . . I remember her. And her sister, Carmella, too. She was a real pistol, that one."

"She still is," Dom says with a smile, thinking *pistol* is as apt a description for his aunt Carm as any he's heard. "I never knew my mother and Aunt Carm went to a different church when they were young."

"I bet you never knew a lot of things. That's the problem with you young people. You think you know it all. And you don't like to listen to the ones who really do."

Dom seethes, but manages not to say anything. Who cares if this old man thinks he knows everything there is to know about . . . well, everything? For Mia's sake, Dom will have to just sit here and sip his wine and nod politely.

"So your mother," Grandpa Junie says more gently, shifting gears again, "she was a good girl. Not a pistol. An angel. I always wondered whatever happened to her. I figured she got married, had a family. I never would have guessed . . ."

He trails off, looks down at his lap, and then back up at Dom with genuine, unexpected sympathy. "I'm sorry for your loss, Dominic. I lost my own mother when I was young. I know how hard it is."

There's that familiar lump again; the one

that invariably surfaces in Dominic's throat whenever somebody mentions his mother these days.

Funny, he got through some of the most difficult milestones of his life without her — and without feeling too sorry for himself, either. But now that he's a grown man, the merest mention of the woman he can't even remember just about brings him to tears every time.

"Thank you, sir," he manages to tell Grandpa Junie in a slightly strangled-sounding voice.

"So your mother, I know. Your uncle Cheech . . . I know him, too. And that has me a little worried. A lot worried, I have to say."

Dominic frowns. "Why?"

"Because he can't stay put with one woman, that's why. And because his nephew is married to my granddaughter, that's why."

"But . . . Uncle Cheech has nothing to do with anything," Dominic protests, trying to quell a guilty little voice that reminds him he himself doesn't have the best monogamous track record, either.

"You look just like him. In his younger days, that is. When he had hair."

This isn't the first time Dom has been

told he bears a resemblance to his wayward uncle, but it's the first time he's found himself feeling defensive about it.

"Uncle Cheech is —"

"Why did you marry Mia, Dominic?" the old man cuts in.

"Because . . . I love her."

Dominic allows the first words that come to mind to roll right off his tongue unchecked, knowing it's the only acceptable answer.

But now that it's out there . . .

I love her . . . I love her?

Well, he can't help but feel intensely warmed by the words. Or maybe that's just the wine.

"What about her money?"

"What about it?"

"You knew she had millions when you met her."

"No, sir," Dominic says quite honestly. "I didn't. And if I had, it wouldn't have mattered. The money is not why I'm with her."

Looking unsatisfied — or perhaps unconvinced — the old man tries a new tactic. "Mia says you two have been sneaking around, dating each other, for a long time now."

"Yes."

"How long?"

"Almost a year," he replies, in accordance with Mia's prior coaching.

"Why?"

Uh-oh.

"What did Mia tell you?" he asks cautiously.

"She didn't."

"Oh. Well, ah, sir, we snuck around because Mia knew how you had your hopes set on her getting married, and she was afraid that if it didn't work out, you would be devastated."

"She thought I would be devastated if she didn't marry Cheech Chickalini's nephew?"

"Yes, sir." Dom can't help but feel slightly ridiculous.

"I see." Grandpa Junie sips his wine.

Then he leans forward and lifts a gnarled finger, holding it up mere inches from Dom's face.

"I just want you to know," he says slowly, "that if you turn out to be a gold digger, and if you dare to break my granddaughter's heart, I'll make you sorry. Very, very sorry. Do you understand?"

"I understand, sir," Dominic tells him. "I assure you, that won't happen. I didn't marry her for money."

But that might very well be the reason

she married me, he can't help but think uneasily.

"You married him because of the money," Nana Mona says, shaking her head at Mia as she expertly slices a loaf of Italian bread with vigorous strokes. "I don't believe it."

"I did not, Nana! I married him because . . ."

"Because why?" her grandmother asks, when Mia can't quite bring herself to say it. "Because you're madly in love with him? That's just as bad."

"It wasn't because of that, either." Mia sighs. "You always told me that would be a mistake, remember?"

"So you were listening?"

"Of course, Nana. I was listening." *And watching. Watching my parents' marriage crash and burn.*

"Then why?"

To buy time, Mia opens the silverware drawer, counts out four salad forks, four dinner forks, four butter knives.

"Are you serving coffee and dessert?" she pauses to ask.

"Of course."

Mia counts out four teaspoons; four dessert forks. Then she closes the drawer and finds her grandmother still waiting for an answer.

"What do you want me to say, Nana? That I married him so Grandpa wouldn't cut me off, like you said?"

"Do you really think your grandfather would have done that?"

"Yes," Mia replies without hesitation. Then, belatedly, it occurs to her to ask, "Wouldn't he?"

Her grandmother shrugs, looking down at the crusty remainder of the loaf of bread.

"Nana . . ." Mia tosses aside the silverware and crosses the kitchen to touch her grandmother's arm. "You said that if I wasn't married by Grandpa's eighty-fifth birthday, I was out. Out of the will, out of the building, out of his life."

"That's what he told me."

"He didn't mean it?"

"Who knows? Sometimes he talks. That's what he said."

"You don't think he meant it?"

"Do you really think Grandpa would turn his back on his own flesh and blood?"

"He's stubborn. He likes things his own way."

"So do you. Would you turn your back on him?"

Mia sinks into a kitchen chair, her thoughts reeling.

"What's wrong, Mia?"

"Nothing, I just . . ."

"Never mind," Nana says disapprovingly. "You just realized that you might have married this Chickalini fella for no good reason. Right?"

"No." She shakes her head. "Not at all."

I just realized that I might have almost married somebody else for no good reason. I just realized that if I had been thinking with my head — and not with my heart — I would have married Derek.

It was her heart that made her ask Dom to kiss her. And her heart that sent her chasing after him, sneaking around Mandalay Bay, lying to chambermaids. It was her heart that made her willing to give up all that money. Not her head.

"Then what?" Nana Mona asks, looking intently into her eyes. "What's going on in that head of yours?"

Apparently, not a whole heck of a lot, Mia thinks ruefully. *Not in my head, anyway.*

Chapter Sixteen

"Are you sure we shouldn't have at least told them about us before now?" Mia asks Dominic the following Saturday evening as they step out of a cab on Thirty-third Street, just off Ditmars Boulevard.

Mia has been to this neighborhood countless times in her life. She even worked at Mike's Diner right around the corner. She probably passed Dominic on the street, maybe even noticed his dark good looks.

"No," he says in answer to her question, "trust me, Mia, it's better if we tell them in person."

She smooths the skirt of the prim charcoal suit she chose for this momentous occasion. "But they do all know I'm coming, right?"

"My sisters know I'm bringing a date."

"Just not a wife," she mutters, shaking her head.

"We'll tell them as soon as we get inside. Don't worry."

"I have a feeling this isn't going to be the

most laid-back birthday dinner you've ever had in your life."

"Who needs laid-back?" Dominic asks in return, his expression betraying the answer to his own question.

He does. *He* needs laid-back.

Mia can't help but notice that the last few hectic days at the office and a couple of sleeplessly passionate newlywed nights seem to have worn him out.

Not that he's been complaining. When he gets home to her apartment at night, the last thing he seems to want to do is re-hash his day.

Instead, he wants her to tell him about hers. Which embarrassingly takes all of two minutes.

She's starting to think that her life of relative leisure might leave something to be desired — at least, when held up in contrast to her husband's thriving high-powered career.

For her, the highlight of every weekday is her hour-long high-powered personal training session at the gym with Fuji. The rest of her time is spent assisting her grandmother around the house, a job she once did willingly, and for free.

It was Grandpa Junie's idea that she make it a full-time career.

Yes, Grandpa Junie made it awfully easy for her to stay under his roof, where he could keep an eye on her.

But whose fault is it, really, that this is how you ended up?

You can't blame him for your own lack of ambition. You're a big girl. You could have gotten out. You could have made something of yourself.

Now she can't help but wonder what would have become of her if she had stuck it out through junior college — not to mention waitressing. Or perhaps even filled out that financial aid form Lenore was always pushing at her.

Sheesh, just look at Lenore.

Mia's best friend graduated from college with an accounting degree and now works full-time for the IRS. It might not be the most glamorous job in the world, but it beats being a personal assistant to your own grandmother.

How did I never notice before that my life is so . . . blah?

The days Mia used to while away contentedly now seem endless — and empty. Aside from keeping her plants watered, she hasn't had the heart to spend time propagating new growth.

She hasn't even allowed herself to surf

the Internet while Nana Mona takes her afternoon nap. For one thing, she still hasn't replaced her lost reading glasses. For another, it would bring back unsettling memories of her cyber-relationship with Derek, and her pre-Dominic life in general.

Dominic.

He's the reason she's seeing her life in a new light.

"You can't always take the easy way out, Mia," he said that night in the hotel room, when he was telling her how he himself learned the value of hard work.

So. Is she reevaluating because she wants to live up to his standards?

Or maybe it's just that she's feeling more restless now because she has something to look forward to at the end of every day.

Come on, Mia. Do you really want to base your entire existence on the comings and goings of a husband who might not even stick around?

No. She most certainly does not.

And after this weekend, she's going to reassess her lifestyle — perhaps even make some changes.

But one major milestone at a time, she tells herself now, as she and Dominic approach his father's vinyl-sided two-story house.

Mia finds it easy to picture a young Dominic hanging out on the stoop with a Popsicle on a hot summer's day, or dangling upside down from the branch of that tree in the side yard.

He told her a lot about his childhood last night, in an effort to prepare her to meet his family at last.

Nothing could be more stressful than his initial meeting with her grandparents . . . or so he keeps reminding her. She actually didn't think it was so bad, once Grandpa Junie and Nana Mona completed their individual grilling of the newlyweds and the four of them sat down to a relatively enjoyable dinner.

By the end of the meal, Nana Mona had pulled Mia aside and conceded, "He's a nice boy. I just hope he isn't after your money."

And Grandpa Junie whispered audibly to Dominic on his way out the door, "Don't you forget what I told you."

"What did he tell you?" Mia asked the minute they were alone together in the elevator.

"That if I turn out to be a gold digger, he'll hunt me down and kill me."

"He *said* that?"

"More or less."

Mia isn't necessarily surprised.

Not that she thinks her grandfather is capable of actual violence. Then again, who knows what he's capable of? Just a short time ago, she was convinced he would actually cut her off without a penny.

Now Nana Mona is acting like it was an empty threat.

A threat, Mia can't help but realize, that Grandpa Junie never actually made in the first place.

No, she only heard it secondhand, from her grandmother, and chose to believe it.

Still, how can she even doubt that Grandpa Junie meant business about her being married before his eighty-fifth birthday? After all, he went all the way to Sicily and brought back Vincenzo, didn't he?

But he never really came right out and gave Mia an ultimatum.

Her scramble to find a groom was based on her grandmother's warning — and all right, her own worst arranged-marriage nightmare scenario.

Maybe I went a little overboard, Mia has repeatedly found herself thinking these past few days, as the dust settles.

Come on, Mia. A little?

She donned a wedding dress, hopped on

a plane, and took off for Vegas to marry the first guy she could find.

Why? Why did you do it?

Well, what if it wasn't so much about the money, even then?

What if she simply wanted to marry Derek to save herself any potential heartache down the road?

What if she was secretly so afraid she might meet somebody and fall blindly in love that she pulled out all the stops to make sure that couldn't happen?

Preserving millions of dollars was a darned good excuse for her erratic behavior. But that might be all it was. An excuse.

And now look.

Here you are, married anyway.

But not safely.

Oh, no.

There's nothing safe about her feelings for Dominic Chickalini.

With every day that's passed since they exchanged their vows, Mia has found herself more and more captivated by him . . . and more and more wistful that the vows they took in Vegas aren't real.

All right, they're *real* in the sense that they're legally wed.

But we don't love each other.

At least, he doesn't love me, and I . . .

Well, who knows what it is that Mia feels for Dom?

If it's mere infatuation, that definitely isn't strong enough to sustain a lifelong relationship.

And if it's true love . . . well, that prospect isn't any more comforting. Because true love doesn't always sustain a lifelong relationship, either.

True love can die.

"Are you ready?" Dom asks, and Mia realizes that they've made it to the top step of the stoop.

She's about to officially cross the threshold into Dom's world at last.

"I'm ready," she lies, and he opens the door.

"Uncle Dominic's here!" a young voice trumpets from somewhere within.

Mia thought she was ready. But, finding herself instantly engulfed in a vast human wave, she's caught off-guard by the overwhelming *presence* of the Chickalinis.

Everybody seems to be talking at once, while sweeping both Mia and Dominic along through a blur of entry hall and living room until they reach what is clearly the obvious final destination: the dining room.

"Everybody, this is Mia," Dom announces, once the initial flurry of birthday hugs and kisses has subsided, and once he's admired and tucked into his suit pocket a stack of homemade construction-paper-and-crayon birthday cards courtesy of his niece and nephews.

"Mia, this is . . . everybody."

One of his sisters — the younger one with the makeup and big hair — protests, "Dommy, at least tell her our names."

"How's she going to remember them all?"

"Try me," Mia tells him with a grin.

As Dominic names each of his family members in turn, she tries to notice something distinctive about each of them so that she'll be able to keep track.

Pop: Well, he's the obvious patriarch. He has a thick thatch of gray hair and is wearing a dress shirt that's open to reveal a gold cross around his neck.

Aunt Carm: fleshy face, aquiline nose, housedress.

Dom's sister Nina: pleasantly middle-aged, dark hair. She seems to be running the show here — she checks her watch, goes to the kitchen to clatter some pot lids, and returns in a flash.

Nina's husband, Joey: also pleasantly

middle-aged, but handsome, with graying temples.

Their daughter, Rose: darkly beautiful, with long hair and big eyes that seem to take in every detail when she looks at Mia.

Their son, Nino: fairer than his sister, with a solemn gaze and nice manners.

Dom's sister Rosalie: a little chubby but attractive nonetheless, in stark contrast to her sister's understated appearance. She's all makeup and hair spray and acrylic fingernails.

Rosalie's husband, Tim: hefty build and double chin, booming laugh, ruddy face and hair; the obvious lone Irishman in a roomful of Italians.

Their son T.J.: so shy he speaks in a whisper, wears glasses, and has a paperback book beneath his arm.

Their son Adam: spunky preschooler, with his father's coloring and impish laugh.

Dom's brother Ralphie: lanky and the tallest one in the room; not as classically handsome as Dominic but has an air of quiet, casual confidence.

Ralphie's fiancée, Francesca: curvaceous and pretty; a cross between his sisters, seeming to mirror both Nina's rapid-fire efficiency and Rosalie's flashy sense of style.

"Hey, where's Maggie?" Dominic asks.

"I thought you guys invited her and Charlie and the girls."

"We did," Nina says. "But she called a little while ago and said she was having some pains."

"Labor pains?" Dom asks, and Mia remembers that Maggie is his friend, the one with the two girls and a baby on the way.

How odd it seems that just days ago, she was hearing about Maggie for the first time, and thinking she would never know how it all turned out.

Now here she is, a part of everything. Officially a part of his life.

"She wasn't sure whether it was labor or a false alarm," Nina is telling Dom. "She said she'll keep us posted."

"So do you think you can remember all of us?" Francesca asks Mia, as she lights the first of two tall tapers in the middle of the table.

Mia notices that although she's not even married to Ralphie yet, Francesca is obviously, comfortably, one of them. She can't help but feel envious; she can't help but wonder if she'll ever truly belong.

How can she, when the bond all the Chickalinis so obviously share is love . . . and love is the one thing Mia's marriage lacks?

"It's not even *all* of us," T.J. pipes up in response to Francesca's still-unanswered question. "Uncle Pete and Aunt Debbi and the cousins aren't here."

"They live across the ocean in Germany, because they're in the military," Rose informs Mia with the expertise of the oldest cousin, even as she herds the others toward the children's table that's been set up in the kitchen.

"Yeah, Uncle Pete is a hero from the war," Adam puts in. "He was in Iraq and he got shot, but he's okay now."

"He wasn't shot," Nino corrects his younger cousin. "His battalion took mortar fire, but he was fine."

"I didn't know that," Mia says, turning to Dom as the children make their mass exodus.

He raises an eyebrow at her, as though to remind her that there are many things she doesn't know about his family.

They're things I would know, she realizes, *if we had known each other for any real length of time before we got married.*

Again, she feels a pang of regret as she gazes around the dining room at the assemblage of Chickalinis. She finds herself longing to be one of them . . . truly one of them.

But despite the wedding ring on her left hand — which nobody has noticed yet — she knows she doesn't really fit in.

If they knew that their brother's marriage was based not on a promise of love everlasting, but on an open-door return policy . . .

Well, Mia can't help but sense that they'd disapprove.

But they won't know, she reminds herself, and remembers to paste a happy smile on her face as she accepts a glass of wine from Aunt Carm.

They'll never know.

Not until it's over.

Dom gazes contentedly around the crowded dining room, the backdrop for all momentous Chickalini occasions.

There's even less space in here tonight, as there are two extra leaves in the oblong table. It takes two mismatched tablecloths to cover the whole thing. One is fancy white lace, the other an off-white everyday one so familiar and timeworn that Dominic knows every frayed spot and indelible stain as well as he knows the freckles on his own arms.

The table is set with the good china and already lined with a black-and-gray-speckled roaster pan filled with Aunt Carm's braciola, two CorningWare casseroles that contain Nina's eggplant Parmesan and her baked ziti, and Rosalie's oval red-and-white enamel platter heaped with roasted vegetables.

There's the bread basket that's older than Dominic; the butter dish he had to buy with his allowance after he broke the original when tossing a baseball in the house; the fancy cut-glass salad bowl filled with the usual iceberg lettuce, tomatoes, onions, and bottled Italian dressing.

On the sideboard is Nina's round Tupperware cake carrier that he knows contains his favorite triple-chocolate cake with coconut filling. His sister has made it for him on every birthday for as long as he can remember.

Sometimes, though, the family celebrated without him because he was too busy to show up for his own birthday dinner.

Too busy? Or you couldn't be bothered?

Now he regrets every birthday he failed to spend here, with these people who so obviously love him.

Look at Pop's gray hair. Look at Joey's. Look at little Adam, long out of diapers and talking about kindergarten. Why didn't he realize time was so fleeting? Why didn't he realize there's nothing more important in life than family, and home?

Yes, this is home, he thinks, comforted by the savory aromas, the well-worn backdrop, the cherished, smiling faces.

There's no way Mia can walk into his world and not feel the warmth.

Is there?

He sneaks a peek at her and finds her smiling at Aunt Carm over the rim of her wineglass, nodding at something his aunt is saying.

He relaxes a little . . . until he remembers that they still haven't broken the news about their wedding.

"All right, kids, go sit in the kitchen and we'll fill your plates," Nina instructs. "Mia, you're sitting there, between Dominic and Pop. Dig in, everyone."

As they take their seats and begin to do just that, Dominic searches for the right moment to make his announcement.

Maybe he should wait until dessert.

Or after dessert.

Maybe he should wait until he and Mia are on their way out the door, so he won't have to endure the predictable chaotic fallout for longer than a split second.

Maybe —

"So, Mia, how long have you and Dom known each other?" Rosalie asks above the clinking of forks and the children's laughter in the next room.

"For a while," Dom says, rescuing her.

"And you live in the city?" Francesca wants to know.

"Actually, Mia lives here in Astoria — she grew up here," Dom intervenes.

"Where?" Nina wants to know.

Before Dom can answer the question, Mia laughingly says, "I can speak for myself, you know."

"Yeah, Dommy, let her talk," Aunt Carm scolds. "Who do you think you are, one of us?"

As Mia answers the question, Dom exchanges knowing glances with his father, his brother, and his brothers-in-law. They're all silent, more focused on the food than the dialogue, all quite accustomed to the Chickalini women shifting the conversational gears.

"So you still live in the apartment where you grew up?" Rosalie asks Mia, as she intuitively passes the salt to her husband, who didn't even have to ask but clearly needed it. "What about your parents? Are they still there, too?"

"No, and — I mean, I live in the same

building, just not . . ." Mia trails off and looks at Dom, who realizes she's wondering whether to mention her parents. Or her grandparents. Or the lottery money.

"She lives on a different floor," Dom intercedes, deciding that now isn't the time for any of that.

"What do you do?" asks Aunt Carm.

"What do I *do?*" Mia repeats, looking puzzled.

"For a living," presses Aunt Carm, the professional housewife.

Again, Mia looks at Dom.

He finds himself pushing back his chair and standing up, then tugging Mia to her feet as well.

"Uh, Mia and I have an announcement to make," he says, and clears his throat.

"Now?" she asks in a high-pitched whisper, looking alarmed.

Now is as good a time as any, Dominic wants to point out, but everybody has miraculously fallen silent and fixed expectant eyes on him.

If there's any question he doesn't want to answer for Mia, much less have her answer on her own behalf, it's *"What do you do?"*

He tells himself it isn't that he's ashamed of Mia's lack of a meaningful career, or that he thinks Aunt Carm will disapprove.

In fact, all the women in his family willingly gave up their jobs when marriage and family beckoned. So Aunt Carm will probably applaud Mia's nonexistent employment status. She'll probably think it bodes well for the prospect of a new little grandniece or grand-nephew on the horizon.

So why don't you want Mia to admit that she's her grandmother's personal assistant?

Would you rather be introducing a . . . a swimsuit model?

Of course he wouldn't. He's proud of Mia. Really, he is.

He just doesn't want anybody else to see her as a pampered rich girl, that's all.

"Oh, my God!" Nina gasps suddenly, and presses her hands to her lips.

Dominic looks up to see that his sister is staring first at his left hand . . . then at Mia's.

"You guys are . . ." For once, Nina is rendered speechless.

"They're what, Nina?" Joe asks.

She just gapes and points.

Everybody looks at their ring fingers. For a moment, there's a silence so complete that the kids come running in from the kitchen to see what's going on.

Then a collective roar goes up in the room.

Dom looks helplessly at Mia, but she's already been manhandled out of reach by his sisters and Aunt Carm, who are taking turns hugging her, and crying.

Feeling numb, he shifts his gaze to his father, and finds him watching the scene as though from a detached distance. His expression is bemused and he's shaking his head slightly, off in his own little world.

Dom sidesteps his sisters and touches his father's shoulder. "Pop?"

"Congratulations," his father says, and opens his arms to embrace him. "I'm just glad I lived to see the day. I wasn't sure I would."

Something in his voice makes Dom pull back to look up at him in concern. "Pop? Are you feeling all right?"

"Me? I'm okay. You're the one I should be asking that question."

"Yo, Dominic, you've been holding out on us, you old dog." His brother-in-law Tim, an oversized New York firefighter with an oversized heart to match, swoops him into a bear hug. "What are you doing, eloping to Vegas behind our backs?"

"Yeah, we thought you were away on a business trip, peanut, and here you are tying the knot." Joey, who has always been as much a big brother to Dominic as Pete has, claps him on the back. "Paulie said he saw you in the airport out there, but he didn't say anything about your being with a woman."

"Well, uh, I *was* on a business trip," Dominic feels obliged to point out. "It was my sales conference, remember? And don't call me peanut."

"Sorry, peanut. Business and pleasure?" Joey asks with a dubious tilt of his head. "What are you two doing for a honeymoon? Going to a marketing seminar in Hawaii?"

"No, we just . . ." Dominic takes a deep breath. "We thought eloping to Vegas made more sense than . . . you know. Getting married here."

"What's the matter with here?" Tim asks with a grin. "You thought your sisters were going to take over your wedding or something?"

"He's the only smart one in this family," Ralphie grouses.

Dom can't help but smile. "I thought I'd never hear anybody say that."

"Well, enjoy it, because you'll never hear anybody say it again." Ralphie grabs Dom's fingers in a hearty double-handed shake. "Really, congratulations, Dom. She seems like a great girl."

"Yeah. She is." Dom looks over at Mia, who's surrounded by females, including Rose, and trying to get a word in edgewise to reply to the barrage of questions.

She catches his eye and smiles, looking a little overwhelmed, but happy; perhaps pleasantly surprised by the warm reception.

"So what happened?" Joey asks. "Did you get caught up in the whole Vegas thing and do it on a whim, or what?"

"Kind of," Dom admits. "But I don't know how much *Vegas* had to do with it."

"Are you kidding me?" Tim asks. "It had everything to do with it."

"What do you mean?"

"Everything about that place is surreal. You got the Eiffel Tower next to the Statue of Liberty next to a giant Sphinx. Volcanoes are exploding, fountains are dancing, pirates are fighting." Tim is really warming to his subject. "The brightest lights you've ever seen, the constant noise, the wacky people, all that food at all hours, the heat, the drinking, the money being thrown around . . . that place is nuts."

"You're right. It is," Dom murmurs in agreement, wondering why he never really thought about it that way.

"I can see how somebody could totally lose their head there in the middle of all that craziness," Tim goes on. "It's hard to even think straight. You don't even know what's real and what isn't."

"No," Dom agrees, "you don't."

"Yeah, and people do all kinds of bizarre things out there. All those wedding chapels . . . everywhere you look, there's a wedding chapel, people getting married left and right, probably to total strangers, half of them . . . it's crazy."

Caught up in his tirade, Tim doesn't catch Joe's warning look, but Dominic does.

Joey wants him to shut up because he thinks I'm going to start blaming the whole marriage on Vegas, Dom realizes, half-amused . . .

And half-alarmed.

Maybe there's something to Timmy's theory.

Maybe he really *did* lose his head. Maybe he got caught up in the whole Las Vegas nonreality.

It would certainly be a logical explanation for why a perfectly contented bachelor would suddenly find himself wearing a gold wedding band.

Feeling a tug on his sleeve, Dom looks down to see his youngest nephew, Adam, looking solemnly up at him.

"Uncle Dom?"

"Yeah, buddy?"

"Are we s'posed to call her Aunt now?"

He hadn't thought of that. Somehow, in all the worrying he's accomplished these last few days, he never got past the initial introduction of Mia to his family.

He hadn't pictured her becoming a part of their everyday lives . . . or stopped to wonder what would happen if she suddenly wasn't; if the newlyweds decided to go their separate ways per their original agreement.

No way am I admitting that part to anyone, even after the fact, Dom tells himself now. His sisters and Aunt Carm would have a conniption. Even his happily — and irrevocably — married brothers-in-law would likely disapprove of a marriage that wasn't necessarily based on forever.

"Sure, buddy," he reluctantly tells Adam, who has tugged his sleeve again. "You can call her Aunt."

"Aunt . . . what?"

"Hmm?"

"What's her name again?"

"Oh." Dom smiles, but inwardly, he's chiding himself for dragging his poor family into this charade; for asking them to accept a stranger into the fold — and feeling guilty for their sweet willingness to do so, all of them, from Pop right down to his youngest nephew.

"Her name is Mia," he tells Adam. "She's Aunt Mia."

"I'm gonna go call her that," Adam says, and darts to the other side of the table.

Dom is left feeling more reprehensible than ever.

How could he have been so cavalier about marriage?

He can tell himself that there's an out whenever he wants to take it, but the truth is, nothing will be that simple. Not now that they're back home in New York, meeting each other's families, living under the same roof.

Which reminds him . . .

"Pop," he says, turning to his father, "I guess it's obvious I'm not going to be living here anymore. I'll rent a truck and come clear all my stuff out next week. Okay?"

"Sure, okay." His father smiles, yet there's a hint of sadness in his eyes.

Well, of course. Another one of his children is leaving the nest.

Still, Dom is struck by how . . . withdrawn, almost, his father seems tonight.

"Pop, have you been taking your medication?" he asks, feeling a hint of unfamiliar anxiety popping up in the back of his mind.

Dominic has never been a worrywart like his sisters. Not about their father's health, not about anything. But now he can't help but notice that Pop looks uncharacteristically fragile.

"Yes, I take my medication." Nino Chickalini shrugs. "I'm getting old, Dominic. I take my medicine, and I eat what my sister gives me, and I gave up asking for salt and butter, but it's not helping me get any younger."

"You're not that old, Pop," Dominic points out, wondering when his father last saw the cardiologist.

"Sure I'm old. Speaking of old, it's your birthday," Pop responds. "Your sister made you your cake. I'd say we've got a lot to celebrate tonight. Nina! Ro!" he calls across the table to his daughters. "Get out the good champagne glasses. We need a toast."

"What are we toasting with?" Joe asks. "Do you want me to run next door and get a bottle of Spumante?"

"No, I've got something," Pop says,

going into the kitchen.

Dom watches him walk away, noticing that he's more stooped over than usual.

"Joey," he says, turning to his brother-in-law. "Is Pop okay?"

The twinkle all but disappears from Joey's dark eyes. "I don't know, Dom. His heart has been acting up lately."

Dom knows Joey is thinking of the day, not long after Dom's high school graduation, that Pop had a massive heart attack. If Nina hadn't found him lying on the floor beside his bed in the middle of the night . . . and if Joey hadn't rushed over from next door and done CPR until the ambulance came . . . well, Pop wouldn't have made it.

Dom thinks of that night often. He remembers his own disconcerting reaction when he awakened to his sister's wee-hour calls for help.

It was Joey, and not Dom, who saved his father's life with CPR. Dom took one look at the traumatic scene in the bedroom and raced out of the house.

Yes, he ran. Ran away. And he didn't come back home until long after the ambulance had taken Pop to the hospital.

Even then, he didn't rush over there with his sisters for the bedside vigil. He simply couldn't handle it, any of it, much to his shame.

You were a kid, Nina said afterward, and Rosalie, too. *You were upset.*

His sisters always were willing to make excuses for him.

But Dominic still remembers how disappointed he was in himself, not just for running, but for not knowing the CPR that was necessary to save Pop. He would have been trained, if he hadn't goofed off in class.

He remembers, too, that Pop had let his health insurance policy lapse so that he could afford to pay Dom's college tuition. Dom couldn't help but think that if he hadn't piddled away all the money he made working at the pizza parlor on baseball cards and, later, on girls, he might have saved enough for his own tuition.

"Hey," somebody says, and he looks down to see Mia, leaning into his side, taking in the chaotic din all around them.

Dominic smiles down at his wife, pushing the unsettling, troubling thoughts back into the past, where they belong. "I think you're a big hit with the Chickalini family."

"I love them, Dominic," she says, her eyes shining with joy. "I mean, I really, really love them. They're great."

His heart sinks another notch. "They are pretty great."

"Do you think they like me?"

"Are you kidding? Didn't my sisters just steal you away from me and talk your ear off? Then again," he feels compelled to add, "they do that with just about everybody. The nuns at Most Precious Mother, grocery store clerks, strangers on the street . . . you know. Everybody."

"So you mean they might not really like me?" Mia whispers, sounding a little uncertain, and he instantly regrets trying to dilute the warm reception.

"Relax, Mia, I'm just kidding. Of course they really like you. Who wouldn't?"

This isn't fair to my family, he tells himself, *but it really isn't fair to Mia.*

Despite her claims to the contrary, she *should* fall in love. She should fall in love with somebody who loves her back with all his heart; somebody who can promise her forever. It's what she deserves.

"Your sisters are so thrilled you're married, Dom," Mia is saying. "Oh, and they want to plan a wedding reception for us."

"They what?"

"They want to plan —"

"No, I heard you. I should have known."

He shakes his head.

"What? I think it would be fun."

"Another wedding?"

"Not another *wedding*," Mia says. "Just a reception. You know, dinner, dancing, toasts . . . what's wrong?"

"Nothing." Dom sighs, trying — out of tremendous guilt — to muster some enthusiasm for the idea. "I'm sure it would be fun."

"You don't seem very excited."

"No, I am. I'm thrilled."

Before she can respond, Pop returns from the kitchen, a bottle of champagne in hand.

"This is the bottle Pete sent me from that trip he and Debbi took to France a few years ago," he says. "It's good stuff. Let's open it. It isn't every day that my son turns thirty and gets married, all at once."

Amid much laughter, glasses are filled, and apple cider is hurriedly splashed into plastic wine goblets Nina digs out of a cupboard for the kids.

Then they all stand around the table, glasses raised.

Dom puts his arm around Mia and holds her close as Pop says, his voice a bit unsteady, "I have to admit, I wasn't sure this day would ever come. But if it was going to come, I was sure as heck going to be here to see it. And I know your mother is here to see it, too, Dominic."

He chokes up and breaks off, bowing his head.

Dom feels tears spring to his eyes and, looking down at Mia, is surprised to see them in hers.

"Who knows?" Timmy says jovially when nobody else seems capable of speaking. "She might have even had a hand in it. A miracle like Dominic getting married must've come straight from heaven."

Everybody manages to laugh, but Dominic feels as though he's going to cry.

Especially when he looks up and meets his father's emotional gaze.

"Here's to the newlyweds," Nino Chickalini says, beaming through his tears. "Mia, honey, welcome to this crazy family. *Cent'anni.*"

"*Cent'anni,*" everybody echoes.

Everybody including Mia.

As the others scramble madly to clink everybody else's glass, Dominic looks down at her in surprise.

"What, you think I didn't speak a little Italian?" she asks, smiling. "*Cent'anni.* It's a wedding toast. It means a hundred years."

411

Yes. A hundred years. May your marriage last a hundred years.

The irony, Dom tells himself, as he takes a fortifying sip of his champagne, *is that everybody here believes that ours can.*

Everybody but the bride and groom.

Chapter Seventeen

"Mags! You did it!"

Watching Dominic hug his friend, who just answered her door with a blue-blanketed bundle in her arms, Mia is relieved.

He was so quiet during the cab ride uptown just now that she was worried the visit would be strained. He claimed he was merely exhausted after a full week of work; it is, after all, a Friday night.

But he seems to have instantly relaxed at the sight of new mother Maggie and her tiny son. After relinquishing the oversized teddy bear and several wrapped gifts he bought on his lunch hour, he gingerly moves aside a flap of blanket and gazes almost reverently at the sleeping baby.

"I did it?" echoes Maggie, who is an exceptionally attractive blue-eyed brunette despite postpregnancy puffiness and dark circles under her eyes. "What do you mean? *You're* the one who did it, Dom."

"Um, Mags, I hate to break it to you, but I didn't have anything to do with giving Charlie a son, other than sending big-time

413

testosterone vibes your way."

"No, you doofus, I mean you're married! You did it! Give me that hand." Balancing the baby in one arm, Maggie grabs his fingers with the other and examines his wedding ring. "Wow. It's real."

"Fourteen carat. What, you thought it was gold-plated?"

"Not the ring, the fact that you're married. I mean, I just can't believe it!"

"Believe it," Dominic says, still focused on the baby.

Or maybe, Mia thinks, he's just pretending to be enchanted by the baby so he won't have to look at her. He hasn't made eye contact with her since they met in the lobby of his building. He was late, but he had told her not to come up when she got there.

Today wasn't the day, he said, for him to introduce his coworkers to his wife. Everyone was just too busy.

Mia was left wondering whether he'd even bothered to tell anyone at MAN that he *had* a wife.

Maggie has abruptly turned her attention to Mia. "So . . . you're the glowing bride!"

She smiles, trying not to feel disconcerted by the term.

She doesn't feel like a glowing bride anymore. Did she ever?

Aloud, she says only, "Right. I'm Mia."

"I'm Maggie, and you have no idea how thrilled I am to meet you. Come on in!" She steps back and they cross the threshold into the brownstone.

Mia admires the hardwood floors, high ceilings, crown moldings, a flight of stairs with spindles and newel posts. This is a real home, just as the Chickalinis' place is a home. Just as her own grandparents' apartments — both the cramped old version and the spacious new one — have been homes.

Something's missing in my place, she tells herself. *Even now that Dominic is there.*

Or perhaps, especially now that Dominic is there.

He didn't even bring all his belongings. He kept saying he was going to rent a truck and move everything out of his father's house, but he had yet to actually do that. He only had the clothing he could fit into a garment bag and a suitcase he'd borrowed from his brother-in-law next door.

Now the suits hung in the otherwise-empty closet of one of Mia's spare bedrooms, and the clothes were in the empty bureau. She had offered to make room in the master suite, but he told her he didn't want to cram his stuff in beside hers.

"Charlie's in his office, writing — oh, careful, don't trip," Maggie says, expertly sidestepping a doll in their path, then kicking it out of the way. "He'll show up sooner or later, but I'm under strict orders not to disturb him."

"Where are my girls?" Dom asks.

"Sleeping over at my mother-in-law's tonight, thank God. They were thrilled. They packed everything they own for one night in Bedford."

"Obviously not *everything* they own," Dom comments drily, gesturing around.

There are toys everywhere Mia looks, strewn from the floor of the entrance hall at the front of the house all the way to the kitchen at the back. There, they finally settle at Maggie's insistence, so that she can make coffee.

"Don't go to any trouble on our account, Mags," Dominic says, as his friend places the tiny blue bundle in his arms without asking. "Mia and I are going out to dinner after this. I told you we just wanted to pay a quick visit to see the little guy."

Mia finds herself marveling at the sight of him holding a baby; impressed by his obvious expertise. She has never held a newborn in her life.

"Don't worry, I'm not going to any trouble on your account, Dom. I'm the one who needs the coffee." Maggie measures grounds into a paper filter, saying, "Little Charlie has been nursing every hour around the clock. I feel like I'm sleep-walking."

Mia can relate, having endured a few sleepless nights herself lately.

Part of the reason is her insatiable appetite for Dominic, which apparently is mutual.

Yes, somehow, they have great chemistry in the bedroom.

It's just in the limited time they've had together *out* of the bedroom that things are a little . . . well, less than great.

Not that they're arguing, because they aren't.

It's more that an invisible wall seems to have gone up between them, brick by invisible brick, ever since Dom's birthday party last Saturday night.

He still comes home to her every night after work, although his arrival seems to get later and later. He still brings her bouquets of flowers every night: tulips, or lilies, or roses. And they still make love every night, somehow finding their way into each other's arms even after an abbreviated evening spent together, yet in unmistakable emotional isolation.

And every night, long after her husband has effortlessly drifted off to sleep, Mia lies awake trying to figure out what went wrong and why.

She certainly knows *when*.

But *why?* What happened the night of his birthday to make him retreat emotionally?

She can't help but wonder whether the reality of their marriage hit home for Dominic when he brought her to meet his family.

It can't be that they didn't like her, because she can tell that they did. In fact, one or both of his sisters have called her every day since, just to check in, and to talk about plans for the wedding reception next month.

She just wishes they would stop commenting on how shocked they are that their younger brother actually took the marital plunge. It isn't as though she had any delusions that Dominic was actively looking for a wife when he got on that plane to Vegas. But Mia's confidence in the future of their marriage is severely undermined by the realization that he most definitely had no intention of ever getting married.

Not that she ever really *had* any confidence in the future of their marriage.

Cent'anni?

She's starting to think they'll be lucky if they last *Cento giorni.*

One hundred *days.*

"I want to hear everything," Maggie says, as they settle into a cozy kitchen nook with steaming coffee and bakery cookie pops that proclaim *It's A Boy* in light blue piping.

Mia can't help but marvel at her expertise as she nurses the baby while eating a cookie and sipping coffee above him. She finds herself envying Maggie's obvious contentment in her harried little world. It must be nice to know exactly where you belong.

Nice? It must be pure heaven.

Maggie adds, "And, *ahem,* Mr. Chickalini, I also want to know why I'm not meeting Mia until now."

Dom shrugs in response to his friend's accusatory expression. "There was never a good occasion for you guys to meet."

"Carolyn's wedding would have been perfect. And I know she invited you with a date. You should have brought Mia. But at least now I know why you moped around all night."

"Why?" Dom and Mia ask in unison.

"Because, Dom, you missed your fiancée!" Maggie says in a *why else?* tone. "I mean . . . duh!"

Mia has never met anybody like Maggie before. The woman simply oozes breezy confidence.

"Oh, yeah, well . . ." Dom trails off and shrugs. For the first time, he looks directly at Mia. "I probably should have brought you."

She manages an almost-smile. "It's okay."

She has to remind herself that of course they didn't know each other then, so he couldn't have taken her to the wedding. Still, she can't help but feel a bizarre resentment. The way Maggie is scolding him, Mia can almost convince herself that even if she and Dominic *were* seriously dating, he might not have invited her to the wedding.

"Weddings and Dominic . . . they just don't mix," Maggie said, biting the entire *It's A* off the top of a cookie pop. Around a mouthful, she adds, "I'm glad he's married, but I wish I could have been there to witness the big moment."

"Nobody was there, Mags, so don't feel bad."

"I just don't get why you had to elope."

"Because we couldn't wait. Right, Mia?"

"Right," she murmurs.

"So pretty much overnight, you went from being old *Love 'Em and Leave 'Em Chickalini* to *Race You to the Altar Chickalini.*" Maggie shakes her head. "I always told you that someday, you'd fall in love for real. And that when you did, you'd change your mind about everything you never thought you wanted. Am I a psychic, or what?"

"You're a *psycho,* that's what you are," Dominic says with a hollow-sounding chuckle. Leaning toward the baby, he whispers, "Hey, your mommy's crazy, did you know that?"

"I don't know about him, but I knew that," a male voice says, and Mia turns to see a slightly rumpled, very handsome man who can only be Maggie's husband. On his head is an odd baseball cap with what appears to be a bird's feathered hindquarters protruding from above the brim.

"Watch it, Charlie," Maggie says, and adds, "there's coffee. But we just used the last of the half-and-half."

"That's okay, I'll share yours." He slips into the chair beside his wife and takes a sip from her cup. Then he adjusts the baby's blanket to cover his exposed toes and plants a kiss on his forehead.

"Mia, this is my husband, Charlie, and that crazy thing on his head is his so-called thinking cap — he wears it whenever he's writing. Now who's the psycho?" Maggie holds up her cookie pop so that her husband can take a bite, then says pointedly, "Um, Dom, don't you want to make an introduction?"

"Oh, sorry. Charlie, this is Mia. My . . . wife."

Mia looks at Dominic, then at the Kennellys, wondering if they noticed that the last word seemed to strangle him.

Wife.

Maggie and Charlie definitely noticed. They look at each other, and in that marital telepathy Mia has witnessed between her grandparents, and between Dom's sisters and their spouses, they exchange unspoken . . . well, it looks like *concern,* in Mia's opinion.

They're worried, she realizes. *They're sensing that Dominic isn't wholeheartedly into this marriage.*

But Charlie sounds convincing as he

shakes Dominic's hand and says, "Congratulations. I've been telling Maggie for years that you were capable of finding a wife without her help."

Turning to Mia, he says, "You must know that I met Maggie because she was trying to play matchmaker for Dom."

"He mentioned that," Mia is glad to be able to say truthfully.

"I just felt like he wasn't looking for the right kind of women," Maggie says, woman to woman. "I told him he needed a woman of substance, somebody smart and beautiful, somebody with character, somebody —"

"Somebody like you," Dom cuts in drily. "That's what you said, Mags. You said I needed somebody like you."

"You did," she says with a shrug. "You needed somebody who wouldn't let you walk all over her, and then walk away."

"Walk all over her?" Mia asks, raising an eyebrow as her stomach begins to churn.

"Oh, he didn't do it in a bad way," Maggie says, as though there's a good way of walking all over a person. "It's just . . . well, you must have noticed the Chickalini charm — that's what everybody used to call it, back when we were in college. Dom just had a way of getting people to do whatever he wanted, without their realizing they were being manipulated. He had girls doing his laundry and —"

"Maggie, are you sure we don't have any half-and-half?" Charlie interrupts, obviously trying to shut her up.

"I'm sure. So anyway, I was like the only female in a ten-mile radius of the guy who was immune to —"

"That was a long time ago, Maggie," Dom cuts in.

"Not that long ago," she protests. "You were like that when I first met you, and you were like that until — when did you say you two met?" she asks Mia.

I didn't, Mia thinks, and looks at Dom. Let him answer that one. She's not entirely certain she's capable of speaking at the moment, anyway.

"It was a few months ago," he says vaguely. "So Charlie, you've finally got a son. How does it feel?"

As they discuss the baby, Mia clutches the handle of her coffee mug, hoping nobody has noticed how her hands are trembling.

Maggie's words are echoing in her head.

Dom just had a way of getting people to do whatever he wanted, without their realizing they were being manipulated.

How, Mia wonders, with a sickening sense

424

of clarity, *could I have been so stupid?*

She's upset.

That much is obvious to Dom as he and Mia exit the brownstone and walk toward Broadway to flag down a cab.

All night, she's been going through the motions, from the moment he met her in the lobby of his building.

To be fair . . . she isn't the only one. He, too, has been detached. And not just this evening.

All week, he's been aware of a growing distance between them. Aware, too, that it's a chasm he hasn't been able — or perhaps, willing — to cross. He finds himself stalling at the office in the evenings, rather than hurrying home to his wife.

When he gets there, he can't even bring himself to look her in the eye, afraid that his misgivings might be blatantly obvious.

In bed, with the lights out, is the only time he's felt any kind of connection with her. And that particular connection isn't something he takes lightly. It just isn't . . . enough.

He's a cheater. That's what he is. With this sham marriage, he's cheated his family, her family — hell, he's even cheated himself. But worst of all, he's cheated Mia. She deserves to be loved.

The only thing that's held him back from walking out altogether is the glimmer of possibility that he himself might be capable of falling in love with her. His feelings for her are already much deeper, more profound, than anything he's ever experienced before. They might very well develop into love, over time.

But how much time?

And what if it never happens?

What if —

"I think we should skip the restaurant, Dom. I just want to go home."

Her words jar him back to the moment, but when he glances down at her and sees the look on her face, it takes him a few seconds to even comprehend what she's saying. At least, verbally.

Her expression relays far more than words ever could.

"But . . . we haven't eaten," is his lame reply, as his thoughts careen wildly like Julia and Katie's beloved bumper cars.

They've reached the corner.

Maggie stops walking, turns away from him, gazing uptown at the oncoming traffic as though she's searching for a cab. Searching for a ready escape.

"It's okay," she says, her back to him. "I'm not hungry."

"Well, we can get takeout on the way home, and —"

"Dom —" She interrupts herself abruptly, turns to face him, and takes a deep breath.

Oh. Oh, no.

Looking into her dark eyes, he knows what's coming before she says another word.

"I think that I should go home alone, and you should . . . you should go to your father's, or your sister's, or something. At least just for tonight. I think —"

"But Mia, we —"

"Let me finish. I think you need some space."

He opens his mouth to protest, but she shushes him with a raised hand and adds, "We both do. We both need space."

He shakes his head, gazing at the traffic whizzing down the avenue. "Why do we need space?" he asks Mia, inexplicably needing to stop the inevitable. "Space for what?"

"Space to think things through. Space to decide whether this" — she waves her left hand, the one wearing the gold fourteen-carat band — "is what we really want."

"I thought we both decided that it was," he finds himself saying, even as he wonders what the hell he's doing. She's giving him his out. The out she promised him. The out he should be taking without question.

After all, you specialize in running away, he reminds himself bitterly, and clamps his mouth shut.

"No, Dom, you were doing me a favor to help me out of a bind. And now that it's not about my losing a fortune . . . well, you're free to go."

Free. He's free.

Is that what she wants?

She wants him to go?

She really was using him, then, to get to the money?

He swallows hard.

"You know, Mia, you've always just settled," he hears himself saying to her. "You've always taken the easy way out. Is that what you're doing now?"

"What are you talking about?"

"With work, with school . . . you've never had to fight for anything. You've never —"

"And you *have?*" she shoots back at him. "You and your Chickalini charm? What have you ever fought for in your life?"

He opens his mouth to argue.

Then he closes it.

Because she's right.

His feet carry him to the curb, where he faces oncoming traffic with a raised hand, glad she can't see the tears that are pooling in the corners of his eyes.

As he stares blindly into the blur of headlights rushing past him, a mere couple of feet from where he stands, he flashes back to a long-ago day, a childhood day.

"When your true love comes along, you'll know it," Pop said.

I might know it, *Dom thought,* but no way am I going to do anything about it.

No way, no how. He didn't want to turn into a sad, lonely old guy crying in a pizzeria. He wanted to be a New York Yankee, a superhero . . . the kind of man who would never, ever cry in front of his son, or anybody else.

"Dom . . ." Mia touches his shoulder.

He shakes her off. "Step back," he says hoarsely. "Get on the sidewalk. There's too much traffic."

"But —"

"Get back, Mia. Be careful."

A cab swerves toward them, cutting through traffic from two lanes over. It pulls to a stop a few yards past them.

"Come on," Dom says, striding toward it, aware of her scurrying along beside him.

He opens the back door for her, and she climbs in.

Rather than climb in after her, he slams the back door closed and knocks on the driver's window, gesturing for the guy to roll it down.

He does, and Mia does the same in the backseat.

"Dom, what are you doing?" she asks. "Get in."

He shakes his head, puts two twenties into the driver's hand, and tells him the address of Mia's apartment.

"We're both going to Astoria," she protests. "This is silly. At least ride over with me so that we can figure out —"

"No, I have no idea where I'm going right now," he says, and means it literally — and figuratively.

"But —"

"Look at me, Mia," he says gruffly, and puts his face down close to hers. "I'm not going to just run away. Okay? And neither are you. I'm going to call you. Tomorrow. Please be there. And we can talk."

She's silent.

"Mia . . . I really will call."

She shrugs.

"When I call, will you be there?"

She hesitates. Then says without conviction, "I'll be there."

Seeing the doubt in her eyes, he says, "I promise I'm going to call. I *promise*. Do you believe me? Do you believe that I'm not running away?"

"I believe you," she says, but he knows it's a lie.

As the cab pulls away, he watches the red taillights until they disappear.

I'm going to call her, he tells himself, walking aimlessly down the block. *Of course I am. I'm going to fight for her, dammit.*

Why? She doesn't believe in love, and she didn't marry you for love . . .

Right. He didn't marry her for love, either. But that's different, because . . .

Because why? Because it's you? Because the rules are different for you?

Come on, Dom, how can you blame her?

How, when his own reasons were no more noble than hers?

But people change. Love happens to them, and they change.

It can happen to him, and it can happen to Mia. In time. It can happen to them together, or . . .

Or she could walk away and find somebody else tomorrow. Somebody who will love her the way she deserves to be loved.

Maybe I should go after her right now, he thinks suddenly. *Maybe space isn't what I need. Maybe it's the opposite. Maybe I should —*

His cell phone rings suddenly in the pocket of his suit coat.

As he reaches for it, his heart leaps at the possibility that it might be Mia. Maybe she's come to the same realization. Maybe she doesn't want to spend even one night apart, either.

Then he remembers that she doesn't have a cell phone, that it was lost with her bag in Las Vegas, and his heart sinks.

It must be about work, he tells himself, flipping it open and glancing at the Caller ID window.

But it isn't work.

And a moment after he says hello, the bottom falls out of his world.

Chapter Eighteen

More than a week has passed since Mia last saw her husband.

He didn't call, as he promised.

She isn't surprised. She knew he wouldn't.

She knew, but she had hoped anyway. Hoped his word might prove to be as solid as the ring on his finger, even if the marriage it symbolized wasn't.

"Maybe it's better this way," she tells Lenore, as they sip coffee at an outdoor café on Astoria Boulevard on an Indian summer Sunday morning after Mass. "Maybe it'll be easier for me to let go of a jerk than it would have been to let go if he were a great guy."

"In that case, he's definitely a jerk," Lenore tells her, with a firm nod of her bleached-blonde head. But her brown eyes, behind her wire-rimmed glasses, are uncertain.

"In that case?" Mia echoes. "You mean, you don't really think he's a jerk?"

"I don't know. I want to believe that he

is, but . . . to tell you the truth, Mia, you've kind of been a jerk, too. No offense."

"No offense taken," she says wryly. "Believe me, I feel like a jerk."

"But with you, it's different," Lenore says quickly. "I mean, you were blinded by the whole money thing."

"That doesn't make it any better. That makes it worse."

"But he might have married you for your money. *That's* definitely worse than you marrying some willing guy just to keep your money. Except . . ."

"Except?" Mia prods impatiently.

"Except it really doesn't sound like he's that into the money. You said yourself he wouldn't let you pay off the gambling debt on his credit cards."

"He said he didn't want me to, but then he said I could."

"Because you insisted."

"Right, but . . ."

"But what? You can be a real bulldozer when you want to, Mia. Admit it. Sometimes you don't take no for an answer."

"Listen, Lenore, I was willing to give him the benefit of the doubt right up until the end. Until he made a promise that he obviously had no intention of keeping."

"Maybe he got hit by a bus. Did you ever

see *An Affair to Remember*?"

"The one with Cary Grant and Deborah Kerr? Or the remake with Warren Beatty and Annette —"

"What difference does it make? The point is, maybe he had a very good reason for not calling you. Maybe you should call him."

"I did," Mia admits, looking longingly at the raspberry turnover she just spied on a neighboring diner's plate. "I called him earlier this week. At the office."

She couldn't help herself. She wasn't even sure what she would say when he picked up. She only knew she couldn't let him go without a fight.

You know, Mia, you've always just settled . . . you've always taken the easy way out.

"And?" Lenore prompts her.

"And I got his voice mail. He said he would be out of the office for the remainder of that day."

"So? Maybe he got hit by a bus, like I said."

"If he was lucid enough to call the office, he was lucid enough to call me, don't you think?"

"I guess." Lenore sips her coffee thoughtfully. "So that's it? You just called him that once?"

"At least I tried," Mia says grimly.

Some fight.

Maybe she could have tried a little harder, but . . .

But he didn't try at all. She can't let herself forget that.

Lenore sighs. "Well, I guess he really is a jerk. I could have told you that right from the start and saved you a lot of trouble, because I'm really starting to believe that all men are jerks."

"Not all men. There are a few good ones."

"Name one."

"Fuji."

"Name one heterosexual one."

"My grandfather."

Lenore rolls her eyes. "Name one heterosexual, single, nonoctogenarian male who isn't a jerk."

Mia hesitates. "I can't."

"That's because they don't exist. Listen, Mia, you're better off without this guy. Just like I'm better off without my ex-husband. Because . . . what are you looking at?" She looks over her shoulder, following Mia's gaze to the plate on the next table.

"That raspberry turnover. I can't help it. It's like it's calling my name."

"It's calling my name, too. You want to

order one? We can split it."

"No, thanks."

"Come on. It looks really good."

"It looks great, but no."

"One little taste can't hurt."

Oh, yes it can, Mia thinks glumly, shaking her head. *One little taste can be devastating.*

"Here you go, Mr. Chickalini." The nurse bustles back into the room and hands Dominic a blue plastic bag.

He looks up dully. "What is . . . ?"

"All of your father's personal effects are in there."

"Oh. Thank you."

He swallows so painfully he must have visibly winced, because the nurse touches his arm gently and asks, "Are you all right? Can I get you a glass of water, or call somebody for you?"

"No, I'm . . ." He shakes his head, unable to speak, and heaves a shuddering sigh. "I'm okay."

He looks back at the bed where just minutes ago, his father drew his rattling last breath. Or perhaps it was longer than that; perhaps over an hour ago.

He has no way of knowing what time it is, or even what day it is. They've all run together since he took up his bedside vigil on the Friday night Joey called him with the news.

His father had suffered a massive heart attack and had been rushed to the hospital.

It was bad, really bad, right from the start.

Yet somehow, Nino Chickalini lingered. Lying in the ICU with thin threads of oxygen tubing stretching beneath his aquiline nose and across his sallow, sunken cheeks, he came and went in the days that followed. He would sink into unconsciousness for long, frightening stretches of time, then awaken to inhabit a fragile state of consciousness that was even more frightening.

He's fading, Dominic thought more than once, looking into his father's glassy eyes, listening to his labored breathing, bending his ear to parched lips to hear faint words that might very well be his last.

His father was dying before him, dying with every labored, precious breath he took, and Dominic was powerless to help him. There was nothing he could do. Nothing but be here.

I won't run away this time, Pop, he vowed silently, over and over, clutching his father's weak white hand. *This time, I'll be here with you every step of the way.*

And he was. When he managed to sleep, he slept sitting up in the chair beside the bed, and when he bothered to eat, he ate here. He left only a few times to go home for a quick shower, and to pick up a few of his father's things. A framed photo of Mommy, a rosary, a book, a shaving kit. Things Pop might look for and need, if he started feeling better.

Somehow, it helped Dominic to bring those things, even though he knew, deep down, that his father wouldn't be getting better.

His aunts and uncles came and went, as did his brother and sisters and sometimes, just briefly, their children. They came with crayoned artwork Nino couldn't see and poignant questions nobody could answer; questions that more than once sent Dominic's sisters sobbing into the corridor. Pete and Debbi were traveling in Europe and had yet to be reached.

Father Tom came. He came to administer last rites, and then he came, often, to sit with Dominic, to hold his hand and pray with him.

He noticed Dom's wedding ring at one point.

"Her name is Mia," Dom told the kindly priest. "And I'll need to speak to you

about an annulment when things settle
down."

"What happened, Dominic?"

He merely shook his head and said, "It
was a mistake from the start. And it just
didn't work out."

When he put her in the cab that night,
he had every intention of calling Mia. But
somewhere in the midst of his family crisis,
he simply let go. He did his best to push
the nagging thought of her from his mind.

A few times, he did consider at least
calling to let her know what had happened.
But he was too emotionally drained to
even hear her voice. His father's hospital
bedside was no place to address a marital
crisis.

And anyway, he had nothing left to offer
her. Everything he had, every ounce of
strength he possessed, was directed toward
his family now. He had to be strong for his
father, for his sisters, for Ralphie, who was
taking it harder than anyone.

"Can I call you a cab, Mr. Chickalini?"
the nurse asks, and he slips back to the
tragic present with a heavy sigh and a
heavy heart.

"No, thank you."

He trudges slowly down the corridor
that has become second nature to him in

these last days, carrying the blue plastic bag, dreading the task that lies ahead: informing the rest of the family that Pop has passed away, then making the arrangements for the funeral and burial.

As he steps out into the chilly September evening, the fresh air hits him full force — and so, all at once, does reality.

Pop's gone.

Overcome by a sudden, primal sorrow, he stops short and clutches a lamppost for support.

"No . . . Oh, God, oh, Pop, no . . ." An anguished sob escapes him, and it's all he can do not to collapse right there on the sidewalk of the bustling boulevard.

Vaguely aware of curious pedestrians, he tries desperately to get ahold of himself.

He takes several deep breaths, staring down at the sidewalk, watching his tears splat on the dry concrete around his shoes. He doesn't even have anything to wipe them with. His father always told him he should carry a starched white handkerchief in his pocket, but he never did. That was too old-fashioned.

"Nobody carries handkerchiefs anymore, Pop."

"Well, you should. You never know when you might need one."

No, Pop. You never know.

He wipes his eyes on his sleeve and looks up, up at the hospital where his father's body is being transported to the morgue; up past the roofline.

Thousands of stars are suspended in the inky night sky. Seeking comfort, Dom searches for the brightest one. They all seem to be glittering with equal brilliance tonight . . .

Then he spots it: a single, luminous light almost directly overhead, more resplendent than ever before . . . and, streaking across the sky toward it, the radiant path of a shooting star.

He nods, gazing at it in awe until tears flood his eyes and he has to look away.

They're together, he tells himself. *Together at last.*

When he glances back up at the sky, there's no trace of the shooting star . . . if it was ever really there at all.

Yet a strange sense of peace seeps into him as he begins the long, lonely walk home.

Waiting for Fuji on the steps outside his building, Mia opens the copy of the *Astoria Times* she just picked up at the newsstand. She flips idly through it, thinking not about house fires or car accidents or civic groups, but about Dominic.

Does he really think he can just walk away without officially ending their marriage?

Sooner or later, they'll have to connect, whether he wants to see her or not. They'll have to discuss an annulment or divorce; he'll have to pick up his things. Her closet and bureau still hold his clothes.

And clothing is the least of what he left behind, she thinks, viciously snapping a page and tearing the corner as she turns it.

She wonders how much longer she can feign normalcy for her grandparents' sake. After coming up with a week's worth of excuses about Dominic's whereabouts, she's certain they must be growing suspicious.

Maybe she should tell them he got hit by a bus.

Or maybe she should just admit the truth: that he abandoned her mere days into their marriage.

No.

Grandpa Junie would go ballistic.

So? What do you care? It's not as though Dom's coming back. What difference does it make if Grandpa finds out he was apparently right about him from the start?

She cares. She doesn't know why, but she does.

Maybe out of sheer stubborn refusal to let her grandfather say *I told you so.*

Or maybe because she's clinging to a foolish shred of hope.

Hope? Ha. She hoped for how many years that her parents would come back to her, and did they?

She turns another page, asking herself how she could have been so stupid. How could she have gone and done the very thing she swore she never would?

I didn't, she protests feebly. Futilely. *I'm not in love with him.*

I'm just . . . just . . .

Just in love with him, she admits in resignation. Hopelessly, madly in love with him.

She can hardly blame him for not loving her back, can she? Look at her. She's utterly useless. She has no real job, no independent source of income, no pride, no motivation. Nothing has ever really mattered to her but . . . but . . .

But orchids, she realizes.

And with that, from somewhere deep within, an utterly unexpected idea sparks to life.

Orchids . . . ?

Orchids.

Shaking her head as if to rid herself of the bizarre thought that's beginning to form, she looks around. Still no sign of Fuji.

She blindly turns another page of the newspaper . . .

And is struck by something far more unsettling than orchids.

Above a hauntingly familiar photo of a man she met only once is the chilling headline *Astoria Businessman Succumbs After Illness.*

The pews of Most Precious Mother Roman Catholic Church are filled with mourners. So many people have turned out to pay their final respects to Nino Chickalini that they're standing three-deep in the back.

But Dominic, facing forward throughout the funeral Mass, didn't grasp the presence of the enormous crowd until now. He was too caught up in Father Tom's moving eulogy, and in keeping his own emotions in check when all he wanted to do was break down and cry.

Now, as his grandmother wails uncontrollably for her firstborn son, Millicent Millagros begins to play the Prayer to Saint Frances, Pop's favorite hymn.

Dominic and his siblings begin the slow, final walk down the aisle behind the coffin adorned with roses.

Caught off-guard by the sheer volume of friends and family filling the church, Dominic bows his head, overcome by the compassion of others and his own sorrow.

"Make me a channel of your peace," Millicent sings, and Dom can hear Aunt Carm sobbing loudly nearby.

It was Dominic who chose that hymn and all the others; Dominic who carefully selected his father's best suit and shirt and tie; Dominic who tucked a small photo of his mother into the breast pocket before delivering the clothes to the funeral director; Dominic who decided that he should be buried wearing the wedding ring he had never removed.

He drove to the airport to greet his older brother's flight from Germany; he arranged for the postfuneral luncheon at Pop's restaurant; he contacted the newspaper with the obituary information.

"You really came through for us, Dommy," Nina said, her voice clogged with emotion as she pulled him aside at the wake last night. "For us, and for Pop. Are you sure you're okay?"

"I'll be fine," he lied.

"What about Mia? Maybe you should have at least told —"

"No," he cut in. "I shouldn't have."

He had already told Nina and the others that his short-lived marriage was over. That he got caught up in the excitement of Las Vegas, just as Timmy said, and made an impulsive, stupid decision. That he's better off, much better off, alone.

Alone.

Yes, he certainly is.

As they slowly processed down the aisle behind the casket, he's aware of his grandmother moaning in her wheelchair as the nursing home attendant pushes her along; his sisters being held steady by their husbands' arms; of Francesca's protective grip on Ralphie's wrist; of Pete leading the way stoically, hand in hand with Debbi and their children. But he can't bear to look, really look, at any of them. After endless days of keeping the family from falling apart, he can't bear to see the brunt of their stark, awful grief; can't bear to reveal his own.

Only when he senses they've reached the back of the church does he dare to raise his head.

That's when he sees her face.

Only for an instant, before one of the

altar boys throws open the vestibule door, obliterating his view . . .

But she was here.

Mia.

Here, with tearstained cheeks and sympathetic eyes that met his for a fleeting moment.

He turns back, searching the throng for another glimpse; finding nothing.

Like the shooting star he may or may not have seen the night his father died, she's gone . . . if she was ever really here at all.

Why would she be? he wonders, swiping at his overflowing eyes with his sleeve.

Then, his heart quickening a bit, he wonders . . .

Why wouldn't *she be?*

If she somehow found out about Pop . . .

Well, she would come. She would come, because no matter what had happened between them, she's his wife. Perhaps in name only, but his wife nonetheless.

As he steps out onto the sidewalk into gray autumn rain, the church bell begins to toll in the steeple overhead.

It's a mournful sound, punctuated by pattering raindrops and heels tapping on concrete; by the murmured condolences and hushed sobs of the exiting congregation.

But Dominic hears only the echo of his

father's long-ago words.

She was my one and only true love. Somebody like her doesn't come along more than once in a lifetime.

Somewhere deep in Dominic's broken heart, a faint, fragile shimmer of hope has taken hold.

Chapter Nineteen

October

Normally, Mia welcomes the unexpected buzz of the building's security system. Once in a while, a family friend will unexpectedly drop in for coffee. Of course, sometimes it's just a UPS deliveryman with something she ordered; other times, it's somebody who's come to the wrong address.

Even that doesn't bother her on a normal afternoon. Anything to break up the monotony of killing time during her grandmother's afternoon nap upstairs.

But when the buzzer sounds today, she's not just killing time. She's seated at her dining room table, course catalogs and enrollment forms spread out across the polished surface. They're from an online ornamental horticulturalist course she just discovered. If she's accepted — and if she completes the course of study — it might lead to a career that employs her favorite hobby.

Who would have guessed that a passion for orchids might lead her to discover her life's vocation? And why didn't she ever think of this before?

Because, Mia, you've always just settled. You've always taken the easy way out.

Dom was right.

But she's ready to roll up her sleeves and get to work . . . even if it takes years.

And it will, if she eventually goes for her master's degree in horticulture.

Reluctantly putting aside her paperwork — and her newfound enthusiasm for academia — she crosses to the foyer to answer the buzzer.

Maybe it's her lost luggage, which the airline recently discovered in North Dakota. They had promised to have it shipped overnight, but it has yet to show up.

Or maybe it's just Grandpa Junie, having locked himself out again and forgotten where he's hidden the spare key.

He's done that twice in the last week alone.

"I always knew I'd go senile one of these days," he said the second time. "Half the time, I'm lucky if I can remember where I live."

Mia assured him that he wasn't really senile, although she was starting to wonder.

Privately, she couldn't help but acknowledge that his forgetfulness was helpful. At least he's stopped asking her about Dominic every day, either accepting the excuse that Mia's husband works long hours and is rarely around, or perhaps having forgotten that he even exists.

Nana Mona still asks, though, and still looks worried by her granddaughter's evasive replies.

I can't keep up the charade forever, Mia tells herself as she reaches out to press the intercom button. *Sooner or later, I'll have to tell them the truth.*

Yes, even if it leads to a litany of *I Told You So's.*

Even if it leads to being disowned and disinherited.

Somehow, now that she's found a career goal, her grandfather's money doesn't feel nearly as crucial. She'll figure out a way to support herself, to get through school on her own. It might even feel good to take sole responsibility for herself for once in her life.

But when it comes to the marriage . . . and Dominic . . .

Well, she can't seem to let go quite so easily.

Especially after meeting his gaze at the funeral and finding it utterly bereft. His desolate eyes have haunted her ever since.

She doesn't know what to do about that, though. She might have forgiven him for not calling now that she knows why he didn't, but she can't ignore his failure to reach out to her in his time of need. She could have been with him during his father's final days, to offer support and friendship, if nothing else.

Well, he saw her at the funeral. She knows he did. And more than two weeks have passed since then.

She's starting to forget what he looks like. She's starting to forget what he sounds like. She wonders if, in time, she'll allow herself to forget him altogether. It would sure as hell be a lot easier than living the rest of her days haunted by his memory.

"Who is it?" she calls into the intercom.

Silence.

Then an unmistakable voice — a voice she hasn't forgotten after all — answers, "It's me."

Dominic could have taken the stairs, he supposes.

But waiting here for the elevator to descend to the first floor buys him just a little more time to figure out what he's going to say.

You've had weeks to do that, he reminds himself, as the elevator doors slide open at last. *Haven't you figured it out by now?*

No. No, he hasn't.

He's spent days searching for just the right words to say to Mia, but the right words are as elusive as that shooting star he thought he saw the night Pop passed away.

The truth is, as he steps into the elevator, he has no idea what to tell his wife.

Carefully cradling his precious burden in his left arm, he presses the button with his right. The doors slide closed and with a bump, he's on his way.

What if he gets there, is face-to-face with Mia at last, and finds himself at an utter loss for words?

That won't happen. You've rehearsed a few things you can say.

Yes.

Things like, *I should never have taken vows I wasn't sure I could keep.*

And, *You deserve a marriage that's one hundred percent real.*

And, *I wish things had turned out differ-*

ently for us, because you're special to me and you always will be.

All of those things are completely honest.

None of them seem to convey the depth of his regret and longing.

But it's too late for more soul-searching. He's reached her floor, and the doors are opening, and he can't hide away in here another moment.

It's time.

Time to face her with his apology; time to listen to whatever she has to say, and then . . .

Time to say good-bye.

He walks down the corridor toward her door, thinking wistfully of the handful of times he returned after work, briefcase and bouquet in hand, to jokingly say, "Honey, I'm home."

She's holding the door ajar for him.

He sees her hand before he sees the rest of her.

Her left hand.

And there's still a gold wedding band on her fourth finger, just as there is on his.

But . . . why?

Maybe, like him, she just couldn't bring herself to take it off yet. Maybe she was waiting for him to confirm the inevitable.

Well, here he is . . .

And there she is.

His breath catches in his throat when he sees her. She's wearing jeans and a flannel shirt, her dark mane pulled back in a pony-tail, her face scrubbed free of makeup. And . . . glasses?

She's wearing glasses. How can he have known her — been married to her — and never have realized that she wears glasses?

It only proves that this whole thing was a mistake. Deliberate sham marriage or not, it was a mistake. They're strangers who got caught up in a surreal situation, and it's time they called off the charade and moved on with their normal lives.

Only . . .

Only, looking at Mia, he suddenly can't imagine his life feeling normal without her.

"Hi," she says softly, her expression rid-dled with uncertainty.

"Hi."

"I'm so sorry about your —"

"It's okay," he says, and takes a deep breath. "Were you there? At the funeral? Because I thought I saw —"

"I was there."

He nods. "I thought I saw you. Thank you."

"Come in," she says, and holds the door wide open.

He steps into the foyer. She closes the door and leads him into the pastel living room.

He never spent any time here in their short time living together. Now it seems oddly decorous to be taking a seat on the cream-colored sofa, his cellophane-wrapped gift for her balanced on his knee. He's obviously no longer the man of the house; he's a formal temporary visitor.

Who are you kidding? That's all you ever were.

She sits beside him and touches his arm. "Are you all right? I know how much you loved him. I know . . . well, I know how hard it must be."

"I'm all right," he manages to say. Then, after a pause, "No. I'm not. I'm not all right."

He tries to fight the emotion that wells up inside, but it's impossible. A choking sob escapes his throat; tears spill past his lashes.

"Oh, Dominic . . ." She pulls him close. "I'm so, so sorry."

He says nothing, just literally cries on her shoulder . . . the last thing he ever intended to do.

Finally, he pulls himself together and reaches into his pocket for his father's handkerchief — only to see that she, too, is crying.

"Hey," he says softly, dabbing her cheeks with a corner of starched white cotton. "It's okay. He's with my mom."

He's with the love of his life, and they'll never be apart again.

Dominic's throat is tight with emotion as he looks away from Mia. His gaze falls on the gift he brought, and he hands it to her. "This is for you. I saw it in the florist shop when I was ordering funeral flowers, and . . . and I thought of you. So I went back for it this morning."

"Thank you." She takes it from him and her eyebrows furrow slightly as she apparently realizes that it's a plant.

She carefully pulls away the cellophane wrapping . . . and gasps.

"How did you —" She breaks off, shakes her head in disbelief as she stares at the pale pink blossom atop a long stem. Then she asks again, "How did you know?"

"What do you mean?"

"It's a phalaenopsis — an orchid. My favorite kind of orchid."

"You have one by your bed," he tells her. "Every morning when I woke up . . . *there* . . . I found myself looking at the flower. It looks just like a butterfly. And when I saw it in the shop, I thought of you. I figured you might like another one."

"I would." She nods and sets the pot carefully on the marble table, staring thoughtfully at it. "Thank you, Dominic."

He senses that there's more she wants to say, but can't.

Why not? What's holding her back? And why is she staring at the orchid? He never expected a simple potted plant to get to her this way.

Well, if she can't speak, he can. And should. He should tell her everything he wanted to say before she starts asking questions, or making accusations, or . . . or says whatever it is that's causing that enigmatic expression.

"Mia," he begins after clearing his throat, "there are some things you should know about me. About how I feel."

"How . . ." Her voice is barely audible as she turns back to him expectantly. "How do you feel?"

Looking into those dark eyes of hers, he suddenly knows.

In that instant, he knows.

He knows exactly how he feels; he knows exactly what he wants to say.

It isn't *I'm sorry.*

And it isn't *Good-bye.*

It's . . .

"I love you."

As the words spill from his lips, he realizes he's never before uttered them aloud. Never in his life.

"I love you," he says again.

Mia presses a trembling hand to trembling lips — her own, and then his. She opens her mouth mutely, then closes it again.

He takes her hand and kisses it. "You don't have to say anything," he tells her. "I know you don't believe in —"

"No, I do," she blurts, looking almost as surprised by the outburst as he is. "I do believe in . . . love."

Pulse pounding, he asks, "You do?"

"I do, because . . ."

He holds his breath, not daring to believe it can be possible.

"Because," she says fervently, "Dominic, I love you, too."

And there it is, then, there at last.

His shooting star — a million shooting stars, all at once, exploding in his soul.

Epilogue

December

High above Ditmars Boulevard, the steeple bell is ringing. In the hushed sanctuary of Most Precious Mother, every pew is full; people stand three-deep in the back of the church.

On the altar are dozens of flickering, luminescent white candles, pale pink orchids, and a pair of Christmas trees simply trimmed with white lights.

Standing in the chilly vestibule at the back of the church, Mia shivers as Millicent Millagros begins the opening chords of the Wedding March.

"Are you cold, Bella?" Grandpa Junie asks, dapper in his tuxedo.

"Not cold. Just . . . excited."

Beaming proudly, her grandfather offers her his arm.

Mia takes a deep breath, glad she isn't wearing that too-snug white gown and constricting corset this time around.

Today, she has on a simple white dress

and white satin slippers that don't hurt her feet. In her hands she clutches a bouquet of white orchids.

"Are you ready, Bella Mia?"

"I'm ready, Grandpa," she whispers, and takes a step onto the satin runner that stretches ahead the length of the church.

Mia searches beyond the familiar faces at the opposite end — Nana Mona and Lenore, Nina and Rosalie and Maggie, a row of handsome Chickalini men lining the altar in tuxedos. She gazes past the scores of family and friends and flashing cameras, past Father Tom waiting in his white celebrant robes, searching . . .

Then she sees him. Her beloved Dominic, the man she married once in haste — and is about to marry again . . .

This time, for keeps.

Dominic's head is held high, his gaze serenely fixed on her as she walks toward him down the aisle. A white orchid is pinned to his lapel.

When at last they reach the altar, Grandpa lovingly places her hand into Dominic's warm grasp.

The old man leans forward to kiss Mia's cheek, then takes his place beside his own bride, Nana Mona, in the front pew.

★ ★ ★

As he gazes into Mia's eyes, Dominic knows without a doubt that this time, it's right.

This marriage is the real thing.

No contingency plans, no *Get Out of Jail Free* card, no doubts.

Nothing but vows that are meant to be honored . . .

And love.

True love.

He smiles at his bride and in his head, he hears the echo of his father's voice.

Cent'anni.

In his heart, Dominic answers with un-wavering conviction.

Yes, Pop. Cent'anni.

About the Author

WENDY MARKHAM recently celebrated a milestone birthday with her first trip to Las Vegas, where she saw her first desert sunset, tasted her first deep-fried Twinkie, and hit her first slot jackpot all in one weekend. Somewhere in the midst of all that decadence, *Bride Needs Groom* was born. Wendy is now looking forward to returning to Vegas to promote the novel. When she isn't signing copies of the book, you can find her in front of her lucky Wheel of Fortune slot machine with a bucket of quarters in one hand and a deep-fried Twinkie in the other.